George Augustus Sala

Make Your Game; or, the Adventures of the Stout Gentleman

The Slim Gentleman, and the Man with the Iron Chest

George Augustus Sala

Make Your Game; or, the Adventures of the Stout Gentleman
The Slim Gentleman, and the Man with the Iron Chest

ISBN/EAN: 9783337179878

Printed in Europe, USA, Canada, Australia, Japan

Cover: Foto ©Raphael Reischuk / pixelio.de

More available books at **www.hansebooks.com**

MAKE YOUR GAME.

MAKE YOUR GAME;

OR, THE

ADVENTURES OF THE STOUT GENTLEMAN,
THE SLIM GENTLEMAN, AND THE MAN
WITH THE IRON CHEST:

A Narrative of the Rhine and thereabouts.

BY

GEORGE AUGUSTUS SALA,

AUTHOR OF "THE BADDINGTON PEERAGE;" "TWICE ROUND THE CLOCK;"
"LADY CHESTERFIELD'S LETTERS TO HER DAUGHTER;" "GASLIGHT
AND DAYLIGHT;" "LOOKING AT LIFE;" "A JOURNEY DUE
NORTH;" "WILLIAM HOGARTH," ETC., ETC.

LONDON:
WARD AND LOCK, 158, FLEET STREET.

MDCCCLX

PREFATORY REMARKS.

As this little book is neither a treatise on Metaphysics, a dissertation upon the Origin of Species, nor an exposition on the law of Vendors and Purchasers, the Author ventures to hope that for once his good friends the critics will forbear to train against so tiny a monticule of writing, their great guns of analysis and demolition. It may occasionally be excusable—if for no other reason than for this, that a plenitude of talent may sometimes weary, and that a dash of triviality may refresh—to publish a work which has no higher ambition or pretence than to while away an idle hour. One can't be always reforming the constitution, or squaring the circle; and he who can do neither is unwise to make a pretence of achievements beyond his capacity.

With the view of averting invidious misapprehension, the Author thinks it expedient to mention that

the three travellers he has delineated in the following
pages are not in the slightest degree intended as portraits of any three given personages with whom he
happens to be acquainted. Such a disclaimer does
not, perhaps, affect the public; and the very extravagance of the characters drawn is in itself a guarantee
for their non-existence in actual life ; but the explana-
tion *does* affect the Author himself, his personal
friends, and *their* friends ; and as they, as well as the
public, may turn over the leaves of " MAKE YOUR
GAME," it is but a matter of justice to put such a
disclaimer on record. Certain characteristics possessed by the author's fellow-travellers, and a good
many more characteristics which they certainly did
not possess, were shaken up in his mind, very much
in the fashion of the counters in a bag at the game of
lolo, and were afterwards impartially distributed
among the ideal personages who " made their game."

Since Mr. Spurgeon has returned from Baden-Baden
with a full, true, and particular account of the mysteries of *Roulette* and *Trente et Quarante*, there is no
need, perhaps, for the author to tender any apology
for having described the chief gambling place of Ger-

many. He has made his travellers play at the tables, in simple candour, and simply because, in the course of the three visits he has paid to Hombourg, he has observed that nine-tenths of the English visitors to the Kursaal do so play. And, while repudiating any graver general "purpose" than that of amusing, he has endeavoured to deduce from the adventures of his shadowy tourists a tiny scrap of morality, to the effect that the moths who flutter round the garish lamps at the Kursaal of Hombourg-von-der-Höhe, and its kindred Hades, almost invariably singe their wings; and that the chances at *Roulette* and *Rouge* generally turn out edged tools, with which those incautious enough to play with them are apt to cut their fingers, sometimes very dangerously.

London, September, 1860.

CONTENTS.

CHAPTER VII.

CHAPTER VIII.

CHAPTER IX.

CHAPTER X.

MAKE YOUR GAME;

OR,

THE ADVENTURES OF THE STOUT GENTLEMAN, THE SLIM GENTLEMAN, AND THE MAN WITH THE IRON CHEST.

CHAPTER I.

FROM THE TOWER OF LONDON TO ROTTERDAM ON THE RHINE.

THE remaining days of August could be counted on the three last fingers of a man's hand, and there was positively Nobody in London—not a soul. Everybody had gone out of town. When I say Everybody and Nobody, it will be perfectly well understood, of course, that the two millions, or thereabouts, of units who figure in the Registrar-General's reports, and who can't, and often don't go out of town from year's end to year's end, are the Nobodies I allude to. The Everybodies must be counted by thousands only. There was nobody in Rotten Row; no dandies leaning over the rails; no ragged tramps, with sun-baked bare feet and shapeless hats, coming to squat on the grass, and, hugging their tattered window-knees, and gazing moodily at the dashing Amazons and the dashing carriages, radiant with varnish, and blazing with heraldry. Young Ultimus Homo (son of Lord Worldsend) was, indeed, compelled to remain in town. His arduous duties as a Treasury clerk— ("Why can't they shut up the Tweasuwy when gwouse-shooting begins?" asked young Ultimus Homo of Lady Clara Formosa's miniature-locket, close to his noble heart)—these duties detained him— atrocious tyranny! from ten to four, every day. He hired his usual Park-hack—modest younger brother— from Mr. Quartermaine, and rode sadly past Apsley House; but he shuddered at the base of Achilles' statue (at which no ladies were staring) to see the deserted "Wotton Wow," as he called the ride in his mild Mayfairian dialect. The ghost of "Skittles" might have haunted the place, so silent was it : and with a sigh, and a smothered exclamation of "dweadful baw," young Ultimus Homo turned his horse's head down Grosvenor Place. *Atra cura* sat behind him as he passed Tattersall's, at the entrance of whose yard were no panting Hansoms or champing mail phaetons. The dead wall of Buckingham Palace garden looked as mortuary as a whole Merthyr Tydvil mine full of door nails; the flagstaff of the Palace was bare ; the Bird-cage Walk held no birds; no aristocratic Mordecais sat in Storey's Gate; there was nobody in Parliament Street, nobody in Whitehall; and so wretched felt young Ultimus Homo that he might have been driven to the desperate act of riding his steed over the rotten palings of Westminster's moribund bridge, and perishing in a quicksand of mud, like Edgar of Ravenswood, had not the horse been the property of Mr. Quartermaine, not his own ; and had not the bright thought struck him of looking up young Roger de Bootvoir, whom a tyrannical Commander-in-Chief compelled to wear a muff cap and a red frock, and to cry "Sho'er humph!" on certain days in the week. Roger was yawning terribly, gazing through a back window at that dingy brickkiln, Marlborough House, and the two subsequently partook of the dinner provided with such splendid liberality by a grateful government for the officer on guard and his friends at St. James's Palace.

This brief apologue may serve to show you how empty London was. Nobody at the clubs save the whitewashers, and old Colonel MacCrabe, who is on the committee, and remains in town to see that the waiters don't steal the spoons, or the steward make surreptitious presents of Moselle and Burgundy to his friends. Nobody at the opera houses, save the stage-doorkeepers and the fleas in the grand-tier boxes. Nobody in Regent Street or in Eaton Square. Nobody at the Blue Posts. Nobody at the Royal Institution, in Albemarle Street. Nobody in Belgravia, Tyburnia, Bromptonia—nay, even in Bloomsburia and Camdenia. Her gracious Majesty gone out of town (little princekins dabbling in the sea by this time). British aristocracy gone out of town. Gay young bachelors, popular in society, gone out of town. Law, yes, *suprema Lex*—bench, bar, attorneys, solicitors, the very tipstaves and criers, gone out of town in a body. Rich tradesmen departed with their wives and families. All the inhabitants of all the squares— save Gough Square, Salisbury Square, St. Helen's Square, and Red Lion Square, which, according to the notions of general society, are no squares at all—gone out of town bodily. "Gone!" This last beautiful quotation I have taken from one of the most striking works of the late George Robins.

On the other hand, "out of town" was crammed —Brighton gorged, Hastings overflowing, Margate lodging-house keepers dreaming of huge investments in the funds, and visitors dreaming of being tried for the murder of extortionate lodging-house keepers. Pale ale at the "Trosachs" half-a-crown a quart. Ninety per cent. added to the charge for looking at the waiter at Patterdale, Windermere, and the Lake hotels generally. The three Legs of Man kicking up their heels with delight; and the tailless cats bitterly regretting that they have not stumps, even, to wave —they put up their backs instead—at the shoals of tourists invading the Castle Mona. The bugler on the Lake of Killarney blowing away his lungs, pocketing half-crowns, and selling impudent fictions to an unheard-of extent. Hastings, Oatlands Park, Scarborough, Teignmouth, the Isle of Wight (there were no beds to be had at all at Ventnor, and the harbourmaster had serious misgivings, from the numbers of yachtsmen and lady promenaders, for the safety of Ryde Pier), Torquay, Lowestoft, South Wales, Southsea, and Gravesend—yes, dear little semi-watering place, something between a diminutive herring and an overgrown whitebait, you shall have a place here for the sake of Rosherville and Windmill Hill—were all crowded to excess. London's blood had retired from the heart, and tingled with feverish out-of-townishness at the extremities. Yet the mighty heart on Thames's bank kept its gigantic pulsations with tolerable regularity, nevertheless.

A great many trains, steamboats, pleasure tours of every description, and to every part of the continent of Europe, were advertised, with reduced fares and other advantages. Oddly, everybody didn't seem at all inclined to go abroad, and comparatively nobody went. *Pension* keepers at Boulogne, *café restaurant* proprietors on the Paris Boulevards, hotel landlords from Calais to Civita Vecchia, from Cologne to the Lake of Constance, murmured, and clasped their hands. Cooks wept scalding tears into vacant stewpans; chambermaids looked sadly at beds already made, and needing no re-making; waiters whistled as they went for want of some one to cry "*Vla! M'sieu!*" to; and the columns of empty hotel ledgers laughed to see the sport. But all whispered with rage and terror the ominous word "passports." The passport difficulty was making the fortune of our own delightful watering-places at home, and the Milor Anglais was a *rara avis* on the Continent.

It was at this dead season of the social year that it occurred to three mysterious individuals, whom I will christen once and permanently the Stout Gentleman, the Slim Gentleman, and the Man with the Iron Chest, to yawn fearfully, to fling down journals, weekly and daily, to declare, stretching their arms recklessly, that there was " nothing in them," and to asseverate that they were getting intolerably rusty. They had had too much of the " mill," these three individuals said ; darkly hinting, moreover, that if they continued grinding much longer, the millers might fall, through

THE STOUT GENTLEMAN, THE SLIM GENTLEMAN, AND THE MAN WITH
THE IRON CHEST.

weariness, into the hopper, and be ground to flour, admirably suitable for the famous Fee-fo-fum to make his bread with. The Stout Gentleman declared plainly that he wouldn't stand it; the Slim Gentleman began to be observed frequently in sequestered nooks, pondering over maps, guide-books, railway time-tables, and steamboat advertisements, in a secretive and scrutinizing manner; and the Man with the Iron Chest intimated his intention of emigrating to the antipodes, and not returning till he was mayor of Melbourne, unless a three weeks' continental tour was very speedily arranged. Unluckily, the Mill, of which all the three individuals were more or less men, was a mill that never stops; the sails *must* go round, wind or calm, even if the miller's men have to hang to them to make them rotate. The mill is a paper mill, and grinds a curious compound of pens, ink, brains, and manual labour, into a certain thing called printed thought; and some people say that the mill in question (the millers have to work very hard, are not very handsomely paid, and their names are—oh, no! never mentioned!) is stronger than the Honourable House and the Right Honourable Board; that it is situated (a remarkable mill this) in the Fourth Estate of the Realm, and that it moves the world. I, who am Nobody, don't think that it does, but people say so.

There was a considerable difficulty in persuading some outside millers, *de bonne volonté*, to relieve our three individuals for a season; for, by an odd coincidence, everybody connected with mills was yawning, complaining of hard work, saying that August was near over, and the weather was magnificent, and that they *must* go out of town. At length substitutes were found to take up the burden of the popular air of " When the wind blows, then the mill goes;" and our three heroes—having seen their portraits, you will acknowledge them to be heroes indeed—met in solemn conclave, over some iced beverage, some undeniable regalias, and a vast pile of maps and railway guides, to consider the knotty point as to whither their steps should be directed.

The stout gentleman, who had been recently married, and was accumulating honeymoon over honeymoon with the fatal facility of one who has begun to accept accommodation bills, was modest in his views, and suggested Pegwell Bay, at which there was a shout of derision.

"We can get donkeys, thin bread and butter, and shrimps, and plenty of them, in London," the slim gentleman remarked, sarcastically, rattling some money in his pocket, at which metallic sound the man with the iron chest, who was out of cash that afternoon, writhed.

"Well," urged the stout gentleman, "there's Herne Bay—only think of the pier! There's Southend—only look at the sand and the society. There's the Undercliff—"

"Bosh!" cried the opposite parties. "We've three weeks before us: an age. The Continent, of course; and as far away as possible."

"But the passports!" objected the stout gentleman.

"Bother the passports!" interrupted the man with the iron chest, who was remarkable for the democratic vehemence of his political opinions, and was always complaining of poverty, "*are we not all personally known to the Secretary of State for Foreign Affairs, and haven't we all got bankers?*"

This was conclusive. A continental trip was decided on, and the only point now remaining for settlement was the country to be distinguished by the presence of the three tourists. The stout gentleman, now quite abandoning home influences, and determining to be a gay rover for twenty-one days, blithely suggested the Mediterranean. The slim gentleman said calmly that he had been considering the practicability of patronizing the Peninsular and Oriental Steam Navigation Company, with Malta as a goal, but that he was afraid that it could not be done in the time ; " for one *must* look in at Naples, going or coming, you know," he said.

The man with the iron chest, on being asked for his opinion, gave it with some acerbity. He said that in the first place he wished he was at Jericho ; next, that his two friends might go to Hong Kong. He had a fancy, he continued, for visiting Typee or Omoo, if the celebrated islands (if they were islands) in question, described by Mr. Herman Melville, really existed. If that werë impracticable, he should like, he said, to visit Bucharest, because there, he had heard, you could go to the Italian Opera for fourpence halfpenny, and he had a great curiosity to see a live Hospodar, to say nothing of a Waywode or a Kaimakan. Finally, he expressed his entire willingness to proceed to any part of Europe fixed upon, barring only the Italian town of Bergamo, hateful to him, he said, for many reasons. Upon this, the slim gentleman, clearing his voice, uttered these remarkable words—

" UP THE RHINE."

" We've all been up it and down it," grumbled the man with the iron chest (who was so ready, you will recollect, to agree to everything), " and one of us too often."

" But the Rhine, by way of Rotterdam," insinuated the slim gentleman.

" There's something in that," the M. I. C. deferred. " I was never at Rotterdam."

" Rotterdam !" the stout gentleman cried, enthusiastically. " Go for Rotterdam ! It must be such a queer place. Only imagine ! Real Dutch cheeses, blooming in all their luxuriance, under their native sky !"

"They don't grow on trees," muttered he of the chest.

"No, they don't," the stout one answered, good-naturedly; "but crab-apples do, grumbler. I say again, go for Rotterdam! It will be inconceivably jolly! I have been to Zealand, and had a peep at Holland. You'll all like it. Dutch pugs, Dutch dolls, Dutch prawns, Dutch drops. Dutch clocks."

"And Dutch metal?" the slim gentleman inquired.

"And Dutch metal, as you like. We'll only stop there a day; but we shall see real burgomasters, real galliots, real dykes, and taste real schnaps. And who knows that, with our facility for acquiring languages, we may not come back perfectly able to speak double Dutch backwards on a Sunday! What a triumph that will be over our classical friends! Let us go to Rotterdam, my children."

"And thence?"

"Thence," said the slim gentleman, glibly talking like a book—a railway guide-book, at least—thence by rail to Utrecht and Emerick on the Prussian frontier, you know. Then to Cologne—remember the Three Kings and the Eleven Thousand Virgins."

"Ha!" exclaimed the man with the iron chest.

"Sleep at Cologne or Deutz, whichever you like. Then, the next morning, take the RHINE STEAMER, and spend a whole day among the magnificent scenery of that noblest of rivers. Arrive at Mayence late at night; up the next morning and across the bridge of boats to Castel, and so by rail again to Frankfort-on-the-Maine."

"Frankfort's on the Oder," remarked the stout gentleman.

"There are Frankforts and Frankforts," the slim one continued, "and this is on the Maine. Splendid city, Frankfort. Rothschild's house, St. Paul's church, Danneker's Ariadne, the Jew's street—"

"And the Frankfort lottery," the iron-chested man

observed. "I had a ticket in it once, and ought to have won a ruined castle on the Rhine and the title of baron, only I didn't. Somebody else always does."

So the Rhine tour, as sketched out above, was fixed upon; and the first stage of the journey was to be, it was announced, from St. Katharine's Wharf, over against the Tower of London, by steamer, straight away to Rotterdam. "A long sea-voyage," demurred the stout gentleman—who was not proof against sea-sickness; but his companions (no better sailors than he) rallied him, and told him that, even if the *mal de mer* attacked him, it would do him good. So they parted—these three—promising each to bring as little luggage, and as much good spirits, as possible, and unanimously appointing the slim gentleman treasurer, the iron chest man secretary and bookkeeper, and the stout gentleman auditor, during the expedition.

Many tears were shed that night, and a tremendous quantity of tobacco smoke had to be emitted, and promises made respecting certain new dresses to be purchased three weeks thence, before peace could be restored in certain British households. The man with the iron chest appeared in polite society that evening with inflamed eyes, and a small pellicle of skin scratched or chipped out of his left cheek, just beneath the temple. He spoke darkly of one Her, with a large H. The acquaintances of the slim gentleman remarked that he was slightly pensive, though philosophically, and that he whistled "The heart bowed down." The bride of the stout gentleman (who did not show till morning) caused to be conveyed, by special messenger, to the man with the iron chest, this appalling reminder: That there were to be no "Carryings on" (as if *he* ever carried anything on!) and that he would be held personally responsible for any vagaries (more especially defined as "Philanderings," such as looking at pretty girls, or dancing at village feasts with shepherdesses in striped stockings) committed jointly or severally during the excursion. What, asked the M. I. C., passionately, had he to do with it? He afterwards calmed down, and remarked that it had ever been thus, from childhood's hour. Some subsequent and touching allusions to a young gazelle, with a soft black eye, were laughed down by his auditors in the most unfeeling manner.

Are not half a dozen sentences necessary—not to give the preceding lives and adventures of the Remarkable Three, but to give just an outline of their exterior characteristics? I won't detain you long. First, then, it seemed to be the special mission of the stout gentleman to go through this vale of tears laughing at, but more frequently with, everything and everybody. His laughter was so genial and so contagious that he frequently received imploring missives from dramatic authors, offering splendid inducements if he would only attend the first representation of their works—comic works, be it understood; for the stout gentleman was just as prone to laugh at a tragedy as at a comedy; and Ballyrook, the author of "Boreas and Stavidides, or the Lacedæmonian Grandmother," in five acts, always ascribed the lamentable failure of his drama to the cachinnatory presence of the stout gentleman in a private box; but a one-act farce was considered safe with the stout one in the second row of the stalls. The stout gentleman lived on his talents, his private property, and his good humour, all of which were inexhaustible. He liked good dinners, was partial to pipes and cigars (medium flavour), was an amateur chemist, alchemist, and natural philosopher, sketched very well in ink and crayons, and only hated fools when they were mischievous.

The slim gentleman was a cynical philosopher—a Diogenes who lived in a polished mahogany tub, with hoops gilt. He was a capital judge of Rhine wine (the stout gentleman liked hock, but preferred claret), and did not admire the works of Mr. Martin Farquhar Tupper. His enemies—we all have enemies—said of the slim gentleman that he lived on suction, for in London no man ever saw him dine. He was on the sunny side of forty and the shady side of twenty, so you can be in no doubt about *his* age. The travellers' ages united might just turn the corner of a century.

As to the man with the iron chest, he was a mystery. He didn't live on suction, though he declared occasionally that he had a valet-de-chambre, in the shape of a vulture, which lived upon *him*. But how could a man with a vulture gnawing at his vitals be so full in flesh? Prometheus with ensanguined side is feasible, but who could form a conception of Prometheus with a red nose? No one knew exactly where the man with the iron chest lived. He gave contradictory addresses—sometimes said that he resided at the West End; and the most reasonable chance of finding him was to lie in ambush in a certain dark, mysterious, and deserted little arcade, between Wellington and Catherine Streets, in the Strand, where he sometimes gave audience to ambassadors, on affairs connected with the paper mill. He was not punctual, and was addicted to writing from the "*Poste restante*," in Timbuctoo, to apologize for not keeping that last appointment in Waterloo Place. Some people said that the man with the iron chest had an income of five thousand a year, and that he kept a yacht, and rode to the Queen's hounds; others that his diet consisted mainly of fried fish, and that he slept on broken ginger-beer bottles. He was very mysterious, but not picturesque, for he had, you see, *such* a red nose.

The iron chest, with which his name must be ever associated, was even more mysterious than he was. It was an ugly black box—not a mediæval iron chest of the George Colman or Wardour Street type, but with a considerable quantity of metal about it. It was half covered with parti-coloured labels relating to foreign railways, or to " Bristol Up," or " Brighton Down," and half-effaced initials in red chalk. You were always meeting this iron chest. You saw it grimly looming in the left-luggage departments of railway termini: you met it on platforms, thoughtful porters pasting fresh labels upon it; it flashed past you on the roof of rapid cabs in Cannon or Union Streets; it stopped the way at steamboat landing-places; and wherever you met it, the man with the red nose was sure not to be far distant. Rumour said that both man and chest had once been met with on Hampstead Heath, the man vainly endeavouring to persuade a donkey-boy to hoist it on a side-saddled ass for conveyance to " Jack Straw's Castle." What did it contain? Title-deeds, gold, bank-notes, rags and bones, manuscripts of tragedies in many acts, or poems in many cantos? Who shall say? The man when questioned gave evasive replies, and if pressed, was rude. He could be very rude. When the authorship of " Junius's Letters " is disclosed, and the secret of Caspar Hauser's parentage revealed, the mystery of that iron chest, and of the man that belonged to it, will perhaps be solved.

It was high noon, on a bright and gloriously-warm end-of-August day, when the adventurous Three stood on the deck of the first-class steamer *Batavier*, which was panting and pulling, fuming and fretting, to get away down the river, and, like a salmon just of age, plunge into the Northern Ocean. Only, the *Batavier* was bound for Rotterdam, a haven which salmon, save in a dried and kippered form, eschew.

Such a noise and apparent confusion there was! Two steamers' decks had been crossed ere the deck of the *Batavier* could be reached, and goods and passengers were so mingled and so moving, that you had a difficulty at first in distinguishing whether it was the passengers who were being shot down inclined planes, or lowered into the hold, or packing-cases which stamped about in travelling-caps, and full of queries as to the destination of their berths. Very hot day, as I have said; yet there was a whole Manchester warehouse full of rugs, wrappers, shawls, and great coats, on ladies' and gentlemen's arms. The passengers would not have been English else. Not a very full complement of travellers either. Those wearisome passports may have had something to do with checking the flow of emigration, and Rotterdam is not usually the place where a continental pleasure tour begins. But plenty of merchandise, both light and heavy. Not a cattle-boat, luckily, though, in some pens forward, there were a few sheep, and two donkeys with their foals. Much loud stamping and gesticulation, accompanied by language not wholly complimentary, took place, as the starting-bell began to ring. Porters, who had carried trunks aboard, demanded extravagant remuneration; and the somewhat unusual spectacle was seen of a Hansom cabman, in full vehicular costume, on a steamboat deck, delivering a tremendous philippic, to which Cicero against Verres was but as the address of a small attorney to a county court judge on the disputed question of a milk score, against a fare who had tendered but a shilling for the journey between London Bridge Terminus to Thames Street. The fare, however, happened to be a man of the world—a cautious little individual in a plaid suit, and carrying a thin umbrella—such men are generally wary, so he calmly kept the shilling in his outstretched palm, bidding the cabman take it, summons him, or take a trip to Rotterdam with him. exactly as he chose. And, as the parting bell was ringing somewhat sharply by this time, the cabman, who had left his vehicle on Tower Hill, in charge of a shoe-black of doubtful looks as to honesty, took the shilling, with many grumbling opinions, that " money would never burn in such a stingy cove's pockets;"

and departed, kicking several trunks in an angry and contemptuous manner, expressing a wish that things in general might be " blowed," and offering to fight a peripatetic vendor of cheap periodicals on the wharf, for " luck."

So cast away ropes and fastenings, and slowly heave this strong ship round ; and now see her threading her way through the maze of vessels, boats, and lighters in the pool, thickly beset on all sides, yet moving with a caution of management that is as the instinct of an elephant, putting now one now the other of his huge paviour's rammer feet forward, and piloting his huge bulk through the crowded bazaar of a Hindoo town.

Away, away then, my three merry men—they are all laughing, and have made up their minds to laugh, as Mr. Scrub remarks, " consumedly ;" but forget not to peer through the glorious cobweb of masts and spars, of sails and rigging, of flaunting flags and loose tackle, the reticulations of whose network grow larger and larger, as the steamer glides into the midst of the channel. Now she is free. You, London smoke, you, inky clouds from countless funnels (those little steam-tugs are really the most vicious, grimy, vapouring little craft afloat), you cannot veil the blue and cloudless sky to-day. And to see the sun showering gold—a generous giant !—upon the meanest, dingiest objects ; upon warehouses bulging with goods, doors in their upper storeys gaping as if for breath ; huge bales swinging lazily from gibbet-like cranes, bales poised in mid-air, like Mahomet's coffins of mammon ; upon maritime churches, with Union Jacks flying from the steeples ; upon the groves of masts lying in distant dockyards ; upon crazy little summer-houses, built by retired master mariners, and not unreasonably termed "follies ;" upon unaccountable water-side dwelling-houses, built by nobody knows whom, and nobody knows when or why ; upon private wharves littered with broken-up ships' timbers and broken spars ; upon pyramids of casks, and batteries of sugar-bags, and black mountains of coal, just disgorged from the clumsy lighters : upon the distant bridges seen through London's arch—cut sharply by South-wark's black iron span; the tiny penny steamers, the dancing wherries. The polluted river has even a transient gleam of blue on its surface to-day; the great pillar with the flaming top, the blue dome of St. Paul's, are solemn and regardful of the whole gay scene ; and chief shines the bright sun upon the grand old Tower, calm and torpid—a gray stone tortoise, heedless how many thousands of tons weight are put upon it, how many broad-wheeled wagons of rolling centuries pass over it, and leave its granite carapace uninjured. Yes, Monsieur Crapaud, that is the Tower of London ; that is the only fortalice of which London can boast. You will observe that plain brick dwellings and warehouses are mingled with hoary bastions and crenelated tourelles, the White Tower only rising proudly above all : that sentries are pacing along terraces that might be wharves; that Traitor's Gate is blocked up; that guns peer from between casks and piles of timber. That is a way we have in England—to mingle the shop we keep with the very scant martial show we make.

Our three travellers, alive to the exigencies of the occasion, had each adopted a peculiar suit of travelling costume. The stout gentleman was resplendent. Look at him, and admit that he was a credit to the *Batavier*. That flowing mantle—light though warm, ample though convenient—possessed equally the characteristics of the Spanish grego, the Mexican poncho, the Arab bournous, the more modern Inverness wrapper, and the "upper Benjamin" of the old "Charlie." He wore, moreover, a gorgeous courier's pouch of large dimensions — a pouch of softest leather and brightest framework and lock, and which being opened, disclosed multifarious crimson morocco niches, furnished with tobacco, toilet appendages, small articles of cutlery, his cigar case (Algerian wheat-straw, embroidered with amber beads), a passport case, with plenty of blank leaves for *visas*, and the precious document issued by the Secretary of State for Foreign Affairs, a passport countersigned by the Netherlands Consul, and only obtained, it need scarcely be said, by the extensive personal interest possessed, and the high consideration enjoyed, by the stout gentleman at the Foreign Office. A felt hat of the aristocratically wide-awake pattern covered our stout one's brow; a diamond ring glittered on one finger, a cluster of watch-chains dangled from his waistcoat button-hole. He had a sketch-book in one hand, and a priceless meerschaum pipe (if its scientific colouring is to be taken as a test of its value) was seldom absent from his manly lips. And—let me not forget that—crosswise with the patent leather strap that held his courier's pouch, was suspended by a modest silken cord a gourd—a gourd, sir, yellow, and untanned, such as you may see in Mr. Philip's pictures of life in sunny Seville. This gourd had a little cork and a little vent-peg, and, true to the traditions of its Iberian birthplace, it contained some most excellent Amontillado sherry, which the stout gentleman affably dispensed to his companions. He had a gold pencil-case, he had a gold pen-holder, he had a portentous morocco pocket-book, doubtless full of bank-notes and letters of credit. He was the pearl and pride of gallant young Englishmen taking their pleasure abroad. He laughed unceasingly, he told droll anecdotes, he sang snatches of merry songs, he spoke up quite boldly to the captain, slapped the second mate on the back, and called the steward "Theodore" before he had been ten minutes on board. But he was very stout. The man with the iron chest (he had been sitting on that coffer since its arrival on board on the back of an ancient porter, who grumbled horribly on receipt of his fee, and said that he "warn't used to carryin' coffins with paving stones inside") was slightly jealous of the magnificent "make up" of his stout friend, who, however, always anxious to pour oil on the troubled waters, promised to let him wear the gourd or the courier's pouch, whichever he preferred, all up the Rhine.

The slim gentleman, as became his philosophical temperament, was attired in a plain frock, a black neckerchief, and trousers and waistcoat of the ordinary check pattern. The common stove-pipe hat was at the back of his acute head; indeed, he looked very like a gentleman who was going into the City on business. Well—hadn't he come into the City in order to embark on board the *Batavier*, and wasn't going abroad his business just now? He was precisely the sort of equable individual who would have turned up in the trenches before Sebastopol, on the steps of the Astor House, New York, or at Shepherd's Hotel, Grand Cairo, in exactly the same costume, and with exactly the same unruffled demeanour.

As for the man with the iron chest, it had seemed good to that inexplicable individual to attire himself after the manner of an English groom who had taken to the society of gentlemen professing the noble science of self-defence. The stout gentleman christened him Jemmy Shaw on the spot. The slouching cap, the trousers tight from the knee downwards, and the remarkable monkey jacket of a thick, hard material, which he triumphantly declared "couldn't be cut with a knife," were as sporting as they were pugilistic in appearance. The slight hirsute appendage which he permitted to appear on his upper lip — being "otherwise clean shaven," as the celebrated literary gentleman observed of the other celebrated literary gentleman—gave him rather the guise, the slim one whispered to the stout one, of Jack Sheppard with moustaches.

As for luggage, the stout and slim gentlemen had each brought a handsome and shapely "solid leather" portmanteau. The third traveller would have belied his na me, had he carried aught else beyond that memorable iron chest.

"At all events," the slim gentleman remarked, rubbing his hands, "we shall know what that chest contains, when it comes to be examined at the custom-house at Rotterdam."

"Perhaps," was the brief reply of the man with the iron chest.

No need, I think, to describe, for the nine hundred and ninety-ninth time, the petty incidents of a steam-boat passage down the river, and across the German Ocean (the pretension of calling it an ocean!), to Rotterdam—how the three wanderers passed Erith, and Gravesend and Tilbury, and made sage remarks about railways and steam navigation; how they expatiated on the beauty of the weather, and the calmness of the water (oh, fallacies of hope! and vanity of human wishes); how they moved the steward to bring a little tray on deck, bearing biscuits and cool refreshments, of which they partook, smoking, chattering, and signalling, by voice and finger, familiar places on either bank; how, at about three in the afternoon, they were summoned to dinner—they were getting towards the Nore light-ship by this time—and though the sea was still very blue, and the sun very bright, the water was not *quite* so calm as it had been in Limehouse-reach; how they partook of a dubious soup, that was rather mock-water than mock-turtle, and eschewed that inevitable boiled mutton, wisely adhering to beef; how they manfully ordered a bottle of red port wine, after sundry libations of bottled stout, and drank to and with the captain. I might fill columns with the narrative of these often-recounted

adventures. Dutch painting might perhaps be tole-
rated in the description of a voyage to the shores of
Holland; but I am afraid that I should "make"
neither my readers' game nor my own were I to indulge in very minute detail.

But no matter to whatever length this chapter
runs, something must still be said about the FAWN.

> "The wanton troopers, riding by,
>   Have shot my Fawn, and it will die,"

sings Andrew Marvell in his exquisite pastoral. She
was not this Fawn; nay, nor the White Doe of Ryl-
stone, nor Dryden's "milk-white hind," nor Shakspeare's leathern-coated stag that wept such piteous
tears, and whom the melancholy Jacques watched.
She was not the hart that desireth the water-brooks;
nor the stricken deer that the herd had left, and the
maiden bade come home to her bosom; not the wild roe,
which the individual who declared his or her heart to be
"in the Highlands," desired to chase; not the gazelle
which the author of "Eöthen" took up tenderly in
the desert, and placed across his saddle-bow, looking
lovingly into the darling's eyes. What is the good of
my expatiating upon what she was *not?* I tell you
that she was a Fawn. If she resembled any pictured
fawn, it was the pretty creature that the little girl is
tending in Edwin Landseer's picture. But besides
being a fawn, she was an exceedingly pretty girl, and
a passenger on board the *Batavier*. Oh, those melting velvet eyes of hers! Oh, that timorous mouth,
that imploring mouth, that seemed to join its cherry
lips in supplication, saying, "Don't kiss me, please,
because it isn't proper; but if you *can't* help it, and
must do it, wait, oh, wait! till papa has turned his
face to the binnacle!" Such a tender, trembling,
svelte, and graceful form she had, such little hands
and feet peeping in and out, "like little mice," to use

Sir John Suckling's hackneyed but delightful simile. She wore a shawl—a Cashmere shawl—only fawns can wear shawls now with grace, in these days of jackets and mantles, and the amplitude of her skirts was gauzy and ethereal, not crinoliny.

The fawn had a sister, who would have been exquisitely beautiful, if the fawn herself hadn't been there. As it was, the man with the iron chest, who had fallen desperately in love with the fawn immediately after beholding her for the first time, was unkindly requested by the stout and the slim gentlemen, to confine his visual attentions to the sister, and not under any circumstances to admire the fawn, regarding whom his two friends had agreed to quarrel amicably between themselves. They always treat the man with the iron chest in this unkind manner. They pick out for him the most hideous sweethearts—toothless old hags, that might do duty as Macbeth's witches, hump-backed women, crones with noses redder than his own, women with one eye, women old enough to be his grandmothers. It is very hard.

The fawn's papa was a terrible old buck, of military appearance, with a grey whisker, a tight stock, suggestive of strict discipline, and a very kicking downstairs looking pair of boots. But for all his stern demeanour, he evidently regarded his two daughters as the apples of his eyes. The pretty creatures refused to descend to the saloon, and declined dinner altogether, though he brought them up tit-bits and tiny neguses cunningly mixed. They evidently feared the demon of the ocean, the mother Cary's game-cock, sea-sickness. So they snuggled close to one another on deck, and the fond papa covered them up with cloaks and shawls, beneath which their graceful forms were still salient, like the rounded members beneath the veil of the draped Diana. There was a lady's maid, who should have attended to them; but the poor creature gave up the ghost of seawomanship before she reached Gravesend, and, until the ship arrived at her destination, remained in a pitiable state of collapse, requesting ever and anon during the day and night some passing sailor to "throw her overboard." I think I have told you enough about the fawn to make you think it not very unreasonable on the part of our three travellers to adore her on the spot, from the apex of her delightful hat to the tips of her pretty *chaussure*. There were two English schoolboys on board, going to resume their studies at some boarding-school at Andernath, I think, on the Rhine— frank, honest, ruddy, well-spoken lads, full of cheery good humour and modest self-reliance. They were quite as much in love with the fawn as the three

THE "FAWN" AND HER SISTER.

tourists, although they had not yet assumed the *toga virilis*, and it was a perpetual game of hide-and-seek between these infatuated men and boys to obtain the best glances at the fawn.

Shortly after dinner it began to blow pretty sharply. Shortly after four it blew much harder. Half an hour afterwards it blew great guns—Paixhan guns— then Armstrong's, then Whitworth's, then monster mortars, then powder magazines. It seemed to have blown its hardest; but it didn't lull, and blew harder.

The stout gentleman was still courageous long after Margate had been left to the right, and the steamer was steering north-east by something. He ascended

Stout Gent.—"IT IS SO MUCH BETTER UP HERE."

the paddle-box, conversed with the captain, and became quite nautical. But it blew very hard, and the stout gentleman had to hold on very firmly by the handrail.

"It's much better being up here than on deck," cried the stout gentleman, jovially. But he did not so loud or so frequently as it grew later. He did not puff at his priceless meerschaum quite so persistently. He had a little arsenal of specifics against sea-sickness, from creosote to filberts. Not that *he* was about to be sick. O dear, no! The specifics were for his friends, you know. Large-hearted philanthropist! But the steward brought him a great many cups of tea—seven, I think—and by-and-bye, there came a subtle rumour aft that the stout gentleman had ordered brandy, neat.

I will not dwell at any length upon the horrors of the night on board the *Batavier*. The steamer pitched dreadfully, and when she didn't pitch, she rolled, which was about equivalent to being fried after being boiled. I think I shall best avoid invidious distinctions by saying that all the passengers were sick. The fawn and her sister were quite prostrate, and their papa, though looking like a Marius among the ruins of Carthage, had a bad time of it. The stout gentleman was bravely ill, and afterwards gloried in the fact. The man with the iron chest disappeared altogether. He was sought for in the saloon, but unavailingly; and from a series of indistinct moans being heard during the night from behind a tarpaulin-covered mound of merchandise, it may not be unreasonably conjectured that the man with the iron chest was lying *perdu* there, like an indisposed baboon. As regards the slim gentleman, he behaved with his usual philosophical composure. Nobody could tell exactly whether he had been ill or not. He quietly doubled himself up, his head touching his knees, at about five P.M. The stout gentleman considerately covered him over with a cloak ; and there he lay, moving neither hand nor foot, and refusing to open his lips to man or woman, till about eight the next morning, when, after a terrible passage of twenty hours, the steamer arrived at the Boompjees of ROTTERDAM.

It had been calm, however, for an hour and a half previously, while the steamer had been gliding on the flat bosom of the sluggish Maes. Low, sedgy banks, dykes ; oddly-coloured, quaintly built houses, mostly red and yellow ; alders and pollard willows ; narrow canals, revealing ships far up the country ; tall poles, piers, roomy galliots, with dark brown sails ; odd river-boats that indistinctly reminded you of the junks and lorchas of China and Japan you had seen in rice-paper pictures ; these had gradually marked the approach of the three travellers. But when, at last, after a mere nominal examination of passports and searching of luggage—they did not even condescend to open that ominous iron chest—by some very peaceable-looking *douaniers*, moustached, not whiskered, at the landing-place—when, after respectfully drawing on one side, till the poor trembling fawn, her sister, and the major, her papa—I am sure he was a major—stepped on shore ; when the stout gentleman and his two trusty colleagues positively landed on the quaint and crowded quay of Rotterdam, the stout gentleman threw up his stalwart arms, and burst into a mighty peal of laughter, the like of which had not been heard from his lips since the steward brought him his seventh cup of tea.

"Hurrah !" cried the stout gentleman, quite forgetting his sea-sickness and medicine chest of specifics. "In Holland—hurrah !"

CHAPTER II.

FROM "VULGAR VENICE," BY EMERICK AND UTRECHT, TO COLOGNE, IN PRUSSIA.

"I don't see much to hurrah about, because we are in Holland," the M. I. C. remarked, somewhat tartly, when the stout gentleman had ceased cheering. "The Dutch were here before us, I believe; and those pretty girls (Fawn and sister) are turning round to stare at you. Pray be reasonable, if you can."

Now, the man with the iron chest's mode of landing in Holland had not at all resembled the grandiose arrival of Cæsar in Britain, or of William of Orange at Torbay. It had offered a far greater similarity to the manner in which that other William—the Conqueror—landed, according to report, on the Sussex coast. For he stumbled on crossing the plank from the custom-house barge to the quay; and, I grieve to tell it, first saluted the soil of Holland with his nose. Picking himself up, and rubbing that abraded member—which was redder than ever—in a rueful manner, it did not tend to restore his equanimity to see his stout friend thus rejoicing. As for the slim gentleman, he had frequently complained, when on board the *Batavier*, of not being able to find his sea-legs, and now he seemed equally unable to find his land ones, lurching and shambling about, and holding on to imaginary bulwarks in a very undecided manner.

At this juncture the stout gentleman was taken into custody. Not by the soldiery, or by the emis-

VIEW OF ROTTERDAM.

saries of the Burgomaster of Rotterdam, nor by some wary detective policeman sent by special steamer to catch him alive as the stout proprietor of some fat bank which had turned out to be a corpulent swindle. No; the stout gentleman was as free from guilt as the Man of Ross, or M. de Voltaire's Huron. But he was captured, nevertheless, by a detachment of little round-faced, square-built boys, attired very much in the fashion of the London shoeblacks—not the parti-coloured "brigade" boys, who brush during the day, and attend beautiful lectures with dissolving views at night; but the little irregulars, flying in rags, who take to shoeblacking as a relief from crossing-sweeping, as an attractive from starving, and a preservation from thieving. These Batavian Bedouins seized bodily on the stout gentleman, and made him at once the captive of their brushes and blacking bottles. Each foot had soon its attendant imp, brushing away at it till the stout gentleman's corns became incandescent; two more set to work (let us hope with clothes brushes innocent of Day and Martin's "sootpots," as blacking is called by Mr. Carlyle) to warm the marrow of his abundant dorsal vertebræ; a cohort hovered round his voluminous person, with difficulty only restrained from blacking the famous courier bag, and breathing upon and polishing to extreme brilliance the stout one's black kid gloves. But thy tutelary genius was there, O Houbigant-Chardin! whose "eight and three quarters" are four and sixpence per pair, and the profanation was prevented. The stout gentleman, whom I fully believe to possess confidence equal to that of Lord John Russell—a little man, but said to be ready to undertake the command of the Channel Fleet, and to perform the operation for the stone— and who, for his (stout) part, I thoroughly believe, would gleefully have consented to write a five-act tragedy, ride upon a rhinoceros, sing Rode's air with variations, eat a leg of mutton and a pound of candles for a wager, square the circle, discover the longitude, and go into training to fight the champion of England for two hundred pounds a side and the belt:—the undaunted stout gentleman proved himself fully equal to this trying emergency. The shoeblacks at his feet had each their block. On the foot-shaped pedestal surmounting either block bravely stood up the stout gentleman. Wide apart stood his manly limbs, proud flashed his eye, beaming as Lesbia's famed in T. Moore's lyric. But he was as modest as great, and putting his hands in his vast pockets, cried, "Brush away, my pippins," at which a Low Dutch cheer arose from the ragged boys, and one, the linguist of the party, cast himself at his feet, crying, in imperfect accents :—

"Oh, Anglish shantlemans, Anglish shilling give."

"He looks like the Colossus of Rhodes," said the man with the iron chest, enthusiastically regarding the stout one.

"He looks like the sign of the 'Goat and Compasses,' " said the slim one.

"The little ragamuffins know how to charge, however," remarked the stout gentleman, as he descended from his double pinnacle of glory. "Four young Dutchmen have made a demand of a shilling apiece."

"Give them a shilling amongst them," suggested the M. I. C.

"Give each boy a penny, and box the ears of the rest," was the stern advice of the slim gentleman—a man of business he, and the terror of cabmen.

The stout gentleman, however, concluded to split the difference; and flung a handful of English coppers among the shoeblack crowd, remarking that he could not box twenty boys' ears, but that the pennies might hit twenty boys' heads. The luggage being hoisted on a truck, of very Dutch construction, half-way between a wheelbarrow and a railway-truck, the travellers proceeded along the quay towards the hotel which the slim gentleman, who was quarter-master-general of the forces, had *said* that he fixed upon as their first caravanserai of rest and refreshment. I say that he said he had selected it; but I am afraid he had ulterior motives. They were pursued, though not in any uncomfortable degree, by the usual outlaying squadrons of hotel touters with their limp cards and Babel *baragouin*, of French, German, Dutch, and English mingled. There was one very tall, stout, with a pasty face, a nose of decidedly Jewish dimensions, bright yellow sabots, and an exaggerated muslin cap or bonnet on his head, something like that erst worn by "Souter Johnny," who positively rained cards—they came from his sleeves and his collar like bouquets from a juggler's hat, and fluttered about the three travellers, and who vociferated in Talmudical Dutch that he was "Anglish Jack, real Anglish Jack;" whereupon he was informed that he might be English Jill, or English anybody, but that the Three would have nothing to do with him or the Rabshakeh Hotel in the Sheeni-Straet.

"On your arrival in a foreign land," was the didactic remark of the man with the iron chest, as they pursued the line of the quay, the wheelbarrow luggage truck trundling along before, "you are ordinarily received either by policemen, Jews, or boys. The traveller who reaches London Bridge terminus, scarcely emerges from the arcade before he is surrounded by tattered urchins forcing on his notice oranges or cigar lights, and insisting upon turning cartwheel somersaults before his travel-wearied eyes. On crossing the Russian frontier into Poland, hordes of red-bearded Jews hang upon your skirts, and frantically strive to drive hard bargains with you in Hebrew Sclavonic. Eastern travellers will tell you how, landing on Alexandria's sandy shore, gangs of Arab boys, hideously afflicted with ophthalmia, at once surround you, absolutely forcing you to ride on enormous donkeys, and pressing you to purchase chips of brick from the pyramids of Ghizeh and portions of Cleopatra's great toe. Passing the Flaminian gate at Rome, even, shock-headed, black-eyed young ruffians will tell you in sonorous Campanian that they are descendants of the Colonnas and the Orsinis, and that they are in want of five bajocchi. At Hong-Kong—"

At this recondite allusion, the companions of the man with the nose began to murmur among themselves disparagingly, and say that it was all very well for him to talk guide-book, but that, after all, it was very easy to become a great traveller, in words, by staying at home, and reading-up "Murray;" and that some people gained a great reputation as tourists, whose greatest travelling achievements had been a five-shilling trip to Boulogne. Disdaining these objections, the man with the iron chest was proceeding to dilate upon the social aspects of China—he had been observed perusing Wingrove Cooke's book very attentively of late—when the stout gentleman made a sudden start, folded his arms as though his foot were on his native heath, and his name—well, never mind that; and declared that he would not budge an inch further.

"I told you so," the slim gentleman said to the M. I. C. "With your confounded boring stories about—"

"It isn't that," broke in the stout gentleman; "let him go on. He is soothing, if not interesting, and I can sleep as I walk. It's something quite different, which have I will, and so make no mistake about it, kind sirs. It's *schnaps!*"

"Schnaps!" echoed the slim gentleman, contemptuously. "I want Rhine wine."

"Schnaps!" re-echoed the man with the iron chest, rubbing his nose. "It's rather early for schnaps, isn't it?"

" Never too early for a good deed," was the conclusive reply of him full in flesh. " We are in Holland, and must do as the Dutch do. If nobody else will have schnaps, this young man will."

A little, low-browed, ogling shop, with a bull's-eye wrench in the centre of each pane, a profusion of fresh-coloured painted wood-work, and bright brass utensils inside, offered itself invitingly to the three travellers just between the " Contora," or office of a " *Schiffbracker* " — " Shipbroker or shipbreaker ? " queried the M. I. C.—and the establishment of a gentleman who sold washing-tubs and scrubbing-brushes. The slim gentleman refused spirituous refreshment at so early an hour, and before breakfast, so he stood at the door taking mental notes of Rotterdam, and jingling the silver change in his pockets as usual. The stout gentleman, with that manly frankness which distinguished him, strode into the shop, and called for a glass of schnaps, with a voice like the sound of a trumpet. It was here he commenced the exercise of that system of tactics in the way of foreign languages, which subsequently made him so remarkable during his travels on the continent of Europe. The system was admirably simple, consisting merely in confining himself to the use of the Anglo-Saxon tongue, slightly modified as to its grammatical construction ; pointing to the object forthcoming when visible ; making appropriate pantomimic gesticulations in the manner of Fenella in the *Muta di Portici*, when the object was not forthcoming ; but always speaking in a loud, determined voice, and gazing stedfastly at the shopkeeper, waiter, or other person to be addressed. The success of this novel system—far surpassing in merit, according to our stout friend, those of Hamilton, Robertson, and Ollendorff—was as satisfactory as it was surprising. Thus, when the stout gentleman, after tossing off his *petit verre* of schnaps, smacking his rubicund lips, and declaring that it warmed the cockles of his heart, and took the taste of the *Batavier* out of his mouth, said boldly to the leathern-capped proprietor of the schnaps-shop: "Will you have another one yourself, old boy?" nodding, winking, smiling, pointing, and raising imaginary glasses to his lips, the proprietor (who had a pimple on one side of his nose like a small crab-apple, and was smoking a fat, flaccid cigar, bent downwards like a boomerang) nodded and grinned his assent, filled, and drank off his *petit verre* with an affable grunt of "*vod zandé, Moozoo*" (the egregious Dutchman, to mistake the stout gentleman for a Frenchman!), and handed him, in change for an English shilling, a small avalanche of diminutive Dutch pfennings and stuyvers. "Adieu to the broad, thick, honest coinage of the British Isles," sighed the man with the iron chest. "'Tis only on the Continent that you can understand the meaning of the Infinitely Little." This philosophical reflection did not, however, prevent him from entering the little shop, but in a furtive and sneaking manner, saying that he was going to see what o'clock it was, and taking care to pick previously sundry small copper discs, which he said "would just do," from the generous palm of him who was not slim. He caught his companions up a minute afterwards, was observed to wipe his moustache covertly, breathed hard, and proffered the remark that in some of the Dutch liquor shops you could have a peep at the newspaper for a couple of stuyvers.

"Can you read Dutch?" asked the slim gentleman sternly.

The man with the iron chest replied evasively that it was not a language to be despised, for that the English had found it most useful in their recent intercourse with Japan, the treaty having been, in fact, drawn up with a Dutch duplicate.

"Well, well, my children," interposed the stout gentleman, anxious to avoid dissension, "Dutch is not so much our theme now as victuals. This humble, though sufficiently capacious interior," he added, tapping his vast waistcoat, "feels—after the *Batavier*, and the cruel behaviour of Neptune, god of waves—as though twenty full-grown tom-cats had been boarding and lodging in it for a fortnight. Breakfast—excessive breakfast, of the meatiest kind, is required forthwith. Yonder halts our many-galligaskined friend with the luggage at the door of the Hotel Van Dunk. 'Tis now nearly nine. At twelve we start per train for Cologne. We must have at least two hours for the examination of Rotterdam, and a report on the moral and material condition thereof, and not a minute must be unnecessarily lost. Go then, therefore, thou owner of the chest, order extensive breakfasts, into whose composition beef, hot coffee, and wine of Bordeaux shall enter largely."

"Yes; and see that the luggage is all right, and pay everything, you know," volunteered the slim gentleman.

"Strictly accounting to us for thy disbursements," the stout one added, by way of rider.

"And meanwhile we will sacrifice to the Graces," the slim gentleman concluded gracefully. "I feel terribly in need of a warm bath."

"And am I to have no time for washing?" the man with the iron chest asked piteously. Those unfeeling persons, his travelling companions, jocosely bade him scrape himself, rub himself against the iron chest till his flesh shone, make himself clean and tidy with his fore-paws, after the manner of a rabbit. The stout gentleman, fertile in nicknames, called him "Bunny" on the spot. But the end of it was, that they all had warm baths and clean shirts, and two of them well combed and brushed locks, when they sate down to breakfast in the long, low, barely furnished *salle à manger* of the hotel half an hour afterwards. Two of them, I say, were so neat as to hair; the man with the iron chest was popularly believed to comb his hair with a fork, and had ordinarily a rigid tress or *plumet* erect on his occiput like the scalp ornament of a Cariboo Indian.

The *salle à manger* was not inviting in appearance. Mercator appeared to have been drawing the rough designs of fresh charts on the table-cloth; and an indescribable smell of tobacco-smoke, dried fish, washing-day and cheese, lingered about the apartment. It was the genuine Dutch smell, the stout gentleman, on the strength of his one visit to Zealand, remarked. The windows, bare of curtains, looked into a damp garden, where were some rickety round tables and chairs, painted a faded emerald green, and in the centre a mildewed, broken-nosed cast of the far-darting Phœbus, on a cracked wooden pedestal, with some votive offerings in the shape of tobacco-pipes, shattered, lying among the weeds at his feet. At the dining-table in the *salle* a dark man in a brown great coat, with a high collar, sat smoking a cigar of evil odour, and reading the " Ammsterdammische " something. A few feet off, a shaky old lady, with a bonnet like an illused band-box, was spilling and slopping rather than drinking coffee over a copy of the " Rotterdammische " something else. At the bar at the end of the *salle*, among the coffee cups, liquor flasks, and tin pots, a very ill got-up waiter, pale and flabby, and with a white neckcloth so twisted and frayed that it seemed as though he had half succeeded in accomplishing suicide by suspension with it, but had repented in time, cut himself down, and taken to wearing it like a Christian cravat again, was listlessly chalking accusations of gulden and stuyver scores against the guests at the " Hotel Van Dunk." He, too, was smoking; and presently there entered to him a red-tufted man in a plaid jerkin (though of no possible Scottish clan pattern—it was more like a rainbow gridiron), who made no secret at all about his being the " boots " of the establishment, and dully brushed away at a lady's *brodequin*, as he talked to his fellows, and smoked. They all smoked the same rank pipes, or smouldering, leaf-peeling, dropsical cigars. And all the doors were open, and heavy-voiced men answered the frenzied ringing of bells with "*Er kommt, minheer*," from subterranean apartments, but did not come nevertheless.

Beefsteak for breakfast intolerably tough. The man with the iron chest (a connoisseur in butcher's meat) indignantly declared it not to be beef at all, but grilled gutta percha; the stout gentleman humourously dubbed it "lengthened hardness long drawn out," and suggested that it would make capital endless strap for a steam-engine. The slim gentleman was silent, but stuck his fork into the recalcitrant viand vindictively. Men knew that when that ominous expression was visible on the slim gentleman's philosophical countenance, he generally locked up his cheque-book for a fortnight, and showed you the key when you wanted twenty pounds to buy an "Encyclopædia Britannica." The travellers tried eggs, in whose shells Lapland witches had apparently been to sea for some months, addling the contents in a demoniacal manner. The bread was sour, and yet heavy; the butter was the genuine "Dutch Tub," yellow as a judge of Sudder Adawlut, and strong as a Calcutta Bheestie. There were dark grounds for complaint in the coffee; the so- called Bordeaux had an unmistakeable taste of a domestic cruet, generally flanked by the salad oil; and the sugar grated between the teeth like sand (which it very probably was), or a bad pun.

"As a general rule," the M. I. C. remarked, hewing at his steak till his nose shone like a fog-signal, "in all towns extensively engaged in the colonial trade, the groceries are detestable, even as in seaports you always get the worst fish. Take Bristol, take Glasgow, take Belfast, take Havre, take—"

"Take your Pinnock's 'Catechism of Geography'

away," cried the stout gentleman, rising from the
table, and flinging his napkin indignantly from him.
"The 'grub' (he was very idiomatic) is simply execrable. Come, children, let us take a walk about
Rotterdam, and then get out of Holland as fast as
ever we can. I should be starved to death here in a
week."

They knew very well how to charge, if not how to
cook, at the Hotel Van Dunk. The breakfast, and
some slight toilet conveniences, cost fifteen shillings
sterling. It was not the first hotel in Rotterdam : it
was second-rate in everything but price. Why, then,
did the travellers, possessing as they did among them
a large meed of experience in the ways of continental
hotels, patronise the Hotel Van Dunk? Why did
the slim gentleman say that he had selected the Hotel
Van Dunk, when he had in reality, and in the first
instance, fixed upon the Hotel Van Clam? For this
simple reason—that they all had watched disappear
within its ample portal the military papa, the Fawn,
her sister, the lady's maid, and the luggage of that
interesting party.

"The major seems a jolly fellow, and a perfect
gentleman, says the artful stout gentleman."

"We may breakfast with the Fawn," said the man
with the nose, whom the schnaps (which he denied
having consumed) had rendered sentimental.

"He has his eye on the lady's maid," cunningly
suggested the machiavelian slim gentleman. The Man
has solemnly assured me that he hadn't; that throughout his journey his devotion to Her (with a large H)
remained unaltered, and that "when Time hath be-
reft," I really forgot the immediate sequel; "the
thought should be madness," to some one whose name
has escaped me. But the three travellers, with their
several temperaments, were all destined equally to be
deceived. The major and his olive branches, indeed,
entered the hotel; but they didn't come down to

breakfast. They shut themselves up in the first-floor front, and appeared to require no sustenance beyond warm water, which was brought to them hot and hot in brass pails.

"*Of* course I knew it would turn out so," the M. I. C. exclaimed bitterly. "The shepherd in Virgil grew acquainted with Love, and found him a native of the rocks."

"A crib from Johnson to Chesterfield," whispered the stout to the slim.

"Wait for the wagon," continued the M. I. C.; "pass the flower of a lifetime in waiting for it, and it is ten to one that it will pass you with a disdainful creaking of its broad-tired wheels when you want to 'take a ride.'"

It was a fine day in Rotterdam, a hot day, a blue-skied, sunny, bird-singing day, and the travellers had two hours before them to inspect the curiosities of the "vulgar Venice." They very wisely, I think, came quite unprovided with guide-books or itineraries (save the slim gentleman's collection of time-tables and steam-boat fares, which he kept in his portmanteau, and studied in the silence of the night season, while his companions slumbered), and jocundly declined the services of a *valet de place*. They preferred that things should "turn up;" and a fresh foreign town is a paradise to a person of the Micawber creed. Something is sure to "turn up" at every half-dozen yards' distance. "To take a guide or a guide-book with you, when you are sound in intellect and limb," was the profound remark of the stout gentleman, "is not more absurd than would be the act of a professed pedestrian who should strap two wooden legs to his healthy knees." (Applause.)

I do not propose to follow these three modern wise men of Gotham, step by step, in their peregrinations : but I think I can give the best notion of their several opinions of Rotterdam, by extracts from papers which have come into my possession, in the form of special reports from those unauthorised special commissioners.

"Rotterdam on the Rhine, Maes (or Meuse), and about five hundred rivers besides, I should presume, from the leaky and streaky appearance of the ground plan:"—this I decipher from the notes of the stout gentleman, notes curiously intermingled with pencilled references to "stunning schnaps"—"pretty girl in blue and yellow hair"—"such a fool of a waiter"—"Dutch landlords all thieves"—and rough pictorial sketches, which have been eminently serviceable in the illustration of this narrative:—"Rotterdam is a very queer, quaint, out of the way, bustling, cheerful, cheesy old place. Clean as a new pin, and as handsomely ugly (you know what I mean) as a Skye terrier or a Chinese dragon. It has been called, from its multitude of canals and the boats thereupon, a 'vulgar Venice.' To me it is a sort of picturesque Wapping, mingled with Chester with the streets laid under water, augmented by any number of Liverpool warehouses painted in staring colours, and finished off with a dash of the willow-pattern plate. Pagodas, indeed; queerly shaped windmills; triangular bridges, with fat women and fatter children going over them; odd concentric patterns in glowing hues on window-blinds; junk-like boats with fan sails; porcelain tiles painted with blue devices; huge jars at house doors; abundant flower-pots; and ivory toys, fans, chessmen, dyed feathers, and brocaded silks in shop windows, abound. The wharves are cumbered with tea-chests, and pottery of the most remarkable shapes and hues. There is the oddest mixture of the Celestial" (or, more probably, of the Japanese element, my stout observer) "combined with the native cheese, red-herring, and clay-pipe characteristics of this broad-backed people. Everything is so clean *outside* the houses, that you might imagine the tiles on the roofs to be swept every day,

and the cats warned under heavy penalties to wipe
their feet on specially-provided roof-mats; the road-
way (where roads exist) to be hearthstoned as well as
the doorsteps, the boats on the canal beeswaxed (they
are oiled and frictionised), the mortar scraped and
pointed, the lamp-posts black-leaded, the green win-
dow-shutters fresh painted, the quays washed with
soap and water, the cranes and shears dusted with
feather brooms, the merchandise polished with a cha-
mois leather, the area-railings (the Dutch have area-
railings) rubbed up with whitening, and the sails of
the yawls and galliots fresh bleached, ironed, starched,
and mangled every half hour. I can understand now
that sermon of the Dutch pastor, who told his con-
gregation that heaven was a country very flat, and
with plenty of dykes, canals, windmills, cow pasturage, and summer-houses, and where there was nothing
but nice washing, and scouring, and rubbing, and
polishing, and dusting, for ever and ever. I should
like, after this sample of the cleanliness of Rotterdam, to see the clean village of Broek, where, it is
stated, there are polished brass spittoons at the street
corners for smokers, and the cows' tails are tied up
with blue ribbon. And yet, Rotterdam, from its vast
commercial traffic, is said to be the grubbiest town in
Holland. Of its inward *propreté* I am not qualified
to judge, from the shortness of my stay; I shall be
enabled to give more amplified particulars when we
pass through it on our way home ('Oh, yes! I dare
say,' was the observation of the slim gentleman, when
this report was read at a breakfast-party Wittenage-
mote some mornings afterwards; '*I* mean to return
by Calais'); but from the sample presented by the
salle à manger of the Hotel Van Dunk, I grieve to be
compelled to incline to the opinion that the Dutch
sepulchres are very considerably whitened. Moreover, there is the smell of fish, smoke, and cheese,
mingling perpetually (he was only two hours in Rot-

terdam) with the not ambrosial odour of the mud in
the canals. As to the Dutchmen, they are a sleek-
headed race, who incline to the wearing of caps, are
stolid in facial expression, slow in gait, look all like
first-cousins of Mynheer Van Dunk, Rip Van Winkel, and Peter Stuyvesant: and although I did not
remark as to any notable preponderance of nether
habiliments hanging outside the ready-made clothes'-
shops, or read the name of 'Ten Brock,' or ten pair
of trousers on any signs or door-plates, I could not
help noticing that substantial lumbar development on
the part of the population generally, which, apart
from their industry, ingenuity, and perseverance, may
have been another reason for drawing a simile between the Batavians and the beavers, who also con-
struct dykes and dams, are thrifty and provident, and
are great in caudal appendages. The younger Dutchmen attempt to grow moustaches, and fail lamentably
therein. They are not so unsuccessful in the cultiva-
tion, on their extensive cheeks, of whiskers of about
the size and hue of a cutlet from a leg of mutton, well
done. The Dutch-women are fat but comely, adipose
but affable. The younger girls have a decidedly 'buy
a broom' appearance, and in the display of gray and
striped stockings, offer legs 'open as day to melting
charity.' I cannot describe to you the odd beaten
gold head-plates of the Friesland girls, because I did
not see any during my stay in Rotterdam. The dogs
are fat and well to do, and look as though they had
funded paunch, and stores of skewers laid out on
good security. It being warm weather—although I
am sure a Dutch dog must be far too stupid to go
mad—muzzles were generally worn by these interesting animals; muzzles, some in the form of a par-
rot's cage, others of a strawberry pottle in wire,
others of a coal-scoop. I could not discern one symp-
tom of aberration of mind among them, were it not
haply in a bandy-legged cur that barked furiously at a

very elegant and picturesque *gorda españole* (the cox-comb!) which I wore suspended from my left shoulder —but the prevalence of muzzles gave one a delightful sensation of security respecting one's calves—a sensation for which one cannot be sufficiently thankful. As to the Dutch children, they are always one hundred years old on the day of their birth. They draw in philosophy with their pap, and deliver discourses on ethics in *plat Teutsch* and in their cradles. I am not aware that the babies in arms smoke pipes; but I know that the little boys of five and seven years old calmly discuss those calumets of peace as they proceed to school. Indeed, I believe that the privation of tobacco is one of the weightiest punishments in the Dutch juvenile penal code. These children are the gravest, quietest, most solemnly funny little people I ever saw. Not melancholy, not cowed, but simply serious, pre-occupied by thoughts of vast speculations in marbles; anxiously expectant of huge consignments of hardbake and toffy from the Dutch East Indies, and bent upon superhuman acquisitions of Dutch dolls. I made a hurried sketch of one of these Lilliputian sages, and as I vouch for the fidelity of the presentment, the reader will be enabled to admit that I have not exaggerated the sagacious sobriety of these small philosophers. I would gladly say more concerning Rotterdam, but the villanous odour of the herrings, the cheese, and the tobacco-smoke produced so appreciable an effect upon my duodenum, that I was compelled to resort, for purely medicinal purposes, to schnaps, which—" Here the stout gentleman's report abruptly breaks off, and after the last word a slight scorching of the manuscript is visible, as from the contact with the butt end of an ignited cigar, together with a curious circular blot of a hue somewhat darker than the paper, apparently produced by some foreign liquid.

" Rotterdam," writes the owner of the iron chest,

DUTCH BOY.

in his reckless manner, " may be regarded as one huge PIPE. The people smoke, the chimneys smoke; everywhere dense fumes are being emitted from tubes of all shapes and lengths. I can imagine on a wet day how the horses, the dogs, and the low banks of the canals must smoke too. I am, myself, accustomed to smoke the very best cigars obtainable for credit or money; and as good cigars are almost unobtainable abroad, I determined on my landing at Rotterdam to give up cigars for a season altogether, and addict myself to a mild course of meerschaum pipes. I entered a tobacconist's, in a narrow street behind the high church, and asked to look at a pipe. I never saw such a pipe-shop in my life. It seemed as though ten thousand Haarlem organs of tobacco pipes, rolled into one, had been stacked in the narrow *magasin*. They hung from the ceiling, clustered in the corners like the *fasces* of the Roman lictors, covered the counter, littered the

INTERIOR OF A DUTCH PIPE SHOP.

floor, cumbered every available inch of room, packed
in casks and cases. I was frightened at the pipes. I
asked, meekly, for a small piece of meerschaum; and
the squat proprietor (who spoke a little indifferent
French, interspersed with genuine Dutch) levelled,
one after another, the muzzles of alarming pipe-bowls
at my head. I chose one small-bowled pipe with an
ebony tube, for which the squat proprietor charged
me five francs. They take all descriptions of money
in this city of pipes, and I found things dear in Rotterdam. I was fortified by the assurance of the proprietor that the pipe would not exude essential oil,

and by his vociferated asseveration of '*er schtinkt nicht, er schtinkt nicht;*' but I found, before I was half way up the Rhine, that my genuine meerschaum perspired unpleasantly and smelt abominably. One or two other things more I have to say about Rotterdam; first, of the cleanliness, which I really believe in, and which is common, I know, to all Dutch towns. The retail trade in brooms, shovels, dustpans, and pails done in Rotterdam seems enormous. On my way to the pipe-shop I passed down one narrow street —almost a lane—where nearly every other shop was devoted to the sale of besoms. It was as though the outskirts of the village 'Much Birch,' in England had been suddenly denuded of their underwood, and the broomsticks were sufficient to mount a whole legion of witches on their way to the Sabbath on the Blocksburg. I think the small children of the shopkeepers in that narrow street must have slightly ticklish times of it when the demand for birch-brooms is slack. Next, as to the bridges. You know those uncomfortable little pontine arrangements in the Liverpool docks, which suddenly swing away from you as you are about to set foot on them to allow the huge Australian clippers and Yankee emigrant ships to pass, and keep you, sometimes, an hour and a half from your dinner, and staring savagely at unattainable banks of the basin opposite. They manage these things much better in Holland. Barges, and galliots with masts of considerable altitude, are passing up and down the multitudinous canals at every hour in the day, and the name of the bridges is legion. By a very simple and admirably-carried out arrangement, these vessels pass through with the smallest amount of inconvenience to the pedestrian public. The bridges are divided in the middle, and when a tall-masted vessel is at hand the two halves are hoisted by very unornate apparatus of ropes and pullies to a vertical position on either side of the canal. So soon as the vessel has passed, the

BRIDGE ACROSS A CANAL IN "VULGAR VENICE."

halves of the bridge are lowered again to their original position, join, and form a flat surface. A single policeman at either end suffices to work the machinery; but it is curious to see the business-like impatience with which the public at both extremities await the joining of the bridge. When the half, in its descent, is as steep as a *Montagne Russe*, there are already swarms of adventurous men and lads scrambling up it; nay, it is at an angle of a good many degrees when cabs and carts are seen to adventure upon its planks. To get over the bridges seems to be the only thing which the Rotterdammers deem worth being in a hurry for. Of the Dutch soldiers, I may say that they are very stout (not so stout as art thou, my friend) and very peaceable-looking, and that the subaltern officers are, for the most part, martyrs to an insane ambition to tighten their girths, so as to produce wasp-waists. As well might an elephant attempt to wear stays! And, lastly, people must not say that Rotterdam is at all like Venice, vulgar or genteel. It is no more like Venice than Venetian red is like Dutch pink. To institute, even in the hundredth degree, a comparison between this butter-firkin and cheese-rack, and to-bacco-bale-smelling city of fat canals, with their smug alders, and scrubby pollard willows, and demure poplar-edged banks and Venice, is an insult to the Queen of the Adriatic, the lovely, lamentable, delightful, decayed City of the Waters, marvellous in her misery, beautiful in that slow death, which Byron sang, and Joseph Turner drew."

The slim gentleman is supposed to have drawn up a very elaborate report on Rotterdam, which his companions conjecture to have been at once æsthetic, economic, and ethical. He positively refused, however, to allow any portions of it to become public, saying that he would see the stout gentleman and the M. I. C., his friends and fellow-travellers, barbecued before he would read, or allow it to be read. It is supposed, however, that the report contained some disquisitions pregnant with art-knowledge respecting the High Church—a very grim, Calvinistic edifice, of immense size, whitewashed within, having an open wooden roof, and speckled with dark tablets to the stern memory of departed Dutchmen, high church elders, admirals, burgomasters, men cast in a stronger mould than the peaceful traders of the present day; men who were strong in preachments, and counsel, and fighting; in the age when such Dutchmen as William of Orange and John de Witt were heard of, and when Van Tromp swept the seas (O shame for Albion!) with a broom at his mast-head. Vaunting Englishmen, when you brag of the Highlanders in the Louvre, and the Guards in the Champs Elysées, in 'fifteen, remember that Paul Jones has been in the Frith of Forth, and the Dutch in the Medway.

It is also believed that the slim gentleman had some very pertinent things to say regarding the museum of pictures at Rotterdam, which museum is situated in a squabby building of considerable magnitude, containing an excellent collection of Dutch pictures, though not—with the exception of a wonderful portrait of a yellow-haired woman, by Rembrandt—of the *very* highest class. There are some capital Dutch family and "conversation" pieces of the period of our Commonwealth and Restoration—large canvases full of full-lengths of grave, earnest-looking personages, and comely matrons in black velvet and gold chains, and rich-laced ruffs, looking, moreover, like gentlemen and ladies—a look very uncommon among the modern Dutch people. There are some pseudo-Italian pictures, too, which are as execrable as they are ludicrous; and some indifferent drawings by artists whom I will class under the generic name of "Van Duffer." All these things the slim gentleman was observed to gaze very intently upon; and, during the subsequent travels of the Three, he occasionally condescended to let fall some waifs and strays of criticism, implying that more than two boors, two mugs of beer, and an earthen pot were requisite to prove the authenticity of a Teniers or an Ostade ; that other artists than Gerhard Douw painted birchbrooms and birdcages, and that a white horse does not always make a Wouvermanns. It is thought that had the collection in its entirety pleased the slim gentleman, he would have communicated immediately with the Messrs. Van Nameless, the trustees, produced circular notes to a large amount, and bought the gallery of pictures, standing. As it was, he came away without purchasing anything more valuable than a catalogue, with voluminous foot-notes, in the purest Dutch.

At noon, after a circuitous journey along the canals and over the bridges in a roomy old fly, drawn by a pair of horses much resembling Suffolk "punches," save that they wore streaming manes and tails—a fly, on whose roof the iron chest continually bumped, to the great annoyance of the stout and slim gentlemen, and the secret contentment of the man belonging to the chest—the travellers arrived at the railway station, and, in sufficiently comfortable carriages, well lined and padded, but reeking with smoke, took train for Emerick, on the Prussian frontier. On they went, through the lowest of Low countries, by windmills without number, not all of them employed in grinding corn, but in pumping water from the marshy lands, and so constructed that they could be removed without difficulty from place to place, as the exigencies of drainage required. On they went, by canals that could not be counted, so numerous were they—some broad and deep, some mere narrow skeins of water; for here canals supply the place of hedges between fields. The slow snorting train showed them some of these "canalets," spanned by neatly-constructed bridges about three-quarters of a yard in length ; it bore them by droves of black and white cattle, soberly munching in the oozy lowlands ; by cohorts of soldiers, in their shirt-sleeves, peaceably engaged in haymaking ; by hayricks, with Chinese mandarin hat-looking cupolas, which could be raised or depressed at pleasure ; by fields full of mushrooms, as big as small shields ; by snug farmhouses, barns, and cottages, all very neat and cleanly, all with something English in their appearance, yet with a something else inexpressibly and quaintly Dutch. And so to Utrecht, close to the frontier—Utrecht, a sometime important place, famous for carpets, and velvets, and a certain Peace, about which kings, and diplomatists, and writers of heavy quartos made a notable fuss, and to bring about whose consummation very many thousand brave men (that English army, which " swore so terribly in Flanders," among the number) had died dreadful deaths in ensanguined battle-fields.

But previously, at a station called Wesel, there was an adventure. Our travellers had been remarking upon the paucity of English travellers with whom they had as yet met. They put the reason down, of course, to passports, forgetting that to reach Cologne through Holland is generally considered to be rather an out-of-the-way route. But when the train drew up at Wesel, a real English lady—Mrs. Materfamilias, indeed—with a real English nurse, and, I presume, a real English baby. became visible on the platform, brandishing one of the big paper tickets with which you are furnished on Continental railways, and anxiously desirous of admission into the train. The guard opened the door of each first-class carriage in succession, then of every second-class one, but there issued from every door, and every window, and every chink and cranny of the train, *such volumes of stifling tobacco smoke*, that poor Mrs. Materfamilias started back aghast, and with a suppressed scream. " What ! " she said to the nurse, " go in one of those dreadful

OH, NURSE! NURSE! HOW EVER ARE WE TO GET INTO ONE OF THOSE HORRID CARRIAGES, AND THE DEAR CHILD WITH SUCH A DREADFUL COUGH?

carriages, and the dear baby with such a cold. No, Mary, never!" And she wouldn't get into the train, and the train went on without her; and as all the trains in Holland are as smoky, the unfortunate Mrs. Materfamilias, her nurse, and baby, may be waiting on the platform of the Wesel station to this day.

At Emerick, the frontier, where the Prussian spiked helmet, and the Prussian black eagle, became severely manifest as a head-dress, and a bird that would not, under any political circumstances, stand nonsense, the travellers, to their great and pleasurable surprise, were *not* asked for their passports. They experienced some annoyance, however, from the almost perpetual presence of a Prussian " bogey," in the shape of a new railway guard, who, very different to the tranquil

GERMAN MONK.

Dutch official, had a fierce pair of moustaches, was
here, there, and everywhere, was continually blasting
a horn, and poking his head in at the carriage window, eaten up by a morbidly administrative desire to
look at the "*billiete*," or railway tickets. He came so
frequently, and was generally such a nuisance, that
the stout gentleman began to speculate as to which
fortress he should be confined in with hard labour for
life, if indeed he were not executed outright, for the
offence of throwing a Prussian guard from a train in
motion on to the rails.

At a place called Oberhausen, the travellers saw a
live monk, who did not look at all as though he were
in the habit of mortifying himself, morally or physi-
cally, and was walking up and down the platform with
a tall German, and a short German, one with a very
fluffy hat, and the other with a very "loud" cap, both
of whom were smoking prodigious pipes, and at whose
jokes the good monk was laughing most lustily. It
grew dark soon after this, and the travellers essayed
to sleep, in which task they succeeded, *tant bien que
mal*, with intervals of smoking and chatting, till, at
about 9.30 p.m., they reached the Prusso-Rhenane
suburb of Deutz—which to all intents and purposes
was to them COLOGNE.

Over the bridge of boats, then, in a cab, the lights
glancing in the RHINE. They had had a peep of that
river at Rotterdam, where it was the colour of pea-
soup: but here was the Rhine in the broad and noble
reality. The stout gentleman was so entranced with
the idea of being on the Rhine at last, that when they
were comfortably installed at the Kölnischer Hof, and
a succulent supper, washed down by some moderate
libations of Rhine wine, had been discussed, he, the
stout one, must needs take a walk on the bridge of
boats, and was gaily careering thereupon, a cigar in
his mouth, when he was suddenly pounced upon by
two diminutive Prussian sentries, who with horrid

gutturals and crossed bayonets impeded his progress. The stout gentleman at first thought he had committed some act of Prussian high treason, when the toll-keeper of the bridge came running up and demanded—explaining the demand with two uplifted fingers—the sum of two groschen. The stout gentleman had simply evaded the toll, and on his prompt payment the sentries removed their bayonets from his breast, and he went home to bed a wiser, though not by any means a sadder man.

CHAPTER III.

FROM COLOGNE BY THE STEAMER PRINZ VON PREUS-
SEN UP THE RHINE, TO THE FEDERAL CITY OF
MAYENCE.

I HAVE read in the biography of a late celebrated
wit, that it is impossible to achieve greatness in any
career without habitually rising, during some period
of life, at six o'clock in the morning. The celebrated
wit was not, I believe, the first in throwing out this
aphorism. King Solomon and Dr. Watts have been
eloquent on the evils of sluggardism; and in M.
Raspail's hygienic system (an excellent one, by the
honestest of men), early rising, together with cam-
phor, pickles, and ammonia, must be taken as essential. And have you never heard of the great sect
of " Palingenesists of universal instinct," whose head-
quarters are at Leipsic,* the three principal articles
in whose faith are " No alcohol, no hot water, and *No
beds* " ? It is exceedingly difficult, notwithstanding,
to make a habit of getting up at six a.m. Her Majesty the Queen does it, for the purpose of " walking
on the slopes," but then we are not all queens, and
few of us have any slopes to walk upon. Buy an
alarum, you may say, set it to six o'clock, and put it
underneath your pillow. Yes; that is feasible, and
easy enough; but then 'tis as easy to throw the
alarum out of window two days after its purchase, as
I have known an inveterate bed-presser do. Again:

* A fact. See Léozon-le-Duc.

tie a string to your great toe; affix a leaden plummet
to the other end, lower it through the window into
the street, and pay the policeman to tug it vigorously
at the appointed time. Yes, certainly; but such
things have been, as waking up in the midst of a
pleasant dream, and cutting the string in order to
return to the agreeable vision, which, by the way,
ordinarily terminates in a horrible nightmare. Another plan is to have an ingenious piece of mechanism
constructed, which, at the time you wish to rise, will
discharge a bucket of cold water over you, or pull the
trigger of a loaded pistol pointed at your left ear; but
then, what is easier than to break the mainspring of
the *mécanique*, and shake your fist at it, as you lie

TOLL DEMANDED OF THE STOUT GENTLEMAN.

comfortably in bed?　I really know but two infallible methods for accomplishing the six a.m. feat. The first is to procure—*quocunque modo*—the honestest procurable, but still to procure, say twelve months' imprisonment in one of Her Majesty's jails; you must get up then at six, you know, or the warders and the governor will know the reason why. The second method is to travel continually.　You will need no alarum, no plummet-weighted strings to your great toe, then.

The three pilgrims, bound for Frankfort-on-the-Maine, and thence for some part of the continent of Europe not yet decided upon, bore out, the morning after their arrival at Cologne, the truth of the assertion in the preceding paragraph but indifferently well.　The slim gentleman, indeed, was up and stirring by five o'clock, an hour at which all the three should have arisen; for the Rhine steamer, *Prinz von Preussen*, was to start for Mayence at a quarter past six; and it was to gain a little additional time that they had crossed the Bridge of Boats on the previous night, and slept, not at Deutz, but at Cologne itself, the steamer departing from the city-proper bank of the Rhine.　The slim gentleman — whose toilette was always so quickly yet so neatly accomplished, that his companions declared his suit of clothes to be made all in one piece, buttoning secretly down the side, like the " strip" dress of an equestrian at Astley's, packed with great swiftness—descended to the *salle à manger*, breakfasted in a philosophical manner, called for the bill, and forthwith proceeded to assume, for the first time, that character which, during the tour, so well became him, of the terror of German waiters.　No intricate currency dismayed this philosophic financier. No course of exchange, no "bilan" or "agio," no differential transmutations of thalers against florins or groschen against kreutzers turned him from his purpose.　He had a cunning scent.　He was the sleuth-hound of hotel bills; detected the overcharge—there are *always* overcharges in foreign hotel bills—in an instant, and with an unerring metallic pencil marked the deduction on the margin. It was useless to argue with the slim gentleman; useless to call the three kings of Cologne to witness that the items set down were *ganz recht*. The slim gentleman cared nothing for Gaspar, made light of Melchior, and laughed at the beard of Balthazar. He never threatened to write to the *Times*. He never menaced an appeal to the burgomaster. The metallic pencil pointed calmly and steadily, sure as the needle to the pole, to the excess in charge; and the glibbest of *ober kellners* were vanquished. A terrible man; and were I the defaulting vestry-clerk of St. Duffabox-Undercrump's parish, I would not like that slim gentleman to audit my accounts.

The man with the iron chest had risen too, about 5.30, but not for so practical a purpose. That unhappy person had been banished by his cruel companions to a most incommodious bedchamber, how many storeys high I cannot with certainty say, but it seemed eight or nine—a grim polygon of a place, *full of looking-glasses*, and with, opposite the bed, a dreadful engraving representing the late Napoleon Bonaparte, with a death-like face, a pair of spectral jack-boots, and a shadowy laurel wreath, stepping from a tomb amidst a blaze of sepulchral light, like a gnome from the "grave-trap" in a pantomime. The M. I. C. being naturally superstitious, the effect of seeing so many reflections of red-nosed men tossing in their bed-clothes in the moonlight, together with the Napoleonic apparition, may be better imagined than described. The description would not, perhaps, be so very difficult; but the *Prinz von Preussen* has her steam up already, and cannot wait. It was during this uncomfortable night, too, that the red-nosed man made the acquaintance of a Flea, which he strenuously declared to be the very same flea which had bitten

him in the very same hotel on passing through Cologne two years previously. He knew it, he said, by
a peculiar halt in its gait, owing to his having once
held it for the twentieth part of a second between
his finger and thumb; and it is a fact that the insect
in question boarded and lodged and drank his nightly
magnums of burgundy at the red-nosed man's expense
from that night to the evening they all embarked for
England three weeks afterwards, when it left him
without the slightest notice, and without settling its
by no means small account. The stout gentleman
then suggested, humorously, that the flea was afraid
of sea-sickness; the slim gentleman gave his opinion,
drily, that for that *pulex* there was no passport.
Be it as it may, the man with the iron chest, being
awakened by a chambermaid with sandy hair, dressed,
and should properly then have descended to the
ground floor. There was an impediment, however,
to his doing so in the shape of a remarkably pretty
German girl, with flaxen tresses, who was plaiting
the same at an open casement on the other side of
the narrow street. She was plump, she sang in pretty
German (the street was *very* narrow), her eyes were
blue, she had a dimple on her left cheek, and she had
not yet assumed her frock. The impressionable man
began to murmur something about "*quis multa gra-
cilis,*" and "*cui flavam religas comam,*" and "*simplex
munditiis,*" till, making several false quantities, and
recollecting that he was in Germany, not at Brundu-
sium, he broke forth into a rhapsody about the pretty
girl opposite. "Yes," he cried, "that is Gretchen,
otherwise Marguerite. She asks in plaintive song
whither are fled the days of her innocent youth,
before she knew of Love. Just now she has been
plucking a flower to pieces, murmuring ' he loves me,
loves me not, loves me, loves me not,' till nought but
the stalk and a stray petal remains. *But the last leaf
has told her that she is beloved.* See, she goes to a

quaint oaken casket, and takes forth a necklace. *He gave it to her.* See, she reads a letter. 'Tis from him. O! Doctor Faust, Doctor Faust, how can you have the heart to deceive this simple, trusting, loving creature? Pause, ere it be too late. Bid that infernal counsellor, with the red cock's feather in his cap, and the mocking leer—bid him get behind thee! for he is Satan. Pause, ere the gallant soldier brother be slain—for *thy* sake, Gretchen, beneath thy casement. Pause, ere comes the terrible scene in the dungeon, the awful meeting on the Blocksburg, when thy lover shall see a fair young form, a waxen little baby corse, a thin red line round the neck of his beloved—*thy* neck, O Gretchen—and made by the headsman's axe. Pause, for—" And how long the man with the iron chest might have continued his rhapsody I know not; but at this moment his companions on the floors below addressed him in loud tones, and by the injurious epithets of "sleepy head," and "timber-eyelids," telling him that if he staid much longer he would miss the steamboat.

The stout gentleman *says* that he was "up with the lark." I have no reason to doubt his veracity; but it is certain that, had the chambermaid who aroused him known anything of acoustics, the gurglings, and moanings, and other manifestations, which found their way through the panelling of the door, would not have been barren in indices to prove that our stout friend was then in a horizontal position; and it is certain that the lark had been up a good hour and a half by that time. Perhaps, after all, the stout gentleman did really rise with the delightful little feathered songster, whom Miss Louisa Pyne so accurately imitates in "Rode's variations," and other elaborate twitterings; but then he must surely have gone to bed again immediately afterwards. It was a quarter to six ere the stout gentleman was in a position to commence that grand matutinal duty—shaving. Very rich and rare, and abundant and curious, was the stout one's "shaving tackle." He had a case of razors damascened as to their backs with all the days of the week: only he always shaved on Saturdays with the Tuesday's razor. He had magic strops and Syrian strops; and some peculiar shaving paste with a long Greek name of indifferently grammatical derivation, the which was contained in an oblong crystal sarcophagus, and one small pellet of which, being placed on the chin, moistened, and gently rubbed, speedily produced a rich, creamy lather, as thick and as white as the paint on the face of Mr. Clown. Our friend's expressive countenance was in this pantomimic state, when the door of his apartment was opened, and the idiotic *hausknecht*, or boots, of the Kölnischer Hof burst into the room, ejaculating "*Zu spät, zu spät!*" ("Too late, too late!") and drivelling fearfully.

I say *the* idiotic *hausknecht*, because in German hotels imbecility with the "boots" is the rule and intellect the exception. The landlords seem to take fools from their youth upwards, and breed them to the shoe-cleaning, clothes-brushing, wood-carrying, and trunk-cording business. This one was a tremendous fool, with a shock head of hair like the Dougal Creature, and a terrible grin, so wide and so vacant that, seeing him grin, you always looked round in quest of where the horse-collar might be. The stout gentleman was not at all discomposed at his advent, and was proceeding to make those preparatory feints at himself with his razor, which a right-minded and experienced shaver always tries his hand at before he ventures his blade among the bristles, till the reiterated *zu späts* of the idiotic *hausknecht* caused him to turn round and gently remonstrate with him, in the nearest approach to that functionary's native language which he could command. For the stout gentleman was inoculated with a fixed idea that German was nothing but London slang, spoken with a strong Welsh accent. How far his theory might have been borne out by the boots understanding him is uncertain; for the slim gentleman hurried into the room at this juncture entreating him to make haste.

"Do wash all that stuff off your face," he cried impatiently. "The bill's paid. My luggage is already loaded on the truck. The boat is nearly ready to start. We've a good hundred yards to walk. Walk! we shall have to run them."

"But I haven't shaved," remonstrated the stout gentleman.

"You can shave at Mayence—anywhere."

"But there may be ladies on board the boat," the stout one—always gallant he—objected.

"And we may lose the boat itself, altogether," retorted the slim gentleman, pettishly. "Now do finish dressing—there's a good fellow. Boots, take that portmanteau"—the energetic slim one had swept all the elaborate shaving-tackle into his friend's valise, closed the lid and buckled the straps—"there, that'll do. Dear me! dear me, where is that man with his confounded iron chest?"

It was at this moment that the words of opprobrium, "sleepy head," "timber eyelids," were addressed to the traveller in the regions above. In obedience to the uncourteous summons, he descended a few flights of stairs; but pausing upon a landing higher than his companions, said solemnly—

"It's my belief that this house is haunted."

"Come down!" cried the slim gentleman, impatiently.

"It is well known," the M. I. C. continued, "that in the Schloss or palace of Berlin, the appearance of the '*Weisse Frau*,'—the 'white lady,'—always portends a death in the Royal family of Prussia. When old King Frederick the First——"

"If you don't come down," the stout gentleman

shouted out savagely, "upon my word I'll open my portmanteau again and throw a boot-jack at you."

At this unkind remonstrance, the red-nosed man descended to the court-yard, muttering that he wasn't used to it, and that he had a good mind to part company at once, and make for Bucharest, by the way of Paris, Genoa, and Baden-Baden. It is not easy to see how the stout gentleman's threat could have been carried out, for the idiotic *hausknecht* had spirited away his portmanteau some minutes before. Nor, probably, will it ever be exactly known how the famous iron chest was brought from the garret to the basement; but when the travellers descended, they found that coffer of mystery forming the apex of a pyramid in a truck-full of luggage, with which the idiotic *hausknecht* at once set off running at the top of his speed, giving vent to shrill yet inarticulate cries as he run. At the corner of the street he was observed to stoop his head forward and taste the iron chest, which looked more metallic than ever, with his tongue. Could he fancy that there was anything good to eat inside?

"It must be so," the stout gentleman ejaculated, thoughtfully. "He must have murdered a blackamoor on the coast of Guinea, in the year 1834, and the bones are inside that chest."

It was a very foggy morning. Only one of the travellers, cunning man, had breakfasted. He distributed, indeed, some diminutive breakfast-rolls to his brethren, the which they devoured as they proceeded. It became very soon necessary for their pace to be quickened to a run, for a bell began to ring through the fog with a most discordant clanging, and the idiotic *hausknecht*, looming suddenly in the mist—they had thought him fifty yards distant—warned them with a supplementary yell of "*Zu spät!*"

They were going to throw boot-jacks at him—were they? He was a sleepy-headed, a timber-eyelided man—was he? He had murdered a man, and had hidden the bones of his sable victim in an iron chest— had he? But there was such a thing as NEMESIS, even at Cologne, in Rhenish Prussia, as his obese traducer very soon discovered to his cost. For the unwonted spectacle of three decently-attired individuals, bounding like the wild roe, and waking up the stony echoes of a badly-paved street at six o'clock on a foggy morning, had roused, not the dogs of war, but the dogs of Cologne. Cohorts of those animals started up, from kennels, and back yards, and dubious holes and corners. Savage, ill-conditioned, ragged-eared, gaping-mouthed curs, of no breeding at all, multiplied and magnified by the mist, made their appearance. The slim gentleman soon left them far in the rear; they appeared to disdain the red-nosed man; but they fixed upon the stout gentleman as their special prey. He was their quarry: he was vert and venison to them. They barked at him, they yelped at him, they leaped up at him; they hung upon his skirts; they harassed *him* in the Rear, ha! ha! The man with the iron chest was a Christian, a philanthropist, a benefactor to his species; but he could not help inciting one particularly mangy tyke to the chase, with the encomium "Good dog!" and the slim gentleman afterwards declared—though his statement must be taken with a reservation—that on nearing the steamboat-pier, the red-nosed man, addressing a dissipated mongrel, whose father seemed to have been a turnspit come to grief, and whose mother a poodle in reduced circumstances, uttered these exasperating words,—" *Grrrrrr—at him —wugh!*"

On board the *Prinz von Preussen* at last. Tickets purchased at a little hutch, like the money-taker's box at a theatre; the slim gentleman, with a shrewdness worthy of Escobar, purchasing second instead of first-class tickets. "There is'nt, properly, any first-class at all," he whispered; "only if they can they will

THE STOUT GENTLEMAN PURSUED BY THE CUBS OF COLOGNE.

make you pay for the 'pavillon,' which is a mythical and impalpable part of the boat. Terrible cheats on the Rhine!"

"As King James the First remarked," the M. I. C. added, affably, "when he first saw the judges, the lawyers, the jury, and the suitors in Westminster Hall, they are 'a' rogues, a' rogues.' That is what you mean, I presume."

"Never mind King James the First," retorted the stout gentleman, with unwonted sternness, for his temper was ruffled by his late canine controversy, ' but see to the luggage. That unlucky chest of yours will be charged a ton extra of course, as usual; and do tell somebody I want some breakfast—there's a good fellow."

The deck of the *Prinz von Preussen* did no more resemble the deck of a pleasure steamer than did the weather a time when tourists might reasonably enjoy

THE CAPTAIN OF THE PRINZ VON PREUSSEN.

the pleasure of "going up the Rhine." It was en-
cumbered with merchandise, crates of pottery, baskets
of poultry, and furniture, even to chairs and bedsteads
corded together. Was it quarter-day at Cologne?
and had any tenants of the City of Agrippa and the
town of St. Engelbert "shot the moon" with the intention of levanting up the Rhine to Bonn or Andernach? The stout gentleman at once pronounced
against the fitness of Germans for any species of navigation. "The sailors wear red jackets," he said, pointing conclusively to some fresh-water mariners who
looked like distressed general-postmen who had taken
to holding horses and brushing coats in St. James's-
street, and had emigrated to Rhineland at the close of
the London season. "What can you expect of sailors
in red jackets? You might as well have mariners in
all-round collars. I dare say the man at the wheel
hasn't the least objection to be spoken to. See, he is

smoking a meerschaum. What discipline can you expect in a service where you can speak to the man at the wheel? I'll be bound that the captain wears top-boots."

The commander of the *Prinz von Preussen* was not exactly shod in the manner conjectured by the stout gentleman; but he was nevertheless a most wonderful master mariner to look upon. His costume was of such a hybrid nature, and would take so long to describe, that I think my best course will be to refer the reader to the sketch—somewhat of a fancy sketch, it is true—made of him by the stout gentleman while the man with the iron chest was busy witnessing the affixing of long wooden labels, like bakers' tallies, to the travellers' luggage. On his return to his companions he was complimented on his proficiency in the German language; the stout gentleman adding that he saw it all now; and that in addition to the cockney and the Welsh accent, it was necessary, in order to become an accomplished Teutonic linguist, to introduce a few of the "yach! yach's!" so distinctive of the elocution of the Christy's Minstrels.

Meanwhile, a very damp-looking steward had brought the travellers three cups of exceedingly black coffee; and these, with perhaps a suspicion of cognac, which is very bad and very dear (on the Rhine), and an assortment of the never-failing *butterbrods*, which the stout gentleman characterized as sandwiches which had lost their heads—the top layer of bread being wanting—a sufficiently succulent breakfast was furnished forth. This repast was spread on a damp table on deck, aft, and close to the wheel, the man "at" which was behaving in a most unconstitutional manner, smoking, as has been before observed, exchanging lively *badinage* with any passing mariners, and even grunting forth stanzas of *trink lieder*.

"If I had you on board the gallant *Thunderbomb*, my friend," the stout gentleman, with affected severity, observed, "the gratings should be rigged, and nine dozen your reward, or my name is not Admiral Lord Nelson, K.C.B." "*Herz mein herz warum so traurig!*" (the steersman had commenced that sentimental ditty). "Oh, very well, perhaps you'll oblige me with a light. What on earth are you reading there?"

The last part of this neat speech was addressed, not to the man at the wheel, but to the slim gentleman, who from his note-book was murmuring to himself some recapitulation of memoranda.

"I am simply reading," that slim personage answered, "the list of the fluids you consumed yesterday, from the time we entered the Mäes to the time we went to bed at Cologne, and it is really astonishing to me how any frame could have supported so enormous a liquid consumption."

"Enormous!" cried the stout gentleman, indignantly; "I defy thee. Why, I only took a glass of iced water and a nip of cherry brandy the whole day. Is it not well known that, whatever may be the name on my passport, I am in reality Mr. Pope, of the United Kingdom Alliance, travelling *incognito?*"

"Then I'm John B. Gough," the man with the iron chest remarked, incredulously.

"Say, rather, the 'Frightful example' to illustrate a teetotal oration," added the slim gentleman, with a quiet smile, and pointing to the man's red nose. "But, see! here is the list. That at least is incontrovertible."

"Read, read!" cried the M. I. C., anxious to divert the conversation from his much-defamed nose.

"Ay, read!" said the stout gentleman, defiantly planting his broad back against a bulwark, and vainly endeavouring to discern the left bank of the Rhine through the fog.

"The list shall be read," acquiesced the slim one, clearing his throat with a preparatory "hem." We have here, then—

"IMBIBED BY THE STOUT GENTLEMAN."

"Item : Soda and brandy .... Off the Boompjees.
Item : Four cups of tea .... In the Maes.
Item : One glass Schiedam .... Quay, Rotterdam.
Item : One glass schnaps (to correct the same) .... } Quay, Rotterdam.
Item : Half bottle *pseudo* Bordeaux . Hotel, Rotterdam.
Item : One pint Rotterdam beer...... }
Item : One ditto ditto................. } Rotterdam generally.
Item : Bock bier .... Station, Emerick.
Item : One tankard Baërische bier... Station, Wesel.
Item : One glass cognac and water... Station, Utrecht.
Item : One bottle *pseudo* Edinburgh ale ....
Item : One glass 'Mai-trank' ....
Item : One ditto 'peach tea' .... } At divers stations between Utrecht and Cologne.
Item : One bottle seltzer water ......
Item : One half bottle Geisenheimer
Item : One ditto ditto Assmanshauser .... } At supper, Kölnischer Hof, Cologne.
Item : One *petit verre* cognac.........
Item : One half bottle of Bordeaux.. { As a whet to final pipe before bed-time."

"And he did not burst," the slim gentleman concluded, shutting up his note-book.

VIEW OF THE RHINE AT SIX A.M.

"It is a wonderful catalogue," the red-nosed man said, pensively. "It is Rabelaisian—it is Homeric—it is Garagantuan. It reminds one of the banquet of the three giants, Goulu, Goinfr, and Gouliaf, in the 'Romaunt Roti.' It is wonderful."

"It is the day's consumption of an honest man," the stout gentleman sternly replied. "I am no threadpaper (he glanced disdainfully at the slim gentleman)—no hypocrite of temperance, with a nose that blushes at my own duplicity (the M. I. C. hid his abashed head). Do you want me to die, like John Jones the teetotaller, whose inside, on the P. M., or post-mortem examination, was found to be full of tea-leaves and snow-balls? If nature makes large and stout and handsome men, are they not to be fed? Will an elephant live on a penny loaf and a ha'porth of milk per diem?"

"But you're not an elephant!" objected the slim gentleman.

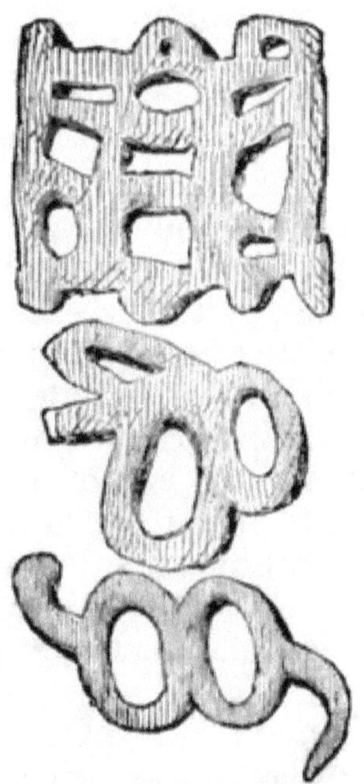

GERMAN FANCY BREAD.

"And you're not handsome," the red-nosed man—
an envious carle—was beginning.

"Silence!" interrupted the stout gentleman. "Go
and make sketches of the surrounding scenery. It's
too foggy, is it? Well, that's your fault. Silence!
—and silence too, that dreadful bell!"

It was decidedly the worst bell that was ever set
ringing. It must have had a hopeless crack in it, like
the Kolokol in the Kremlin, at Moscow; but it had
been clanging dolefully at very short intervals ever
since the *Prinz von Preussen* had left Cologne. The
fog was of a thick, lathery description; so much so,
that the stout gentleman declared that old Father
Rhine was preparing to divest himself of a beard of
some centuries' growth, and was getting his shaving-
water ready.

It was nine o'clock a.m., ere the fog, which is a sufficiently constant visitor on the banks of the Rhine to
induce the belief, without any great stretch of imagination, that one is travelling in the Essex marshes,
cleared off, and revealed the city of Bonn. The stout
gentleman, to whom the fog, or the dog-chase he had
undergone at Cologne, or more probably a vigorous
constitution, had given a tremendous appetite, had, disgusted with coffee and sandwiches, betaken himself to
the consumption of Rudesheimer and bread-and-butter.
He was much struck by the eccentric configuration of
the small, thin, twisted loaves of bread, and comparing
them to handcuffs in fits, doughy cat's cradles, and
the arms of Westminster bent nine-bauble square,
made a sketch of the contents of his plate on the spot.
Nobody paid much attention, however, to the man
with the nose, when he remarked that the fancy bread
sold in Russia was shaped in a similar manner; the
slim gentleman put him down by pointing out that
the identity in conformation was probably due to most
of the bakers in Russia being Germans. A travelled
man, and a wary, the slim gentleman. And so they
came to Bonn.

Which, as everybody knows, is on the Rhine, and boasts an university where the students wear spectacles and jackboots, and fight duels with broadswords, and where his Royal Highness Prince Albert completed the study of his Humanities. The stout gentleman began to murmur a stanzo from Carlo's song in the " Rovers "—

> " Sun, moon, and stars, and world, adieu!
>   That kings and priests are plotting in—
> Oh! never shall I see the U—
>   Niversity of Gottingen."

" I think you are misquoting Canning's lines," observed the red-nosed man, mildly.

" The stanza was contributed by Pitt," the slim gentleman remarked, *sotto voce*.

" And I cannot," the M. I. C. continued, " see the connection between the universities of Bonn and Gottingen, save insomuch that another Royal Highness was educated there; the late Duke of Kent, to whom his royal papa, King George III., allowed the munificent sum of two guineas a week as pocket money. They are more liberal to young princes now-a-days. Heigho! I would that I were a midshipman on board the *Euryalus*."

When the genius of the Rhine suddenly took it into his head to favour the three travellers with a glorious glow of sunshine; when the rapid current turned ceruleau blue; and to leap, and dance, and sparkle in the golden flakes that fell upon it from heaven; when the terraces upon terraces of loaded vines began to show their green and purple splendour on the river's banks—banks that speedily became hills, hills that swelled into steep eminences, eminences that culminated at last into mountains crowned with gray old ruins: the famous MOUNTAINS OF THE RHINE.

As a rule, every castle on the Rhine ought to be at least a thousand years old, with, if possible, a legend and a ghost. If a terrible murder has been committed

there in the middle ages, so much the better. Imbued
with this picturesque creed, it was with deep mortifi-
cation that the travellers' eyes were seared, between
Bonn and the Seven Mountains, by the view of a long
range of white buildings, too evidently brick, stuccoed,
pierced with level ranges of distressingly mathemati-
cally exact windows, and in whose rear two huge and
lofty chimneys, of the received Manchester or Wolver-
hampton pattern, emitted volumes of dense and sooty
smoke.

"A mosque of commerce with minarets of smoke,"
murmured the stout gentleman, discontentedly.

"It's a soap-boiling establishment," said the slim
gentleman, conclusively.

"It's New-castle upon Rhine," the man with the
iron chest exclaimed, thinking he had said something
witty, and looking round for approval. But nobody
laughed; and when he tried to explain by a reference
to Newcastle-upon-Tyne, looks as much in sorrow as
of anger were directed towards him. That unhappy

VIEW OF NEW-CASTLE ON RHINE.

man with the iron chest! he was always putting his foot in it.

Now my dear friends and readers it is fast approaching mid-day, and I put it to your kindness of heart, and your common sense, whether it be necessary for me to describe, step for step, or knot for knot in water measurement, the progress of our three travellers up the Rhine. Goodness gracious! how many hundreds of times that day's journey, from Cologne to Mayence, has been described. Hasn't Tom Hood described it, facetiously! Hasn't Leitch Ritchie topographed it in the most picturesque " landscape-annual " sort of fashion! Haven't Mr. Henry Mayhew's facile pen and Mr. Birket Foster's fairy pencil, brought the Rhine and its beauties, its drolleries, and its legends, home to every recipient of a handsomely-bound gift-book! Have we not " The Rhine," by Victor Hugo! solemn, fantastic, mystical, graphic, and grandiose. We have even had Rhine tours *ex manibus parvulorum;* and Mr. Mark Lemon has thrown his little bag of ballast into this already overladen Rhine-boat. I don't say but that I could —from the notes of the stout, the slim, and the red-nosed ones—give you a sufficiently minute and amusing description of the banks of the Rhine from Düsseldorf to Strasburg, the legend of each particular castle, and the wine-bearing capacity of each vineyard; but I refrain. My space is limited. I am somewhat in a hurry to get my travellers to Mayence; and to tell the truth, I am rather jealous of my secondary position in this narrative. I don't see why these three travelling gents, ordinary people from Fleet Street, taking a three weeks' continental scamper, should have all the talking to themselves. What do *they* know about the Rhine? I won't publish their experiences *in extenso;* for I intend myself to write, some day, a history of *my* impressions on the Rhine; how I went up it and down it, and once very nearly into it. Then shall you read how Cæsar crossed the Rhine and did fierce battle with the half-savage Celts who inhabited its banks; how the Twenty-second Legion, returning from the siege of Jerusalem, was sent by Titus to the Rhine, to continue the work of Martius Agrippa; how Julian the Apostate (a very ill-used man that Julian, as ill-used as Richard III., Robespierre, and Judge Jeffreys) built a fortress at the confluence of the Rhine and the Moselle; how, when Charlemagne cleared away the rubbish of ruined Rome, he laid the foundations of feudalism on the Rhine; how legends strange and weird took root here, grew and blossomed in the voids and crevices of history; how the thickets on the mountain sides were crossed by black hunters mounted upon stags with six pairs of antlers each, and yellow-haired maidens danced and shrieked in sable fens, and red-eyed gnomes dug gold and jewels from the rocky bowels of the mountains, and Wodan, the god with ten hands, vanquished the ten black men of Rigomagum. The strange and wondrous story shall be told you (some of these days) of how the Spirit of Evil rampantly ran riot on the Rhine banks, placing his stone at Teufelstein, and his ladder at Teufel-sleiter, and having the effrontery publicly to preach his infernal Evangel at Gernsbach, near the Black Forest; and of how Urian the demon crossed the river at Düsseldorf, having on his back a huge rock brought from the sea, with which he intended to destroy Aix-la-Chapelle, only being frightened by an old woman, he dropped it in the environs of the Imperial City. It remains there to this day, under the name of the "Lousberg," and on its summit is a summer-house, where I have eaten *schinken* and quaffed Marcobrunner with a Dutchman and a beautiful Jewess, who had eyes like black-currant jelly. Glorious old Rhine, thy hills and valleys are replete with legends, though we behold them but through a penumbra. Like Prospero's isle, thy vine-clad banks and donjon crested precipices are "full of noises;" but they are not of wholesome sound—rather songs of ruinous melody, sung by songstresses whose smiles are perdition; rather bursts of demoniac laughter, issuing from caverns tenanted by bats and dragons.

The Rhine! the Rhine! there are churches, and abbeys, and convents, and quaint timorous little villages, nestling under the lee of the gaunt and grim old castles. Dreadful times those villagers must have had in the days of the fierce old mediæval barons, and Herzogs, and Kurfursts, and Landgrafs, and Margrafs, and Teutsch Ritters. Imagine some ruthless *moyen age* Baron von Abershawstein, sending his steward down every morning to the village with a demand for a hogshead of new milk, nine dozen of fresh eggs, a kilderkin of honey, free from comb, and a marriageable young lady! Imagine the "Rent Day" at the Schloss von Abershawstein! No realization of Wilkie's picture, that. No smug butler drawing corks for thirsty tenants; no substantial breakfast laid for the farmers of many acres; no reduction of ten per cent. on the last quarter. Nothing of the kind. Payment on the nail, or the Baron von Abershawstein would know the reason why. "Pay me; or if you don't—" and the not doing involved a visit to the torture-chamber of the castle. "Rack me the tenant's bones," cried the Baron von Abershawstein; "draw me each of his double teeth; cut collops off Farmer Hodges's cheeks, and grill them for his breakfast; throw Giles Scroggins into the pit among the rats; half-hang Roger Dapple; split Reuben Mayleigh's nose; nail Gaffer Gosling's ear to the castle pump; pour melted lead down Gregory Hobnail's throat—he's three quarters behindhand, is he? the rascal! I'll warm him. *Teufel und wetter! Donner und blitzen. Shelm!"*

The wicked old barons of the Rhine have disappeared; so have their fair-haired, blue-eyed, meek-spirited wives, who sometimes became saints, like Elizabeth of Hungary, irreverently described by Mr. Carlyle as "a very pious but fanciful young woman," leading her husband Conrad, who lived in the romantic old hill castle of Wartburg, "such a life," that he was obliged to go to the crusades in self-defence, "lodging beggars, sometimes, in his very bed, continually breaking his night's rest for prayer and devotional exercises of undue length; weeping one moment, then smiling for joy the next; meandering about, capricious, melodious, weak, at the will of devout whim, mainly." Though the historian of Frederick the Great has evidently little respect for hagiology, I don't think myself that I should like to be married to a saint. Sometimes the fair-haired and blue-eyed wives of the wicked barons did *not* enter for the Sanctity Stakes, but went wrong altogether, with squires and seneschals, and there were terrible to-do's (Legend of St. Gengulphus, *passim*) when the husbands came from the Holy Land, disguised with scrip and scallop-shell, like pilgrims. But they are all gone now. Barons and baronesses, squires and seneschals, Conrads, Hermanns, Ottocars, Albrechts, Ottos, Rudolfs, Waldemars, Brunchildas, Hildegardes, Dorotheas, Gelas, Margarets "Maultasche" (of the "pouch mouth"), Ritas, and Luises. Their castles are eyeless and toothless, mere ruined bankrupt heaps of jagged stones and skeleton anatomy. Time and the thirty years' war—time and the seven years' war —time and the bombardments of the French Jacobin armies—time and the cannon of Napoleon, have riddled those antiquated *schlossen* like sieves. The few that are weatherworthy and habitable are converted into houses of correction. The very convents have subsided into boarding-schools and orphan asylums. Only the churches and the legends remain.

Flow on, then, thou shining river—a fluvial interpellation originated elsewhere, I believe—flow on, past Bonn and the Seven Mountains, with Drachenfels and Rolandseck, with which the storied magnificence and romantic beauties of the Rhine properly commence. Past Andernach, with the little white village of Leutersdorf, and the grand four-steepled church, where the Emperor Valentinian and a child of Frederick Barbarossa—imperial Rome and imperial Germania —lie buried. The republican General Hoche, also, is interred beneath a plain stone in the cemetery of Andernach; and from the top of the hills the eye embraces an immense circle, extending from Siebengebirge (the Seven Mountains) to the castellated heights of Ehrenbreitstein. There are more churches in Andernach. That of the four steeples is Byzantine in architecture; and another, a Gothic one, is converted into a stable for Prussian cavalry. The tourist may see the inscription " *Sancta Maria, ora pro nobis,*" where properly should be written " Horses taken in to bait." Flow on, past the frowning Ehrenbreitstein and Coblentz, fair and smiling city; past Stolzenfels and Marksburg, with its chamber of torture, its secret passages, and dungeons scooped out of the solid rock. Flow on, past the " Mouse," and the sequestered village of Velmich, and the enormous turret of Falkenstein, beneath which is a pit, descending far below the level of the Rhine; and below that, according to the traditions of the peasantry, a volcano, from which at night, and from the summit of the round tower, leap ever-living flames. Into this pit the sacrilegious Seigneur of Falkenstein cast the Prior of Velmich, habited as he was in his sacerdotal vestments, with the great silver bell about his neck given by Winifred, Bishop of Mayence, in the eighth century. Huge stones were cast upon him, and the prior was seen no more on earth; but when Falkenstein's bitter hour was come, the silver bell made its voice heard, and knelled and knelled while he howled his wicked life away.   And year by year, on every anniversary of the lord of Falkenstein's death, the fatal silver bell continues to ring.

"Dear me!" said the stout gentleman, "I wonder at what time of the year he died. I hope it isn't going to ring now. I am sure it would spoil my appetite.

Flow on, then, past the abode erst of Kuno von Falkenstein; past the monticules to which appertain the legend of the gnome and the Canon of Sayn, and of the three little old women who gathered the bunch of thistles on the giant's tomb. Flow on, past the huge, dismantled donjon keep of the "Cat," between which and the "Mouse" lies the little town of St. Goarhausen.

"This is more like Switzerland than the Rhineland," the man with the iron chest ventured to remark, looking at the sombre and precipitous embankments of the river, and the vast crags that purpled the distance.

"It is considered much to resemble the Lake of Jura," the slim gentleman replied, sententiously.

Now, of course, you know that at St. Goar occurs the far-famed gulf of the Rhine, called the "Bank;" between the Bank and the square turret of St. Goarhausen there is only a narrow passage, the gulf being on one side, and the rocks on the other; and a little beyond, in a wild and savage sinuosity, is the mysterious rock of Lurlei, or Loreley, with its thousand granite seats, which, like a falling ladder, descend into the Rhine. The legend of the Lurlei will not bear repeating. Everybody has heard of the young lady, with voice as sweet, and execution as perfect, as Madame Bosio, who entrapped ardent young boatmen to the Lurlei's fatal *parages*, and lured them to their destruction, and whose mocking *fioriture* and derisive *roulades*, exultant over her victims, the peasants declare they oft hear now on summer evenings. My son, you should avoid all young ladies with flowing hair and gauzy attire, who indulge in florid vocalization on rugged rocks; else shall you split upon the Lurlei, and your bark be quite wrecked; yea, even upon the rocks of Portugal-street—and Maher-shalal-hashbaz, and Rabshakeh, and other Israelites of the sixtypercenturions, shall devour you utterly. The Lurlei is now a commercial speculation. It is an echo of great renown. Until recently, an old French hussar lived at Goarhausen, who would wake the echo with a bugle or a horse-pistol as many times as you liked for a few groschen. They usually fire a musket on board the steamer on passing St. Goar; and I think the passengers consider the echo as included in the fare, and would complain bitterly if they were deprived of it.

Now past Oberwesel and Gutenfels and the Pflatz, an old castle rising out of the middle of the river, from whence Lewis of Bavaria used to levy black mail on all travellers along the highway of the Rhine. Past Bacharach, Lorch, and Bingen; and now a golden sunset is succeeded by a mysterious *crepuscule*, and men begin to talk of Biberich or Biebrich, and of arriving at Mayence at ten p.m. But, first, there is Mausethurm, "the Rat," the dreaded Hatto's tower. His two companions shuddered when (from "Murray's Guide") the slim gentleman murmured the legend of the freebooting monopolist of cereals, who was devoured by the rats his own granary had fed.

"I don't believe a word about Hatto and the rats," broke in the M. I. C. "The place is called 'Mausethurm.' Now this may be derived from *maus*, or *mauth*, which signifies custom-house; and in the tenth century, before the bed of the river was enlarged, the Rhine had only one passage, and the authorities of Bingen levied toll upon all vessels that passed. Depend upon it, the tower was a *douane*, and Hatto was a custom-house officer, the rats of whose own conscience, disturbed by a long course of peculation, gnawed him to pieces."

"In the first place," retorted the slim gentleman, "custom-house officers have no consciences; and, in the next, any old woman will tell you that mausethurm is derived from *maus*, or *mus*—a rat. Your custom-house is a rat tower, and your toll-keeper a blood-stained phantom."

The stout gentleman did not join the discussion. He walked aft, and whistled, and shortly afterwards was heard to order cognac and hot water.

I think I cannot better conclude this narrative of a day passed on the Rhine, than by giving short extracts from the several reports of the three travellers, following the initiative of the process I adopted at Rotterdam.

First, then, the stout gentleman, always eloquent upon creature comforts :—

"We dined on board," writes this Sybarite, "under an awning on the quarter-deck, which was delightful, as the panorama of the Rhine still kept unrolling itself"—[How can a panorama unroll itself? Is it worked on the jack-towel principle, by a man behind the scenes]—"while we dined. This, however, had its drawbacks, for, through fear of losing sight of a village or a castle, one had to be perpetually screwing the head towards the backbone, to see what we were passing on the opposite bank, and the flies would go into the soup. Besides, I had such a hungry-looking waiter attending on me (he looked as if he had been shut up for months in the kitchen of a *restaurant*, with one of the Rotterdam dogs' strawberry-pottle muzzles on) that I was afraid he would be snapping up bits off my plate every time I turned my head away. They evidently don't give their waiters enough to eat in Germany, and it is dreadful to watch their voracious looks at the food they bring you. Dinner good. Mutton but so-so; but veal excellent, white as a

marchioness's baby. Mem.: Raspberry jam very nice with veal; also currant-sauce with cauliflowers and melted-butter, with hot pound-cake. I do not dislike the German *cuisine.* Besides, they dine at one o'clock, which gives you time to get up a capital appetite for a nice meat tea. Saloon of boat prettily decorated with encaustic panels, representing views on the Rhine. Not a bit like the originals, but very charming. Odd costumes among the passengers forward. We took in a consignment of market-women and peasant-girls, in their ' national costume,' at Oberwesel. *Such* antique silver earrings and brooches, and of *such* quaint form; such lace collars and gold and silver thumb-rings. One peculiar head-dress I sketched, and would have brought the head-dress away with me had I been able to muster sufficient German to ask for it. She could not have refused *me* [fatuous stout man!]: I never saw a young lady with a plated paper-knife, or a silver dagger, through her back-hair before. Does she wear it after marriage? and does she ever comb her husband's hair with it? I know that the partner of *my* joys and woes combs my luxuriant locks with . . . ." Here the manuscript is torn away, and the next legible line begins with:—
" Had an adventure about eight p.m. Wonderful discoveries, those comets. What a philosopher Donati must be! How I *do* wish I could speak German! Curious assortment of luggage forward from the funnel. Our friend's iron chest at a discount, for here were monstrous chests, with hasps like dungeon stanchions, and padlocks like lion's-head knockers, and painted all over with ornamental scroll-work, and birds, and beasts, and fishes. An unaccountable people, these Germans. I saw a carpet bag, too, aft, embroidered with a wreath of artificial flowers in beads and floss silk, and bearing this inscription in German text, ' *Gute Reise*,' which the red-nosed man (how does he know, I should like to?) says means 'A

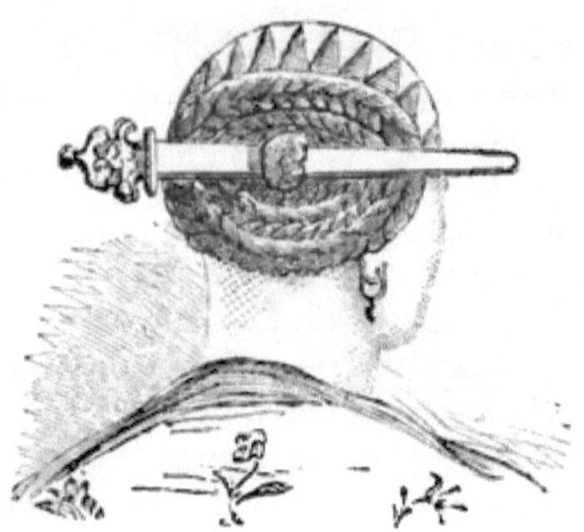

HEAD-DRESS OF PEASANT GIRL.

A LEGENDARY CARPET-BAG.

prosperous journey and a quick return.' Don't like the German language at all. It is absurd, and, moreover, insulting. When they want to say 'Very well,' they growl out ' *Yer fool, yer fool*,' which is rude, and not at all the thing." [Has our stout friend mistaken " *Ja wohl*, for *Yer fool?*"] "The German caps, too, worn by the majority of the men, are most extraordinary inventions. The first rough idea of the German cap was evidently a shovelful of mud thrown on the head, and allowed to trickle down on one side. There is another shaped like a dislocated accordion, another like a fractured sugar-loaf, and another like a dropsical jelly mould. Altogether, I don't think I ever passed a happier day in my life. The veal was really delicious. I went at it three times; but then castles give one such an appetite. We had an Englishman on board, whom I imagine to have been a retired publican. He was checking the castles off with a pencil on his lithographed panorama, just as though they were casks of beer that were being lowered into his cellar, and grumbled horribly because he missed one or two. He declared that it was a swindle, and that he wouldn't stand it. I think even that he threatened to bring an action against the company. At last he broke out in open rebellion, and said he could see more and better castles than these during an hour's omnibus ride in London. 'There's the "Edinburgh Castle,"' he said, 'and the "Ship and Castle," and the "Castle and Falcon," and the "Moro Castle," and there's the "Elephant and Castle,"—and a very good house it is.' He could not be in bad temper very long, however: the day was so beautiful; the scenery so lovely; the birds—but no: we didn't see any birds. However, we enjoyed ourselves thoroughly. What says the poet?

> "'Too late I stayed,—forgive the crime,
> Unheeded flew the hours;
> How noiseless falls the foot of Time,
> That only treads on flowers!
>
> "'What eye with clear account remarks
> The ebbing of his glass,
> When all its sands are diamond sparks,
> That dazzle as they pass?'"

The report of the man of the iron chest is brief and savage. "The men, women, and children on the Rhine," he writes, "are unconscionable villains. If I had been as rich as Rothschild, I should have been penniless ere we reached Mayence, had I bought half the articles I was pressed to purchase. They began at Cologne with guide-books and Rhine panoramas;

on board the boat it was 'Buy, buy, buy!' all day long. I was waylaid on the paddle-boxes by Jews who had brooches with views of the Drachenfels in mosaic; red-headed boys showed me earrings laid up in wool which were 'ver sheap;' and there was a smiling 'tout' on board, one of the regular 'touts' you always meet on board Rhine steamers, and who I believe have regular credentials from the company and the police, and who tried first to ingratiate himself with the stout man (who is vain enough for anything) by telling him that he was like Louis Napoleon. I put a spoke in *his* wheel, however; whereupon he wanted to sell me a musical-box, a meerschaum pipe, and finally a bunch of grapes, which he declared to be real Johannisburg, and to have been given him that morning by Prince Metternich's gardener. I am not certain whether he did not say that the donor was the Prince himself. I would have none of his wares, however, and gave him a piece of my mind; so he fastened himself in dudgeon on the retired publican, and failing success with that traveller, who was too busy counting his castles to attend to him, attacked an English clergyman and company who came on board at Coblentz. He was mooning about the deck with that eternal bunch of grapes all day. I think they were made of wax."

I have only been permitted a view of very sparse fragments of the slim gentleman's notes of the Rhine tour; but the portions I am enabled to publish show, in their strongest light, that individual's financial aptitude, and his Machiavelian acuteness of perception.

"Waiters on the Rhine, thieves," he writes. "Steward of steamboat tried to cheat me out of three thalers, Prussian; convicted him in the act, and told him what I thought of him. He looked daggers; but I looked toe of my right boot, and *meant it*. Mulcted him as a punishment of half his *trinkgeld*, or gratuity.

Left him bewailing his destiny and cuffing his subordinate—a wretched smallbones of a youth, suffering, seemingly, under chronic measles—who washed the plates and brought the pipe-lights. Mem.: All the stewards, all the waiters, and, I verily believe, the whole of the crews of the Rhine steamers, have fathers, or mothers, or brothers, or uncles, or aunts, or cousins, who keep hotels with first-rate accommodation, hot and cold baths on the premises, and *tables-d'hôte* at five p.m. Never have anything to do with them, and light your cigars with the cards of address. That stout man is beginning to show himself in his true colours. I knew him to be as impressionable to the charms of female loveliness as Tupman in 'Pickwick;' but he is now appearing in the guise of a Lovelace, a Lauzun, a Don Giovanni. He was insanely enamoured of the Fawn on board the Rotterdam steamboat"—["He wasn't," the stout gentleman indignantly exclaimed, when the report was read to him; "you were"]—"and to-day he fell madly in love"—["He didn't—you did!" stout gentleman, *loquitur*]—"with two pretty girls—German girls, fair and soft, with mild eyes—one of them lisped—who sat opposite to us at dinner. They were *very* pretty girls—charming girls."—["Aha, my friend!" stout gentleman, *loq.*]—"Our stout friend said that to see the tallest one eat roast veal and raspberry jam was so delicious, that it gave him a pain in the back of his neck. They were sisters, and had a stout, florid mamma with them; also a gawky lout of a male creature in a cap—brother, I hope; sweetheart, if not affianced one, I fear. We (the stout one and I) endeavoured in vain to move that red-nosed one to a proper sense of duty—*i. e.*, to open a conversation with the family in German, introduce us—I mean, our stout friend—and then retire to the forecastle while we carried on a flirtation. We could do it well enough by signs; but then we just wanted half a dozen phrases

THE BEAUTY AND HER SISTER.

of German as a foundation. That ill-conditioned man, however (his nose is getting redder every day), refused to do us this slight service. Our stout friend was not to be discouraged. I found him, about eight p.m., when it was growing dark, in full conversation (if an atrocious salad of English, French, and German can be called a conversation) with the two German young ladies, to whom he was apparently delivering a very elaborate lecture on the comet, which that evening had made its appearance on an unwonted scale of length and splendour. Truly the impudence of some people is wonderful!"

Now you can understand the nature of the "adventure" to which the stout gentleman alludes in his report, and appreciate the sincerity of his wish to be able to speak German.

Ten o'clock p.m.—Fourteen hours on the Rhine, a long day's journey; but then there was that troublesome fog. Assmanthausen, Rudesheim, Schloss Johannisberg, have all been passed, unheeded because unseen; the stars and the comet now usurp the field of view: then the banks of the Rhine are edged for

THE STOUT GENTLEMAN LECTURES UPON THE COAST.

miles by long lines of poplars, bleak, rigid, and lugubrious; the mountains are gradually depressed to a
succession of level lowlands; then comes a maze of
glittering lamps. A great many bells ring; there
is much shouting, much "Yo-heave-hoing," in German, and the three travellers are at MAYENCE.

"What do they let the soldiers wear white calico
frocks for, so late at night?" the stout gentleman
asked, after landing, as two sentinels, habited like
journeymen bakers who had recently enlisted, threw
open the *battants* of the city gate immediately opposite
the landing-place, for the passengers and merchandise
of the *Prinz von Preussen* to pass through. "Surely
they will catch cold."

"Unthinking man!" the M. I. C. replied, sternly;
"those are Austrian soldiers."

CHAPTER IV.

FROM MAYENCE, *alias* CASTEL, BY HOCKHEIM, TO FRANKFORT - ON - THE - MAINE, AND THENCE TO VANITY FAIR, OTHERWISE CALLED HOMBOURG-VON-DER-HÖHE.

THE federal city of Mayence may be described as being, politically, neither fish, flesh, nor fowl, nor good red herring. It doesn't seem to belong outright to any European Power, although two great and one mediocre one—Austria, Prussia, and Bavaria—have an interest in it, and keep soldiers there, making it a capital place to study the varieties of German military costume, and to note the various inflections of the Teutonic language in. Of course, all the Powers are jealous of one another, and the soldiers of the different nations indulge in mutual hatred of the most cordial description. The Austrians call the Prussians donkeys; the Prussians retort that everybody knows that the Austrians are cows; and both fall foul of the unfortunate Bavarians, who are contemned and ridiculed as walking beer-barrels. I am afraid, myself, that the horrible explosion of the powder magazine at Mayence, which we have all heard of, must have been caused by the vindictive desire of an Austrian uhlan to blow up a Prussian jäger, or *vice versá*, or by a conspiracy between the children of the black and the two-headed eagle to send the Bavarian light infantry into the air.

The gate through which the warriors in white holland blouses had admitted our three travellers was the Frei Thor or Free Gate, to build which was demolished the famous old feudal residence of Martinsburg, which, up to the end of the seventeenth century, was the palace of the Kurfursts or Electors. "Bother the electors!" the stout gentleman remarked parenthetically, when this information was imparted to him; "the whole of German history appears to have been turned topsy-turvy by those elector fellows. It's my opinion that the whole Thirty Years' War was nothing but a contested election." There also was the Merchants' Hotel, a magnificent building erected by the notorious "League" in 1317, and which was decorated with the statues of seven electors, and two colossal figures supporting the Imperial crown of Germany. This was razed to the ground during the wars of that enlightened and art-loving people the French, who, it will be remembered, had also the honour of burning up the wretched Palatinate once or twice, and in all ages have been distinguished for politeness, taste, liberality, and also for stabling their horses in churches, making drinking troughs of the holy-water fonts, smoking their pipes in confessionals, and using sacred pictures for musket-targets, leaving behind their line of march burning cottages, uprooted vines, and devastated harvest fields, insulting women, and grinding the faces of the unhappy peasantry. As they used Germany, so they used Italy; so they have used Algeria, so Kertch (our own poor Highlanders getting the credit of much of that Vandalism); and so they would use your front parlour and best bedroom, Mr. Bull, your snug Mechanics' Institute, and neat proprietary chapel, your goods and chattels—from your cash-box to your youngest born's perambulator—if ever they had a chance. And yet these tiger-baboons, who grin with their mouths and tear with their teeth with equal facility, have the assurance to declare that the Rhenish provinces are naturally theirs, and that they are beloved by the Germans. Why, it will be a thousand years ere the Germans forget the murder of Palm, the bridge of Leipsic, the outrage on the followers of the heroic Schill—sent to the galleys when fairly prisoners of war—and the sacrilegious rifling of the Great Frederick's tomb!

There is a bridge of boats at Mayence first built by Charlemagne, and affixed to the piles thereof are seventeen water mills, whose murmur during the night is very romantic and tranquillizing. Indeed, the man with the iron chest, always of a sentimental temperament, declared that he could not imagine a better preparation for bed than a solitary walk on the old bridge, the great pale moon shining placidly above like a benignant empress, fluttering, fleecy, skimmering little clouds paying their court to her, and hurrying away, abashed by the radiance of her countenance; the stars around twinkling with brilliance, subdued but sufficing; the planets a proud aristocracy, coroneted and full of rich domains, down to the "little people of the skies," glittering mildly, mere pins' points of gentility, down at last to the tiny wavelets of the Rhine, sparkling, too, in their humble way, fawning on the great luminary above like bright-eyed little spaniels, glad to catch the smallest reflex of the Mistress Lux, like genteel dwellers in a village in ecstacies at an invite from my lord at the priory, who dined last week with his grace at the hall, who, as each reader of the "Court Circular" knows, is Pinchbeck-stick-in-waiting to her Majesty at the palace. "Yes," the M. I. C. sighed meekly, "that walk on the bridge would be delightful. I don't mind the poplar and alder fringed banks of the river being somewhat formal. The moon, the stars, a mild cigar, a glimmering red light under the hood of one of yonder barges, and memory enough to repeat a dozen lines of Tennyson's 'Vision of Fair Women,' would suffice me."

"There is only one obstacle to your taking such a sentimental stroll," (they were smoking in the hotel vestibule when this conversation occurred), "and that is that the bridge is unfortunately outside the town gates, and that Frei Thor and all are closed at ten p.m."   Thus far the slim gentleman.

"And what the dickens has a bridge of boats to do with a vision of fair women?" asked the stout gentleman, taking the red-nosed man's cigar (without permission) from his lips, and kindling his own extinguished weed at the other's incandescent tip.   He was always wanting a light for his cigar, the stout gentleman, like the people who are always wanting a fresh start in life.   "Besides," he continued, "you know you're nearly as blind as a mole.   You couldn't see the fair women, if they were there, without turning on a policeman's bull's-eye.   You ran against the pretty German girl, who wore her hair parted on one side, while I was explaining the nebulous theory of the comet's tail to her; and I am sure you trod on her toes, confound you!"

"As a rule," the slim gentleman interposed, balancing the minute fragment of his cigar on the tip of a penknife, "girls who part their hair on one side are to be avoided.   Even as a great authority in such matters has declared that red-haired girls should be shunned, being as deceitful as the foxes of the field, so one-sided-haired girls are ordinarily too scientific.   They know all about the 'Vestiges of Creation,' read the 'Old Red Sandstone,' and the 'Testimony of the Rocks;' have a good deal to say about the megatherium, the iguanodon, and the other horrible saurians you see on the lake in the Crystal Palace gardens, and carry little hampers and chips of gypsum and feldspar in their workbags.   The minxes! they should be minding their knitting! Next to the late Doctor Buckland, they think the greatest man in the world is Sir Roderick Murchison.   I knew such a young lady once, who asked me if I had read 'Siluria;' I replied that I had never been there, and she cut me dead immediately afterwards. I fear these scientific girls as much as I should have feared that Scotch young lady—"

"Scotch young ladies are angels!" exclaimed the stout gentleman enthusiastically, emitting a cerulean corkscrew of vapourous nicotine from his lips.

"Who, at least, would not have been rude enough to interrupt me while I was speaking," the slim one resumed, with a severe glance at his companion, "and who was overheard by Sydney Smith, at a ball, to say to her partner, 'What you say, my lord, of love in the *aibstract?*'—but the fiddlers struck up, and he heard no more. Depend upon it, when a girl takes to parting her hair on one side, she will very soon leave off combing it, and then her stockings will come down at heel, and she will be reckoned among irrevocable dowdies. A girl's business is to look pretty and make us love her, and not to know anything about rocks and things."

"I met a lady once," the stout gentleman remarked, thoughtfully, "on a foggy morning, in the Rue Villa Hermosa at Brussels. She was neither young nor pretty. Her hair was parted on one side; she had likewise but one eye, a slight crick in the neck, a halt in her gait, a wrench in her backbone, all the teeth on the left side gone;—and a shawl put on decidedly awry, completed her costume. She was the most one-sided lady I ever saw. She must have been a fierce partisan in politics, and have lived in a room with one window blocked up."

"I *will* speak," suddenly exclaimed, or rather shrieked the man with the iron chest, throwing up his arms wildly, to the intense astonishment of the head waiter, or *oberkellner*, who was smoking *his* cigar, but at a respectful distance, amid a grove of wires from which hung bells, thick as leaves in Vallombrosa.

"Yes; I *will* speak! what has a moonlight walk on a bridge to do with a 'vision of fair women?' It has everything to do with it. To the Poet the images of youth and beauty are everywhere: in the darkness of the abyss, and in the blue, long drawn shadow of the crag: in the floating threads of virgin floss, that are wafted on the summer breeze, and presage brighter days to come. He sees fair women beckoning and smiling on the rocky ledge beneath the Lorelei's crested head. They float down the diamond-furrowed waters, wantoning around the bark that bears the good Caliph Haroun Alraschid. They trim the sails, they guide the helm, they laugh and warble at the prow. They come at night into the student's cell, and clasp him round the neck, kiss his hot brow, and hide the blurred page with frolic hand, and relieve his labour of lore with adorable nonsense. They gather round his lonely pallet, smooth the vexed pillow, and trim the flickering night-lamp, whispering 'Be of good heart. She is coming. She is thinking of you. You shall be loved.' The grosser sense is slain and trampled under foot, as Michael slew the dragon, by the chastened presence of these fair young spirit forms. But one must be a Poet to feel and understand these things.

> "The poet in a golden clime was born,
>   With golden stars above;
> Dower'd with the hate of hate, the scorn of scorn,
>   The love of love!"

I have a red nose, and a waistcoat that wants taking in because the heart beneath is wasting in a slow atrophy, and when I tell women that I love them, they laugh at me. But I am not alone. Give me a river to gaze upon in the moon's quiet light, give me a lamp to look upon a dear old book, and the casket of memory is unlocked, and the inner eyes are dazzled with the sight of the fairest women that the world ever saw. Why, I have the best of all good company! Imogen comes, and Beatrice, and Katherine, the whilom shrew, but quite penitent and mollified now. Gentle, uncomplaining Desdemona, singing ' Willow' to a harp with silver strings, patient Grissell, and sainted Mignon; the Lionheart's fair Berengaria, and Coleridge's Généviève, my hope, my joy, my Généviève—

> " ' Who loves me best whene'er I sing
> The songs that make her grieve.' "

" But, my good friend," the slim gentleman observed, as the red-nosed man allowed his arms to resume a vertical position, " you forget that among your ' fair women' you might have a vision of guilty Beatrice Cenci, of Aholibah, doting on the images of ' those desirable young men ' the Assyrians; of Jezebel with her painted face, leering at the casement; of Donna Lucrezia Borgia making the crust of a venison pasty to poison Maffio Orsini and his friends; of Agnes Sorel and Fair Rosamond, and Madame du Barri, and the naughtiest of fair company. You dote—*vous radotez*, my red-nosed comrade."

" He drank a great deal of Assmannshaüser at dinner," whispered the stout gentleman, " and was helped twice to potato salad. As for his being a poet, he can no more turn a couplet than a mangle, and had to ask me the other day for a rhyme to ' conjecture.' "

" I don't think he's quite right in his mind," was the slim gentleman's reply. " Look at his eye: it rolls." (The M.I.C. had a habit of keeping the other eye closed. It was probably that " inner eye" with which he saw the " fair women.") " Look at his nose: it is perfectly livid. I think we had better have made a trip to Belgium, and left him at Gheel, the town where they take madmen in to board and lodge. All I can say is, that at the first grammatical error he commits in a leading article after we reach home, I'll have a snug little commission *de lunatico inquirendo* out against him at the Gray's Inn Coffee-house."

For the slim gentleman (keep it a secret, if you please) was head miller—the Grindoff, in fact—of a place of torture, where for ten months out of the twelve were doomed to do intellectual penance for their sins, the M.I.C. and other slaves of the lamp. And the man with the iron chest had since infancy laboured under a disability to discover that the nominative case should precede the verb. He looked darkly at the slim gentleman as that individual, having finished his cigar, proposed a walk before going to bed, and muttered that if there were one thing in the world that made him ambitious of reaching a good old age, it would be the possibility of surviving a certain Inhuman Being, and writing that man's life and times.

Though the ill-used individual with the nose could not contemplate the moon from Charlemagne's bridge, he was at full liberty to bathe himself in its soft green light in the streets of Mayence, a privilege of which he availed himself, notwithstanding his fatiguing Rhine journey, till a very late hour at night. Sooth-ing, yet strange, is the utter tranquillity of these continental cities, to one accustomed to the up-all-night life of our huge metropolis. No parliament-house sitting late here, no sub-editor and compo-sitors waiting for the minister's winding-up speech, or the result of the division; no bacchanalian shouts disturb the season of deep sleep; no roisterers return-ing home in cabs make the stones rattle. Everything is still—almost as still as death; and you may hear the town clocks in graduated diapason chime, without that ceaseless accompaniment of the rumbling of dis-tant wheels which, to their treble, marks the bass in London. The cats even seem to keep better hours than in our wicked city ; to be sure, continental cats generally mistrust the high gables of the antique houses, and prefer the kennel to the tiles. No dog is abroad ; for every dog in Mayence is numbered, registered, and *inscrit*, and pays cess and tax. You may say that a low sound, between purring and droning, gently meanders through the air. That can only be the snoring of the good citizens of Mayence, who have been a-bed for hours ; his worship the burgomaster, perhaps, leading the blue-bottle band. Stay ; a foot-fall sounds sonorously. It is the sentry pacing backwards and forwards, before the ghastly white barrack. Men's evil passions are never permitted to slumber. Even at this time of rest for all men, there must be soldiers, helmeted, greatcoated, and belted ; the peaceful moon gleaming with a sharp streak on their bayonets to keep watch and ward over the powder and the bullets, and the grim-muzzled guns with which men rend their brethren. Oh ! but the wolves have ever a fine organization, always a master-beast to keep sentry ; 'tis the shepherds that are faithless to their duty, 'tis the pastors that leave the gates of the fold open, and suffer the flock to become meat for all the fourfooted devourers of the field.

The windows of Mayence's tall houses are blind; few vigils are kept here. In vain you seek for a casement in which glimmers the faintest corpuscle of light. Sages tell us that one human being dies every second. There must be some near their end in Mayence now—a second ago, a second to come. Do they let sick men die in the dark here ? Stay, see, one little dormer window on a sixth storey is illumined. Mortality may be ebbing there ; pain may be near its end ; dark nothingness coming with swift footstep. Anon the window opens—a fat man with a skull-cap, spectacles, and a beard, leans from the sill, puffs vigorously at his pipe, and expectorates on the pavement below. A moonbeam comes and kisses the

silver mounting of his meerschaum. Ah! this is
only wordy Professor Schlaghintern sitting up to un-
timely hours to finish that treatise on Cosmaterato-
logical Glaucoma, as compared with Carcinomatous
Epithelioma, which is to demolish the heterodox kine-
saphist Doctor von Strumplelewachen, of Coblentz.
Cudgel thy brains, good professor; and a good de-
liverance to thee, Coblentz doctor.

O, wonders of the night season! O, wonders of
the moon and stars! O, wonders of the time of
sleep, when the ravelled sleeve is knitted up, and
rugged life is rounded with a dream! But the night
has terrors as well as tranquillity. Friend of mine,
did you never hear a Scream in the night season—
one sudden, piercing, agonising yell? Whence came
it—who gave it? Was it caused by the sharp knife
of the doctor, the dagger of the assassin, by the Word
of Doom, by the sting of long-suppressed remorse?
Or do the dead rise by night? Or is the yell but
fancy—the re-action of nerves too quickly soothed—
a fancy such as musing in bed leads you to believe
that your own name has suddenly been pronounced
imperatively, sharply, distinctly, close to your very
pillow, and when telling you of a weird companion-
ship, you feel conscious of complete isolation?

The three travellers went to bed in one of the big-
gest of the big hotels that front the Rhine at Mayence (*Teutonicè*, Mainz). The Hotel d'Angleterre is,
in size, a trifle under Buckingham Palace, and is a
great deal handsomer. The staircase may be compared to an Act of Parliament, for you might drive a
coach and six, if not through, at least up and down,
its roomy degrees, without inconvenience. "We
supped," writes the stout gentleman, in that collection of reports, which one day, I believe, will be found
as interesting as any of those published, bound in law
calf, by Messrs. Butterworth, "in an apartment about

the size of the Middle Temple Hall—where, by the
way, I ate half my terms at the time when I had
thoughts of going in for the Lord Chancellorship.
There were a dozen gas chandeliers, at least, and we
were the only guests. The slim gentleman even refused to take any supper; and that red-nosed man,
who had become more sentimental than ever, limited
himself to an incongruous repast of black bread
(*pumpernickel*) Gruyère cheese, and Médoc wine. I
am happy to state that the doctrine of mal-assimilation
was triumphantly vindicated in his case, and that he
had alarming symptoms of indigestion, and saw many
ghosts (by his own account) before breakfast time.
I was obliged (for the good of the house, you know)
to sound the final doom of two veal cutlets, and an
omelette *aux fines herbes*. Rudesheimer tolerable:
Macon vieux, but so-so. I was not frightened, only
rather nervous at the magnitude of the apartment.
One tall waiter, with trousers too short for him, a
bulbous nose, and a head very bald and polished.
Curious idiosyncrasy of mine: whenever I see a very
smooth bald head, I have a craving to write my name
and address thereupon. Waiter said (in Germanic
French) that he was an Italian, that he didn't like
' *ze bays*,' and that he wanted to get back to the Lake
of Como. I believe him to have been no more an
Italian than Parmesan (how delicious with macaroni!)
is Dutch cheese. I sang him a little song, and told
him an anecdote or two, which seemed to afford him
but mediocre pleasure. A very obtuse race, waiters.
He said he knew one 'Sir Billi,' of London, who was
a lord and baronet. He had mastered one English
phrase, too, which he repeated with offensive frequency. It was this: 'Vill you av your jaimber-
gandelstig?' Observing at last that it was a quarter
to two, and that the red-nosed man had gone to sleep
with his nose in 'Galignani's Messenger'—I would
not let him retire to rest before me—I took my

'jaimber-gandelstig,' and bade the waiter good night and heaven bless him; but he had gone to sleep, too, and was muttering, stertorously, about 'gandelstigs.' To bed, then: the red-nosed man was so sleepy that he barked his shins eleven times in stumbling up the staircase after me. I slept with a feather-bed atop of me, and dreamed that I was a goose, and that fiends were dancing round me with sage and onions blazing in blue fire. Moral: don't eat veal-cutlets for supper."

For all their late going to bed, the three were up betimes the next morning. You must reflect that their leave of absence from that mill in London was but short, and that three days of it were already gone. The slim gentleman began to evince considerable uncertainty as to whither they should direct their steps after they had visited Frankfort. "We must dine at the table d'hôte at the Hotel de Russie, you know," he said. "Everybody does that. Then we are bound to see Danneker's Ariadne, and the house were Goëthe was born; the Jews' Street, St. Paul's Church, and all the rest of it. Besides, I have a call to make at Rothschild's, and I daresay that red-nosed man will be wanting to speculate in the Frankfort lottery. But after that, where are we to go? Shall it be Heidelburg, and thence through the Bernese Oberland, and across the Alps, by the Grimsel, Furka, and St. Gothard passes?"

"I should like to go to Heidelburg, and see the Great Tun," suggested the stout gentleman.

"We might afterwards make for Strasburg, and see the cathedral, and ——"

"Yes," interrupted the man with the iron chest; "and we could then cross the bridge of Kehl, and make for Baden."

"So-ho! You want to go to Baden, do you, my friend," the stout gentleman replied, with comic severity. "I'll Baden you. No sardines for you this morning, young man."

The M. I. C. had a weakness, almost amounting to an infatuation, for sardines. He had even invented a machine, that was something like a chisel, and something like a "knuckle-duster," for the express purpose of opening the hermetically-sealed sardine boxes. A confiding ironmonger had made one after his model, and the usual result was lively, if not efficacious: the sardine box hopping to the further extremity of the room, dinted, but not opened, and a picturesque fountain of blood spurting from a triangular wound neatly scooped out of the operator's thumb. Three trials of the M. I. C.'s machine were as good, the stout gentleman said, as an amputation. When his friends wanted to vex this ill-used man, they ate up all the sardines at breakfast before his face; and, being modest, and ashamed to order more, he was wont to glare vengefully at the empty dish. He shamelessly avowed his fondness for oleaginous fish. The slim gentleman declared that his favourite beverage was cod-liver oil, as that of some ladies of fashion is eau-de-Cologne grog; and a malicious report was circulated that he had once undertaken a voyage to Greenland in a whaler for the express purpose of witnessing the boiling down of the blubber.

The conversation on the vexed question of their itinerary took place as they indulged in an early morning's walk in the streets of Mayence; the dear, crooked, odd-cornered, tumble-down, choked-up, picturesque lanes that gladden the artistic eyesight in every German town. "Look how gloriously the sunlight and shadow chequer the rough-cast between the blackened timbers of that old house," cried the slim gentleman, enthusiastic for once. "See how capitally that bit of red tells against the dark shadow under the archway."

"It isn't dark. It's blue and transparent, There's an old woman in the shadow peeling carrots. She might have been painted by Gaspard Netscher.

"And those brass milkpails," continued the slim gentleman, not heeding his companion. "See what an exquisite effect of reflected light you get. There; don't you see how the tomatas in the basket are ruddily mirrored in the bright brass! And that puddle, too, I wouldn't have it mopped up for anything. Why, it's a bit of sky fallen on the pavement."

"That flight of steps was never meant to walk up," remarked the stout gentleman, pointing to a staircase, which looked as if a cartful of paving stones had been spilt there.

"Of course it wasn't," rejoined the slim gentleman. "It was meant to be drawn for the Water Colour Exhibition. Look at the greengrocers' stalls! Look at that queer *tourelle* at the corner of the street, all carved and crenelated!"

"It's a watchbox, with a man and a griffin over it, and a doll inside." Thus the stout gentleman—

"It isn't," indignantly exclaimed the slim one. "It's the shrine of Saint Somebody. Look at the jagged pavement, with odd stones of all sizes and all colours. Look at the magnificent collection of old iron on that stall. I tell you the only man fit to draw this street is George Cattermole, and the only man fit to colour it James Holland."

"I wish it didn't smell quite so 'loud,'" interposed the stout gentleman, who was hungry (of course) and wanted his breakfast.

"I wish there were not so many Austrian soldiers in the way; I hate 'em," was the solitary remark of the man with the nose. "If that corporal turns up his nose again at me, I'll make a face at him."

By-and-by, at about nine on the radiant September morning (English July weather), they strolled, still wisely disdaining to ask their way, into the market-place of Mayence. There is in the market-place a queer, fantastic fountain of the German Renaissance, which, besides presenting oddly-sculptured sceptres, nymphs, dolphins, angels, and mermaids, serves as a pedestal for a statue of the Virgin Mary. This fountain was erected by Albert of Brandenburg, in 1540, in commemoration of the capture of Francis the First by Charles the Fifth. There were Austrian soldiers galore in the market-place of Mayence. Unlovely-looking creatures in those Holland blouses; not much handsomer in the coarse, ill-bleached blanketing, in which they are swathed when in full dress. Shaved white bears, the stout gentleman called them; averring, moreover, that they had nefariously become possessed of publican's pewter pots, the which to melt down, and make themselves those dumpy little buttons withal. "And why they don't brand, ' Glass; with care—this side upwards,' on those baggy galligaskins, I don't know," said the stout gentleman.

They "march wide between the legs, as though they had gyves on," these Austrians; and their blared eyes seem hesitating between ophthalmia and cataract. They have large flap ears, unsuccessful mouse-coloured moustaches, and no perceptible eyebrows. Remember that the Austrian, like the Russian officers, are all noble. And by Austrians I mean the real recruits of the Austrian provinces. Emperor Franz-Joseph has many nationalities under his standard: brutal Croats, vapouring Hungarians — these were old Trenck's "pandours,"—half-savage Czechs, valorous but volatile Tyrolese, and borderers. The Austrian proper is a pudding-healed carle, fit only to be sewn up in a white blanket, well beaten with a corporal's stick—within a year or two they yet ran the gauntlet in the Austrian army—and occasionally shot at or bayonet-spiked. He is incorrigibly stupid, and the laughing-stock of all north Germany. They tell stories about the Austrian as we were wont to do in the old jest-books about Teague from Cork, and Sandy from the Highlands—perhaps, with equal injustice. The Austrian soldiers, then, swinging and waddling in Mayence market-place, or staggering by twos, with great buckbaskets full of tin *gamelles* between them, or covetously staring, their silly mouths watering, and trying to finger impalpable zwanzigers and kreutzers in their bankrupt pockets, at the fruit-women's stalls, contrasted very unfavourably with the trim, soldier-like Prussians, with their little moustaches, bristly, well blackened, and fiercely clipped; their bullet-heads covered with short, shiny hair, their quick eyes, and evident look of having been to school. Surely the Prussian infantry, for wheeling, and marching, holding heads up, and shouldering arms, is the very best in, and the wonder of, the world. They understand discipline in the army which the great Frederick perfected, which Napoleon (but it had degenerated) turned inside out at Jena, and which Von Stein afterwards resuscitated to turn the Corsican himself inside out at Leipsic and at Waterloo, under one marshal Vorwarts, whom the "Army Lists" called Blucher. Never came a genius up a trap so opportunely as that Prussian host out of the forest at Soignies, I think. Marshal Vorwarts's—now General von Wrangel's—blue-clad and helmeted babes are standing at ease all over Mayence, smoking their nasty little cigars, and cheapening apples and plums. They always seem to have money to spend, Prussian soldiers. That old Silesian father, now in the landwehr, but who bivouacked in '15 in the Paris Carrousel, may send them a greasy thaler-note or two from time to time. They have savings'-banks in their regiments; the captain treasurer. Said captain is a kind of Grand Llama of Tibet among his men: immediately greater to them than General von Wrangel, than Prinz von Preussen himself, than king or kaiser. You remember the story of Frederick the Great and the sentinel, on the very cold wintry night. "Why don't you smoke?" the king, incognito, asks.—"Against orders—I mustn't;" sentinel replies.—"Oh, but you may; I give you leave."—"Can't help it; I musn't." I tell you, fool, that I will bear you harmless: *I am the King.*" What does the sentinel answer to this?—"The king be——" he says: *what would my captain say?*" Moral: Always obey your immediate superior. It is all very well for your master Sir John, when you are a foot-boy, to pat you on the head, and tell you never to mind about your work; but depend upon it, the next time the butler catches you tripping, he will pull your ears soundly. I have a great respect for the Prussian army; yet I wish nevertheless that the authorities would not dress their drummers quite so much like harlequins. As for their drums, too, they are not drums—they are tambourines, and when struck they sound not sonorously, as honest sheepskin should, but semi-harsh, discordant, metallic, braying sounds. His Royal Highness (not of the Horse Guards, but of Windsor, Osborne, *et autres lieux*) wants, they say, to introduce that tambourine drum into the British army. It won't do. The British army can't get on without the big drum, and I was about to say—without the black man to beat it; but the last time I saw the guard mount at St. James's, the whilom superb Ethiop and gold braid were replaced by a diminutive individual with fawn-coloured moustaches. Another negro, equally scarlet, golden and superb, was wont to bang the cymbals together. Where are those blacka-moors now? *Eheu fugaces!* where is the red port wine I used to drink in the consulate of Manlius? a noble Roman by the way, whom I recommend to the light *littérateurs* of the day, as a change after the Consul Plancus, whose venerable toga they have worn to tatters.

Bavarian soldiers in Mainz market too; burly, jolly, rosy, fresh-coloured, martial-looking fellows enough, with laughing blue eyes, and sky-blue uniforms, and plumed shakoes all on one side—not unlike a species of fancy journeymen-butcher costume. Long-legged Prussian officers, with epaulette scales like gilt oysters on their shoulders, large brass buttons, much like those worn on blue-body coats by elderly gentlemen of a Conservative way of thinking, and trousers lightly strapped over their long-toed boots. They are given to spectacle wearing, and to carrying books, stitched in blue paper, beneath their arms; bearing their heads, moreover, in studious meditation, so sunk on their breasts as to render you apprehensive that they are about to butt at you with the spikes of their helmets.

AUSTRIAN OFFICER AND BAGGAGE.

They know all about Vauban and Cohorn, gabions and counterscarps, the camp of Radowitz and the Treaty of Westphalia. They dine cheaply at table d'hôtes, and eat enormously. "As hollow as a Prussian," the chubby Austrians say. The Bavarian officers don't show so early—perhaps they drink too much of their beloved Bairische beer overnight, and lie abed after early parade. When they do come out, they are very smart, and wear an abundance of cock's feathers; but for the acme of military dandyism, commend me to the Austrians—the officers, mind, not the soldiers. Such white tunics, of the softest, creamiest cloth; such lacquered moustaches, such patent leather boots; such bright buttons, and white buckskin gloves! They almost equal the Russian guardsmen in exquisiteness of appearance. They are proud of not wearing epaulettes. See, they seem to say, how well we can dispense with those vain and cumbersome ornaments! And yet the Austrian warriors are nearly all given to *faire du ventre*, to become corpulent. Here comes one, mincing and ambling, swathed in tight girths, pinioned in stocks and boots of penal splendour. On his arm he supports the delicate radius of a lady. He is bound round about by a fairy circle of flounces and crinoline.

"The Austrian army and baggage," growls the man with the iron chest.

"Humorous, but rude," the stout gentleman replies. "I wonder what on earth they want with so many soldiers in Mayence."

"To blow 'em up, to be sure," suggests the slim gentleman.

"Humorous again, but cruel," the stout one rejoins. "However, I don't think much of either of the three armies. I think I'd undertake to thrash 'em with one arm tied behind me. I wish they'd all go to war with us: Austria, Prussia, and Bavaria."

"And then?" the slim gentleman hinted.

"And then *we'd eat 'em*," was the stout one's conclusive reply.

The stout gentleman was himself busily employed eating, as these remarks escaped him. For besides the soldiers in the market-place, besides the long processions of little girls going to school, tapering from gawky bread-and-butter-looking lasses of fourteen, to the fine end of little toddlekins of three, and watched by videttes of " schwestern " nuns in black serge and starched white veils, with wooden rosaries and downcast eyes; besides the beetle-browed priests who prowled about, glowering furtively from beneath their broad-brimmed hats, folding their big-knuckled hands demurely before them, and dragging their flat splay feet slowly along ; besides the crowds of housewives, old and young, comely and ill-favoured, threading their way through the avenues of baskets, and intent on pomicultural and leguminous purchases—the market-place was thronged by people and things whom I have indeed mentioned last, but who had perhaps the very best right of anybody to be there. Under red umbrellas, then, under pea-green and sky-blue umbrellas —all of a respectable and " gigable " size—under picturesque awnings that might have been built by Messrs. Edgington for a *fête champêtre*, under frail scantlings of wood and tarred canvas, were the market-women : ruddy, bronzed, sturdy, with flaming handkerchiefs bound round their heads ; some with huge flapped straw hats such as the Kabyles wear ; all great in gold and silver ear and thumb rings, fillagree chains and crosses and lockets, and all vaunting their wares in a jargon which even our three travellers, with their slight knowledge of German, could not mistake for aught but an execrable patois. But the fruit—never mind the vegetables—*those* would not bear comparison with Covent Garden : the fruit, my rural friend. The melons seemed to have declared a deadly rivalry with

the pumpkins, and to be determined to outvie them in
size: only, they had taken to drinking (aha! water
melons); and their countenances, like those of most
victims to bibulous excesses, were covered with bulbous excrescences.   As to the pumpkins, they seemed
desirous of emulating the ball of St. Paul's in size.
"When the authorship of the Letters of Junius is
disclosed," observed the stout gentleman, "it will perhaps be known for what purpose market gardeners
grow pumpkins.   One housewife in a thousand may
make a bowl of pumpkin soup: and, in the United
States, 'some punkins' are used to convert into pies.
But what becomes of the residue?   Of what use are
they save to be painted in pictures of still life, and to

THE STOUT GENTLEMAN IN THE MAYENCE FRUIT-MARKET.

look large, yellow, and luscious (and they are *not* luscious, but hard and stringy) in the greengrocers' shops? I would rather have a white elephant to keep than a field of pumpkins. Stay: it would not be a bad idea to have both, because then the elephant might eat up the pumpkins, and you set him ploughing after dinner, as Mr. Barnum did at Iranistan." I will pass over the apricots and peaches, the apples and pears, the damsons and Orleans plums—it was the summer combined with the autumn fruit season. But only consider the grapes! In clusters of five pounds weight, in bunches such as only the vinous imagination of a painter of tavern signs could realize; black grapes and white grapes; grapes transparent, with their clear skins and clearer juice; grapes opaque, with their luscious syrup; huge, melting grapes; little, tender, sparkling Hockheim grapes; grapes everywhere, and quoted at a ridiculously low figure. The stout gentleman not being able to make himself understood, and still less understanding the gabbling market-women, changed an Austrian florin (they had bid a long adieu to thalers and silbergroschen, now) and scattered the measly little kreutzers lavishly among the grape venders. Pounds of grapes flowed in upon him; eager hands were thrust out for more kreutzers; the stout gentleman's pockets, and those of his companions, began to burst, their arms to be overladen, their utterance to be choked with grapes. They had not heart to cry "enough!" The fruit was so delicious. More grapes poured in; and a rumour ran through Mayence (so the stout gentleman suggested) that three English lords were buying up the market. The slim gentleman was in ecstacies. The man with the iron chest, who had been moody since his soliloquy on moonlight, clapped his hands together, and shouted for joy.

"Oh for a screw-press, or a regiment of grenadiers,

to press out all the juice with the goose-step! Dam
up the streets; the market-place would become a
tank. The sun would ferment the whole in an hour,
and that preposterous fountain might in reality run
wine."

"You are talking nonsense as usual," returned the
slim gentleman. "I beg to observe that *I* eat the
grapes for purely scientific reasons. They are wholesome, and are considered an excellent anti-dyspeptic."

"A carpet bag," said the stout gentleman, "is supposed to hold as much as you can cram into it. By a
parity of reasoning, you may eat as many pounds of
grapes as you like, till your ribs begin to crack. Then
it is time to leave off."

"Do you observe," whispered the slim to the stout
gentleman, pointing to the man with the red nose,
who was gloomily munching black grapes in vast
quantities, "*that he eats the skins.* Mark my words
—that man will come to a bad end."

"Better to swallow the skins than to litter the
pavement of the cathedral with them," retorted the
man with the nose, who had over-heard a portion of
the foregoing. "Are we to stay gorging ourselves
with tannic acid? Are there not things in life of
greater moment than grapes? Did we come abroad
to be three porkers in Epicurus' style, or to study
archaeology, and the fine arts generally?"

The cathedral of Mayence is situated close to the
market-place; and the inhabitants appear either to be
exceedingly proud and careful of it, or else to have
forgotten it altogether, for it is built round with an
entourage of sheds, workshops, and even tall houses.
The three wandered about for full a quarter of an
hour before they could find ingress to the fane; and
the slim gentleman distinguished himself by his frequent iteration of his pet pseudo German phrase, "Can
man see Dom?" This, with the occasional substitu-

tion of "Schloss" or "Kunstkammer" for "Dom,"
were sufficient, he said, to carry a traveller architecturally through Germany.

The entrance to the cathedral was found at last, but
through a very curious agency. There suddenly
appeared, staggering among the grapes, a gentleman
of the Hebrew persuasion—his vast "boko" or nose,
his ripe, pendulous lip, his moist eye, and his abundant
diamonds, were eloquent as to that fact—who was
talking to himself in a joyous tone, and executing
perpetual pirouettes on the heels of his varnished boots.
He was splendidly attired, and exceedingly dirty. He
had on a large white neck-cloth, the bow of which was
all awry, and the ends of which hung down limply;
and I don't think that Jewish gentleman could
recover very heavy damages for libel if I were to hint
that he had been partaking somewhat too freely of the
juice of the grape—in a fermented state—on the
previous night. And up all night he had evidently
been. There was about him that unmistakeable appearance of "won't go home till morning—till daylight does appearism," that is not to be eradicated, O
votaries of fast life, lay whatever flattering unction
you will to your souls in the way of soda-and-brandy.
The Hebrew gentleman was profusely polite and
obliging. He knew all about the "Dom," and pointed
out its locality in all four quarters of the horizon,
blandly, but vaguely. Reminded that the building
(which appears to be constructed of old red sandstone,
or of cinnabar, or of fossilized gingerbread) was looming just above the travellers' heads, and that they
wanted to know, not where it stood, but how to effect
an entrance thereto, he suddenly dived down a dark
archway, at the opposite sides of whose mouth a lady
in a checked hood sold sausages, and a gentleman with
a beard braces and meerschaums, and in shrill accents
called on the travellers to follow. Then he myste-
riously disappeared; and the Three, endeavouring to

pursue him, stumbled against a little green baize door, which gave way before them, and in rather a sprawling manner they entered the cathedral of Mayence.

"A most urbane Israelite, that," the man with the nose remarked. "I wish he'd ask me to dinner, and show me the lions."

"He'd want to sell you some rabbit-skins afterwards," said the stout one. "Could you make out what language it was he was speaking? It seemed to me to be a mixture of Greek, Latin, German, English, French, Houndsditch, and Holywell Street. Perhaps he is a Rabbi. He looked very learned."

"He looked very dirty."

"He looked very tipsy," the slim gentleman observed. "I wonder at what Hebrew festival he has been keeping it up. But hush, silence, gentlemen, pray. No, stay; they are repairing the cathedral; don't you see the scaffolding and the whitewash pails? We may converse, in moderation."

They seem always to be repairing the German cathedrals (whose exteriors, by the way, are generally said to have remained unfinished for the last five centuries, or so), and their solemn aisles are continually desecrated by the clanking feet and irreverent talk of English tourists. We lounge in and out of God's house abroad in our travelling suits and railway wrappers, just condescending to throw away our cigars under the carved and fretted portal, as though the grand old piles, the result of the genius, the piety, the honest working faith of a thousand years, had been designed for our special holiday gratification, and formed part of the attractions pointed out at reduced fares in the "Continental route" of the South-Eastern Railway Company. Why do they tinkle those little bells so? how absurd are those lighted candles in broad daylight! what is the priest in his spangled odds-and-ends of dress mumbling? how idolatrous are those pictures and statues! how credulous must be those hooded women, crouching in the tenebræ of the little chapels, and pouring the muttered narrative of their peccadilles into the ear of the listening priest in the confessional! how that incense makes our heads ache! Poor benighted Papists, wretched worshippers of stocks and stones! So we pass on, staring at the saints and martyrs in the painted windows through our eye-glasses, thronging to see the relics as though they were models of the Koh-i-noor diamond, or a mermaid, or a child with two heads, and gaping and yawning, and bargaining with the beadle, and asking if there is "any more to see." Go to, I say, you English tourists; you are not decent, you lack that reverence for solemn things, venerated by millions whose creed is other than yours, which should move you to bow the head humbly in the temple of the Romanist and the Russo-Greek—ay, in the mosque of the turbaned Turk, for albeit his faith is false, it is with his whole heart that he is praying to Allah. Never mind if he grovels on a carpet, and turns his face in the direction of the Kaaba. He is praying, and the mosque is sanctified by his prayers.

"The cathedral of Mayence," writes the slim gentleman, the *ex officio* Ruskin of the party, "was commenced in 978, and finished in 1009. The exterior —somewhat bulbous and Byzantine in contour—is, notwithstanding its strange, underdone, beefy hue, grandiose and imposing. The interior is in a very dilapidated condition; all due, the verger informed me —he had a porringer on his head resembling that of the Lord Mayor's sword-bearer—to the Franzosen, or French. The crop of curses which an inheritor of Napoleonic ideas may reap in his passage through Rhineland is most astonishing in fecundity. Part of the structure, however, was burnt so far back as 1190; and they have been repairing it in almost every architectural style, from florid Gothic to Renaissance, from Byzantine to eighteenth century pigtail, ever since.

There are innumerable tombs lining the aisles, and a
plethora of monuments to the prince-bishops (who
were likewise electors) of Mayence. Some of these
monuments are exquisite specimens of Gothic carving
and floral tracery in stone (looking more like wax or
terra cotta) and have superb canopies, in perfect relief, above them. Others, more redundant in ornamentation, approach nearer to the style of Grinling
Gibbons. Others, the last century ones, are vile *pas-
ticci* of sham Roubiliac and meretricious Vanbrugh:
mere buhl cabinets in stone, and that might as well
have been erected as cenotaphs to Louis Quinze's
marquises as to consecrated bishops. When I looked
at the effigies of these bygone ecclesiastical 'swells'—
their sumptuous vestments, their jewelled crosiers,
the rings and gemmed crosses worn *outside their
gloves*, their embroidered sandals, their rich mitres,
their haughty faces, with the half-closed eyes, aquiline
noses, and double chins, the blazonry of armorial bearings, and the pompous inscriptions in bad Latin beneath, some very neat reflections on the vanity of
mundane things occurred to me. I have forgotten
them now—that stout man kept incessantly chattering; but I am still devoutly thankful that we have no
'prince-bishop electors' in England; that the income
of our episcopal dignities never exceed, if they reach,
five hundred a year; that our good bishops live in
semi-detached villas, grow their own vegetables, consider even the services of a boy in buttons as a sinful
luxury, and never—no, never—interfere in elections,
either for county or for borough.

"They have an ingenious peculiarity in the German
cathedrals," continues the slim gentleman, "whether
as a means of enhancing the revenues of the Dean and
Chapter, or of augmenting the income of the vergers
and *loueuses de chaises*, I am not enabled to state, of
carefully locking the doors after you as you pass from
aisle to choir, or from clerestory to sacristy, and then

bolting. You immediately fall into the predicament
of Mr. Laurence Sterne's starling: ' You can't get
out,' unless, indeed, high mass is going on. There are
always some few worshippers kneeling on the straw-
bottomed chairs, or crouching in the dark confessional
corners—but they have some secret modes of egress
which they keep to themselves. The unhappy tourist
is left to the mercy of the verger, who not till the
imprisoned sight-seer has coughed, stamped, and all
but shouted to attract attention, makes his appearance, jingling a huge bunch of rusty keys, and lets
him out, not, however, without extracting from him,
by nods and winks, and innendoes, a very considerable
toll in silver coin. We were so kept captive this
summer morning in Mayence Cathedral for a full
quarter of an hour; but we—at least, I—did not so
much regret our incarceration; for as companions in
durance we had the veritable pretty young German
laies with their mamma whom we had met on board
the *Prinz von Preussen* on the previous day. They
loked more charming than ever; but by their semi-
suppressed giggling and chattering I conjectured them
 belong to the Lutheran persuasion. The red-nosed
man—confound his impudence!—was absolutely about
to reprove them for their levity; but I soon settled
hat individual's little affair. Our stout friend has
decreed that he s to be placed on half-rations of Rhine
wine for a week. The hardened fellow says that he
much prefers beer; but this is the old story of the
fox and the grapes. The young ladies and their
mamma were unaccompanied by the awkward lout;
which you will say was a piece of good fortune; but
of what avail was it to us? The German belonging
to self and (stout) friend did not amount to half a
dozen words; and the man with the iron chest, who
was really master of a few available sentences, had
turned sulky, and flatly refused to act as interpreter.

So the pretty German girls flitted out of the cathedral, at last, and we saw them no more,"

So back to the Hotel d'Angleterre, and to breakfast (to adopt the style of Mr. Secretary Pepys), and then to paying the bill, and trying to buy some good cigars, and purchasing a hundred as an experiment (which turned out abominably); then, because the day was so fine and the sky so blue, to the consumption of a flask or two of sparkling Moselle; and then, because the day was so hot, to a decided inclination to reclining on sofas, and even on door-steps, and indulging in "forty winks." But to wakiny up manfully, and to more strolling about Mayence' quaint streets, and marking the pretty peasant girls, with their pink and blue-striped stockings (which "did my eyes good to see," said the slim gentleman), and to watching the curious long low drays, drawn by patient oxen, that pulled from the nose, and not fren the shoulder; and then to the hotel again, and o conversing with the bald-headed waiter, who lookd so solitary in the vast *salle à manger* that the stot gentleman called him Robinson Crusoe, and who tol them that three weeks since his Highness Princ Metternich had stopped with his suite for nine day, at the hotel, and was a most affable, not to say charming, old gentleman, and had presented him, Robinson Crusoe, with twenty florins; at which statement the man with the iron chest did not seem the least edified; but remarked, first, that the anecdote about the twenty florins was given merely as an incentive to the liberality of departing travellers; and, further, that he had scarcely ever stopped at a German hotel without hearing that Prince Metternich had been there, or was expected the day after to-morrow. "It's like travelling post in Russia," he said; "the horses are always taken up for Prince Galitzin; and it's my belief," concluded the red-nosed cynic, "that Prince

Metternich is nothing more than an aristocratic bagman. It's all very well to talk about his having ruled the Austrian empire with a rod of iron for years, and refused to pick up Napoleon's hat; but I tell you that he's a commercial traveller for his own wines, sir."

And then, to crossing the Rhine to a *bourgade* called Mainz-Castel, in the dominions of his Serene Highness the Elector of Hesse-Cassel, which, as all readers of Herr von Kotzebue's lugubrious and lachrymose play of the "Stranger" may learn, was fixed upon by that misanthropic recluse, in the turn-down collar and Hessian boots, as his abode, and where he consorted with Francis, and agreed with the repentant Adelaide that there was "another and better world." And then, taking railway, and narrowly missing stepping into the wrong train, which was bound to Wiesbaden, to trotting cosily through a smiling sleepy country whose fat fields were planted alternately with vines and tobacco, and by pudgy little stations, painted in the fantastic stripes with which minor German potentates love to decorate their public edifices, from lamp-posts and railings to sentry boxes and barracks, to FRANKFORT-ON-THE MAINE.

But first to Hockheim, whence comes the delicious Rhine wine known as Hockheimer, abbreviated in commercio-vinous English parlance to "Hock," a designation bestowed as much at random among German wines as "claret" among French ones. And at Hockheim the slim gentleman had a dream. He had been drowsy ever since breakfast, and the sparkling Moselle, and the inclination to somnolence, were shared by his companions. So the "forty winks" about which they had hesitated at Mayence, were prolonged into forty times four hundred, to be moderately statistical; and for miles they slept the sleep of the just. The slim gentleman dreamt. His vision

was of Paradise.   Not that at whose gate Mr. Thomas
Moore's Peri "stood one morn disconsolate," listening
to the springs—

> " Of light within, like music flowing,
>   And caught the light upon her wings,
>   Through the half-open portal glowing."

No—the slim gentleman's paradise was of a more
material kind; and save, inasmuch that there were no
moon-faced houris in it, was akin to that of Mahomet.
It was a paradise of wines he saw; and such a paradise! and of such wines!   All the resources of the
famous cellar of the " Drei Mohren " inn at Augsburg
seemed to have been drawn upon to recruit the ranks

A DREAM OF RHINE WINE.

of the army of bottle imps, who capered and scintil-
lated, and danced and oscillated round his sleep-
deluded eyes. There was Rudesheimer, and there
was Marcobrunner; there was the lordly Aftenthaler,
the ruddy Assmanshaüser, the balmy Liebfraumilch,
the unpretending Pisporter, the refreshing Geisenheimer, the patrician Steinberg Cabinet, the priceless
Schloss Johannisberg, the unattainable (save by Sardanapalus, Baron Rothschild, and Prince Esterhazy)
Imperial Tokay. They gurgled, they fizzed, they
sparkled, they seemed to call aloud to be poured into
Bohemian glasses of strange shape and pattern, and
quaffed incontinently; and the slim gentleman began
to murmur in his sleep for corkscrews and nippers—

IN THE "JUDEN STRASSE" AT FRANKFORT.

till the slow rumbling train came to a halt, and gruff Teutonic voices announced that they had arrived at Frankfort.

In which fair city they made but a very transitory stay : first setting eyes on its cheerful houses about five p.m., and leaving it at eight. Don't give way to disappointment ; don't be impatient. The three travellers were fated to return again and again to the Imperial City ere their three weeks' holiday was in the sere and yellow leaf ; and I reserve for a future chapter the description of the famous " Juden Strasse," or Jews' Street, and the enthusiastic reception which the stout gentleman met with from the children of Jewry ; of the celebrated shambles, where Victor Hugo would have purchased the little pink sucking-pig, if he had known what to do with it afterwards ; of the Medusa and Holofernes Fountains ; of the Collegiate Church, the " Roemer," where the kaisers of the Holy Roman Empire used to be proclaimed ; and the other lions of the city of the Cæsars and the Pfarrthum, and of the enormous financial Entity of Messrs. Rothschild and Sons.

From the station they drove in a roomy vehicle, equally resembling a dropsical sedan-chair on wheels and an omnibus with the middle taken out and the two ends joined together, to the office of the Post ; for both the stout gentleman and the man with the iron chest had been lamenting ever since they left Cologne that no time had been afforded them to post their letters. Both had covered voluminous sheets of manuscript with close writing, crossed and crossed again, in the saloon of the Rhine steamer ; and both expressed considerable nervousness at not having yet committed their correspondence to the letter-box. The stout gentleman hinted that some one in the neighbourhood of Bedford Square, London, would " comb his hair " on his return if he did not write at least four times a week ; and the M. I. C. plainly declared that " blood would flow " if he missed another post to England. As to whose blood was to flow he was not so explicit, but from subsequent allusions to one " Julia," whom he stated to be a Tartar, it was of sanguinary proceedings on that lady's part that he was, it appears, apprehensive.

The post-office at Frankfort is not merely an establishment for the pre-payment of letters, or for the holding of that solace to travellers, a *poste restante :* there is a large court-yard, there are stables and coach-houses, there is a passengers' waiting-room, and a booking-office for luggage ; there are horses, postilions, and certain clumsy, ill-built, lumbering carriages, with heavy wheels, and painted scarlet and yellow bodies, divided into compartments like the old French *coucou* diligences which used to run to Versailles. In other words, from the " Post Bureau," at Frankfort, start mail-coaches and *estafettes* for many parts of Germany. Railways are diminishing their number every year : the Rhine-Necker line, now in course of construction, will, it is anticipated, give them their quietus ; but meanwhile there are yet plenty of places in the interior where the visits of the old abdominous red and yellow stage-wagons are welcome.

The court-yard, at about half-past five p.m., was dotted with travellers, male and female, who presently entered, or ascended the roof of, one of these vehicles, to which were harnessed, *by ropes*, four lank, lean horses, in woful condition, and which was presently driven off with much shouting and whip-cracking ; the outsiders ducking their heads as they passed under the low-browed archway of the Hotel des Postes. But previous to their departure, the companions of the man with the iron chest—returning from the *poste restante*, where they had been to see if by chance any letters had arrived for them—discovered that mysterious Bardolph in close confabulation with a dwarfish gentleman, who, though quite beardless and very ruddy in complexion, looked immensely old. The dwarf was a great dandy, and had very near as large a courier-bag by his side as the stout gentleman. Either he seemed to have taken a great liking to the red-nosed man, or the red-nosed man to him; for the two were talking, and laughing, and gesticulating, and exchanging cigar-lights; and when the dwarf was called away by the *conducteur* to his place in the *banquette* of the departing *diligence*, he shook hands warmly with the red-nosed man, and seemed inclined to leap up, cast his arms about his neck, and kiss him on both cheeks.

"Do you know him?" asked the slim gentleman as

THE DWARF OF THE BUREAU DES POSTES.

they walked away from the Post Bureau. "Is he
Count Beniowski come to life again? Is he General
Tom Thumb's great-grandfather?"

"Never saw him before in my life," was the M. I.
C.'s reply. "He spoke excellent French ; wanted me
to come and take Kirsch-wasser and German sausage
with him, and seemed inclined to ask me to stop a week
with him. He lives in the Friedriche Strasse. Dwarfs,
if you don't laugh at them in the first instance (when
they immediately want to poison you) are generally
very good fellows. He is going to Hombourg."

"You mean Hamburg. It's on the Elbe."

"I mean Hombourg," reiterated the red-nosed

FOR HOMBOURG VON-DER-HÖHE!

man; "and it isn't on any river at all. It's of der Höhe, and it's at the foot of the Taurus Mountains."

"Well, and what more about Hombourg?" asked the slim gentleman, rather superciliously.

"What more!" echoed the exciteable M. I. C. "What more? Happiness more; Youth more; Beauty more; Splendour more; Delirious Joy and Luxury more!

> "'In Xanadu did Kubla Khan
>   A stately pleasure dome decree,
> From which a sounding river ran,
> Thro' caverns measureless to man,
>   Down to a sunless sea.'"

"Stop him, stop him!" cried the stout gentleman. "He's had a sun-stroke; he's been eating opium; he's mad!"

"If this unseemly behaviour continues, and in the most public street of the wealthy and respectable free imperial city of Frankfort," the slim gentleman interposed, "I give you fair warning that I shall immediately return to England, and leave you gentlemen to find your way home in the manner most pleasing to you. Now proceed, if you can, rationally, my rednosed interlocutor."

The M. I. C. proceeded, and so rationally; he gave them (at second-hand from the dwarf) such chastened yet glowing accounts of Hombourg-von-der-Höhe, as a place situated amidst some of the most charming scenery in Europe, and only eight miles distant from Frankfort—as an Armida's garden of dainty and delicate dalliance, where life was a round of feasting, singing, dancing, and merrymaking—that when he had concluded, and the stout gentleman cried "Why not go to Hombourg this very night? we can but come back again, if we don't like it," the slim gentleman did not say him nay; and by common consent they all three retraced their steps to the Post Bureau,

and, at the expenditure of a florin and a half, purchased three tickets for places in the mail-carriage
which was to start for the "Armida's garden of
dainty and delicate dalliance" at eight o'clock that
evening.

They did not dine, however, at the table-d'hôte of
the Hotel de Russie. They partook of their prandial
repast at a French *restaurant a la carte*, where they
dined in a court-yard, at a little green table, under the
spreading shade of some lime-trees. And it is a fact
that, ere dinner was over, the slim gentleman, order-
ing a bottle of Roëderer's champagne, caused his companions to fill bumpers of that exhilarating fluid, and
to drink the following strange toast : " For Hombourg-
von-der-Höhe! for Hombourg, Ho!"

CAPS AND PIPES.

CHAPTER V.

THE TRAVELLERS ARRIVE AT HOMBOURG, ALIAS VANITY FAIR.

THE postilion was a philosopher. I don't say that he had read Ennius, Ælian, Philo, or the Scholiast upon anybody; but he was a philosopher nevertheless. He had garnered up one sage apothegm within that red-waistcoated bosom of his: that it is fitting and proper to make a good beginning and ending—a good entrance and exit in life. Fortune and the Frankforter postal authorities had bestowed upon him a portentous whip with a short stock, and a tremendously long lash, whose crackling sinuosities were horrible to behold and hear. Never did postilion make so good a use of his whip—not a better use, indeed, could any human being make of an instrument of torture whose accursed employment is fading out of prisons and barracks, and families and schools—whose lacerating agency is now confined chiefly to dumb animals, and on those poor brutes even verberated mainly by drivers brutal and unskilful, and which, ere long, this writer hopes will fade away from the world altogether. For no more good ever came of whips and scourges than of racks and thumbscrews. The best use the German postilion made of his *flagellum* was this: that he did not beat his horses therewith. Poor ill-groomed, ragged-tailed, scanty-maned, hollow-eyed animals. with their painfully-defined anatomical development, the rope harness chafing their baggy, rough hides, and their general look of being twin brothers to that lamentable quadruped, standing

VIEW OF HOMBOURG.

on a bleak heath, and taking a Pisgah view of a knacker's-yard at Cow Cross, that you remember in Bewick's splendid, but unfinished woodcut, "Waiting for Death." Small good—only needless aggravation of their sorrows—would it have been to lash those woe-begone ones. So the postilion confined himself to flourishing the whip gaily and incessantly, as the scarlet *post-wagen* rattled over Frankfort's stony streets, brandishing the stock above his head, making the lash gyrate in concentric circles—(and in somewhat unpleasant proximity to the faces of the outside passengers)—and producing a most astounding series of cracking reverberations. The stout gentleman compared them to fireworks, and affected to be able to distinguish between catharine-wheels and Roman candles; the man with the iron chest shamelessly avowed himself to be in an agony of terror; and the slim gentleman (who was in the box-seat—the others were behind) prudently pulled his hat over his brow, and shielded his face with his Bradshaw's Foreign Guide.

"He'll cut my eye out to a certainty," he remarked, somewhat nervously, "I wish, before I'd left, that I'd taken out a policy in the Accidental Death Insurance Company. They gave a pig-jobber the other day ten pounds as compensation for falling out of a gig, and a civil engineer fifty for breaking his shins over a coal-scuttle."

"How would the law affect us if we were to throw the postilion off the box?" the stout gentleman inquired. "There are precedents for such a proceeding. Don't you recollect the case reported in——; well, it doesn't matter; I haven't my law library with me. A sailor had taken an outside back place in a mail-coach, and sat beside the guard, who fancied himself a dab at the French horn, and played a selection of popular airs without cessation all the way from the Bull and Mouth to Highgate Archway. The sailor had no ear, hated music, and repeatedly entreated the scarlet-coated functionary to desist. Guard laughed, and played 'All round my hat' louder than ever. Suddenly there was a dead silence. Coachman, surprised at the dejection of his musical coadjutor, turned round in his box, and, to his horror and amazement, saw his friend's seat in the rumble vacant. 'Where's the guard?' he cried to the sailor. 'Do you mean that confounded trumpeter?' he made reply, cutting a fresh quid; '*I chucked him overboard!*' What if we were to serve the guard in like manner? But they have strange notions of law abroad, and it might be high treason to chuck a postilion overboard."

"You had better take care as to what you are about in a 'free and imperial city,' " observed the M. I. C., with grim significance. "They're the most absolute tyrants in the world; and the Syndic of the Senate is a greater autocrat than the King of Dahomey. If you object to an item in an hotel bill, I believe the Senate banishes you from the city for ever; refusing to marry a tobacconist's stout daughter, if she condescends to make eyes at you from the parlour-window, is imprisonment for life in the dungeons beneath the level of the Maine; smoking other than Frankfort manufactured cigars is fifty thalers fine; and neglecting to purchase fifths in the Frankfort lottery is excommunication."

"You're always bothering about that Frankfort lottery; I think you're an agent for it," the slim gentleman retorted, peevishly. "Hang that whip!" he exclaimed, in painful continuation; "there it is again. One might fancy we were lightning conductors."

But the postilion was a wary man. It was not unadvisedly that I imputed philosophy to him. Rapidly as the whip gyrated, and loud as were its smackings, it did harm neither to man nor beast. It was full of sound and fury; but it signified nothing beyond a

continuous vaunt of **the** speed of the horses, the agility
of the postilion, and what a first-rate turn-out the
Frankfürter-Hombourg Post-Wagen was **altogether.**
It was an invitation for bearded workmen and **plump**
damsels **to come to the casements, and** cry " Ho! the
brave equipage! Ho! **the swift** horses! Ho! the
gallant postilion! May the high, well-born British
lords be generous unto him, **and give him** much
trinkgeld!"

I call him **postilion,** when, **lo! he was a** coachman,
for he sat **on** the box, and **held the** long **reins—**
hempen, pieced with frayed worsted, and **bits of**
ragged chain. And he was **a postilion too;** at least
his costume **seemed** common **in these parts to those**
who rode, as **well** as to **those who drove** post-horses.
A very brave make-up he had now, shiny hat of *cuir
bouilli,* " boiled leather " **they call** oilskin **abroad;**
tremendous **cockade with the free** imperial **city's**
colours: no **ribbons—those were** fripperies fit **only**
for the frivolous French ; **a short blue,** two-inch **tail**
jacket turned up with red, and **with a multiplicity of**
leaden buttons, **all in the** wrong **places, much re-**
sembling the " dibs " **that** school-boys **play** with, and
more the " stage **money,"** the coinage **of** harmless
counterfeit which **the bounteous** lady **counts,** from a
tawdry purse, in the **hand of the** virtuous peasant **in**
the melodrama. **A flaming waistcoat** with an erup-
tion of **butt**ons **thereupon. A** scarlet badge on the
left arm **with an embossed brazen shield, bearing**
Frankfort's **free and imperial arms,—an** eagle **in a**
seeming state **of dubiety whether to have** two **heads**
or one,—probably designed **by way** of compliment to
the rival powers, Austria **and** Prussia, and so making
up its mind **to** looking **like a** griffin **with** some Isis
blood in its veins. A battered bugle, **suspended** *en
bandoulière* **by a parti-coloured** worsted cord, finished
off behind **by two bulbous,** pendulous **excrescences,**
coloured red and white, that were **neither dumb-bells,**

Brobdignagian tassels, nor worsted turnips, but that bore an equal resemblance to all three. Nether-stocks of buckskin, yellow and rigid; and long straight, greased boots like candle-cases. Spurs? no; but spur straps and buckles. It will never do to be poor and seem poor. This is the accoutrement of the German Postilion. He is not so conversational, so full of anecdote, as his French brother of Lonjumeau; he is taciturn, somnolent, almost sulky. His face is very like suet pudding, and he smokes eternally either a rank cigar in a wooden tube, or a cloudy meer-schaum. He wears ear-rings, and a silver ring on his left thumb. His nails are in perpetual half-mourning for the death of the flesh brush. He is, to tell the truth, a stupid lout, and reeks of sauer-krout and bock-bier; but, on the other hand, he does not beat

GERMAN POSTILION.

his horses; does not swear at them, as does the
Frenchman, nor even apply to them such epithets as
"pig's cousin," "Beelzebub's uncle," and so on; but
incites them to their work by uncouth gibberish, now
soothing and now exhilarating. Such is the postilion,
whose name, as a rule, should be Franz, as that of a
German waiter should be Ludwig, and of a German
student Fritz. His attire you will say is sufficiently
gay; but you should have seen him three hours since
when the Three were booking their places to Hombourg. He is curled and brushed and trimmed into a
semi-military spruceness, now; but then he was off
duty, and shambled about the court-yard of the *Posts-
Bureau*, dodging about among the wheels and axle-
poles of the horseless vehicles, a weazened, shabby,
spindle-shanked scarecrow of uncertain age, in a
ragged old stable jacket, and trousers patched and
rent, and a canvas shirt of dubious colour. So have I
peeped through the half-opened door of Knights-
bridge barracks, and beheld the gallant life guards-
man, the magnificence of whose boots and leathers,
the brightness of whose cuirass, and the terror of
whose nodding plume, I have marvelled at as he stood
sentry, his steel scabbarded-sabre trailing, and his
carbine resting on his gauntleted arm beneath the
Horse Guards portico:—beheld him a gawky, common fellow, in bagging shirt and seedy overalls,
trundling a wheelbarrow full of refuse, or sweeping
the barrack-yard with a plebeian birch-broom. Oh,
the virtues of fine clothes! Oh, the advantages of
peg-top trousers and long-waisted coats!

> "Through tatter'd clothes small vices do appear;
> Furs, and rich robes hide all."

In his undress the postilion looked a sorry knave,
very like a haunter of beer-cellars and *tabagies*, and
but passing honest. In his "full fig" he is almost

a government official, is obeyed in his office, and well spoken to by passengers and passing peasants. Oh! the excellence of fine clothes. What would Louis Quatorze have been without his towering periwig and high-heeled shoes, their soles painted with Vandermeulun's victories? Titmarsh has so shown him to you in undress, a lean, forked raddish of a man; no Ludovicus Magnew, but a pinched starveling, *and short in stature*. Take away Dr. Birchmore's master's gown and trencher-cap, with which he awes the trembling scholars nearly as much as with his rod, and with which he impresses the parents and guardians when he offers them cake and wine in the best parlour—what is he, unfrocked, but a brutal semi-illiterate pedant—a vast quantity of Latin and Greek floating about in a vast quantity of bile? Strip off the peer's ermined robes, and a shameful padded old man in stays and a wig totters down Regent Street, leering under the bonnets of the milliners' girls. 'Tis the brass that makes the man in armour at the Lord Mayor's quondam show. Unplate him, and he is but a mechanical varlet; a ticket-porter, or a warehouse sweeper. The very Pope! what is he without the Tiara, the Pallium, and the Fisherman's ring? Only a shivering sexagenarian in a flannel-gown, teased by purple-stockinged dry nurses—*monsignori* and *cammerari!* Sam Johnson sleeping on bulks with reckless Savage for company, and dressed in a ragged horseman's coat, has a plate of victuals handed to him behind a screen. He is not fit to sit down with Mr. Cave's well-dressed contributors, who were so respectable, and of whom nobody hears now. Doctor Samuel Johnson in a suit of well-brushed broadcloth, and his wig new-powdered, dines with Burke and Topham Beauclerc, is toadied by the Laird of Auchinleck's fap son, petted by Mrs. Thrale, and converses even with King George. Great is Diana of the Ephesians: and great also are the successors of Stultz and Nugee. Mr. Shears from Snip Street shall come, to-morrow, to measure me for a new coat with a velvet collar, and a dress waistcoat with a pattern on it like a bow-pot.

To the postilion there was delegated a *conducteur*— a fat man in a fractured accordion cap, and a dark burnous braided all over in the most fantastic manner. He sat by the side of the whipster—the slim gentleman on the other—and had a bugle to himself (the postilion never played on his, and the stout gentleman surmised that it was a "property," one very likely made of pasteboard covered with Dutch metal) from which, from time to time, he discoursed most melancholy music. But he gave it up soon, as did also the postilion his whip-gymnastic and acoustic feats, when a massy gate having been passed through, the last of the stony streets faded into a *chaussée* road—so long, so straight: and the gas-lights of Frankfort were left behind, and the first of the eight miles that lay between that city and Hombourg accomplished. Guard, postilion, and out-sides wrapped themselves in the mantle of silence, the coats and cloaks of a material world, and the environing togas of tobacco smoke; and if the insides didn't go to sleep, I think it a very foolish act on their parts.

For the winds whistled cold, albeit the day had been sultry, and their way, for the first two miles out of Frankfort, lay across a flat plain, which, smiling and fertile enough in the sun, seemed uncommonly bleak and barren now. A long, narrow, straight, powdery road; and the horses plodding therealong in a wearisome, jog-trot manner. No "spanking tits;" no complimentary adjurations to the "old girl" to come up; no recommendation to the off leader to "mind" what he was "up to." The wheels were not greased, the springs were stiff and rebellious; the "axle-pole," notes the stout gentleman, was as thick as a man-o'-war's bowsprit; and slowly and painfully the unwieldy machine toiled along. The fields were very still: only the leaves of the thin trees by the roadside sighed among themselves, and seemed to whisper, "We are gay with our autumn livery now, with orange, and crimson, and purple; but ah! we shall fall, we shall fall! and the unkind November blast will sweep us, and drift us, and send us eddying even from Taunus' foot to Frankfort's barred-up gates."

Four miles an hour—maximum German horse-travelling speed. I suppose this is the *Schnell-post* —the fast coach. As to the ordinary vehicles' rate of locomotion, I presume that it is driven by the Seven Sleepers in succession, and that it is drawn by the foals of the Great Tortoise, on whose back, according to the Hindoo mythology, the elephant stands that supports the world.

Two miles out of Frankfort, the road turns to the left—turns by the tower. Tower very tall and grim, with a slated extinguisher top, like those of the *tourelles* in the old portion of the Paris Conciergérie. Pignons, I think they are called architecturally. Many storeyed is this tower—many storied too, it may be, with ghosts and mediæval legends. Not so much as a dovecot, in this antique Germany, but has its wild tradition. Don't think that the Rhine has a monopoly of these wild stories; that it is alone in its possession of legends as wondrous as "The Pledge of St. Gertrude," the "Swan Tower," the "Solingen Blade," the "Ring of Fastrada," the "Bride of Rheinstein," the "Palatine's Stone," the "Wolf's Glen," or the "Piteous History of Bromser and Gisela." The part of Germany which the Three were now entering, and sometimes called the "Hessian Switzerland," is a very jungle of strange and marvellous remembrances. For the clumsy *post-wagen* is venturing into the green valleys of the Taunus mountains, abounding in healthy springs ["poisonous pumps," growls the man with the iron chest,] and woody uplands, crowned by decaying castles. Like a chain of rusty, honey-combed, worn, half-effaced, dinted, antique coins, these relics embrace the fertile and picturesque country that extends for many leagues along the banks of the Maine. Powerful and illustrious families once resided where the ruins of Königstein, Sonnenburg, and Hohenstein yet rear their haughty, albeit crumbling, turrets; and where the Altking and the Feldsburg raise their lofty heads above the neighbouring hills. Adjoining the "Hessian Switzerland" is the "Nassau Switzerland," where yet exists the village of Eppstein, and the ruins of the immense castle formerly inhabited by counts of the empire, and whose original construction was due, though from circumstances utterly independent of his own volition, to perhaps the most terrible giant that ever existed since the days of Goliath of Gath, Blunderbore of the Midland Counties, and that gigantic Welshman whom the well-known giant-killer, Jack, brought to destruction by means of the artful use of hasty pudding. The story of Eppstein's giant won't take many minutes in telling. Do let me whisper it in your ear, while the stout gentleman lights a fresh cigar, and the man with the iron chest rubs his nose, which he declares is turning red instead of its original blue, and the slim gentleman pulls up the collar of his coat and shivers.

At Eppstein, then, once "upon a time," and even before the time that it was called Eppstein at all, resided a giant, name unknown, huge, savage, and insolent; whose principal amusements were harassing the unhappy shepherds of the prince-archbishop of Mayence, devouring their substance, and kissing their pretty daughters whether they liked it or not; and they did not like it—from a giant:—for this one had four eyes, all bloodshot and flaming, never washed himself, and had a beard as stiff and as strong as Mr. Newall's wire-rope. He was a very drunken giant; and if Mr. George Cruikshank had come that way, would, I have very little doubt, have had him slain and salted, to eat as a whet, like kippered salmon, before his potations. And he was the most insolent giant! He lived in a cavern in the rock at Eppstein; and was the sworn foe of all architects and builders; for if any one attempted to erect a house in his vicinity—were it a lordly castle or a peasant's cot—he would straightway, by the mere employment of his immense strength, pull that house down, and send it tumbling about its owner's ears. "No towers near Taunus," was this wicked Titan's motto. Suppose, for want of a better name, we call him the Giant Rackrent.

Well, it so fell out that Rackrent was compelled to leave the neighbourhood, to assist some of his monstrous brethren near Strasbourg, in Alsace, who had got into difficulties through draining all the beer-casks in the province without paying for them (to say nothing of chucking all the pretty, short-skirted barmaids under the chin, and other misdeeds) and were besieged in their fortress by an army of indignant brewers, beershop-keepers, and fathers of families. Rackrent, the terrific ranger of Taunus' woods and plains, was gone a long time; and the peasants he had persecuted took advantage of his absence to put the brokers into his cavern, for they considered that he owed them many quarters' rent, and seize all his goods and chattels. They found many skulls and bones, a pickled priest, and a smoked monk or two in the larder, lots of hides and fleeces, some chimney-pots, fireplaces, castle gates, donjon-keeps, and odd trifles of that sort, and a vast quantity of gold and silver. They met under the spreading shade of a huge oak to divide the spoil, for news had come that Rackrent had perished for want of beer and corn-brandy in his Alsatian beleaguerment; and dying intestate, they **thought** themselves entitled to administer to his effects. Of course they all **fell to** quarrelling about their several shares; and the *pfarrer*, or parson, had just caught **the** *schullmeister*, or dominie, by the hair of the head, **on the** disputed question of a **silver tooth-pick, as** big as a kitchen-poker, when a **young knight, who gave** his **card**, beautifully **emblazoned** in mediæval **chromo-lithography,** as "Eppo, Ritter" [he **was** descended, Mr. Beaverup, from the Eppos, designed of Kloppstein, whom you will recollect **were descended from the** Schinkensturms of Kalbstein (998), **and one** of whom (circâ **1193)** became allied by marriage with the Von Bopsteins, of Schuesburg, from which illustrious family, as we all know, issued **the celebrated** Boppsius (1601-1678), **who was Professor of** Prevenient Grace at the University of Schwinge**bosen**, and taught metaphysics to his Excrescence Schaffskopf XXXIII., eighty-seventh Landgrave **of** Hesse-Boostein.] Eppo, avowing **utter** indifference **to the** matter in dispute between the villagers, was unanimously, as a knight and a gentleman, chosen for umpire; and he decided so equitably, and so **much to** the satisfaction of all parties, that, although in the morning he had only been the possessor of a light heart and a thin pair of "chain mail greaves," in addition to his knightly spurs, he found himself, **ere dusk set in, the owner, in** freehold, and by the very best tenure—that **of** possession—of a fruitful and **verdant hill, which rose** with a gentle slope from the bosom of the lowlands.

I think that Eppo **must have been bred to the law** in his **youth, and have** completed his education among the Jesuits of Douai or St. Omer (you see I am making **quite** light of chronology in this legend), for he **proved** himself a remarkably crafty customer. Though he would take **no** immediate pecuniary compensation for his award as arbitrator, he had not the slightest objection to receive the many handsome testimonials in kind which flowed upon him. By degrees, too, he got over his reluctance about money-taking, and gradually persuaded the peasants to advance him large sums towards building a huge castle on the summit of the Giant's Rock, whose construction, he assured them, was necessary for their protection in case any of the relatives or friends of the defunct Rackrent should make an irruption in that part of the country. The villagers, who had for years proved themselves wonderfully obstinate in their refusal to render cess and taxes to the archbishop of Mayence, and could only be persuaded to pay tithes and church-rates to their own *pfarrer* by the threat of excommunication, were as astonishingly accommodating towards Eppo. Fear or gratitude led them to grant him all he asked for ; and a splendid fortress was built, with the giant's quondam cave beneath for a wine-cellar, and a neat well-shaft beneath that, stocked with rats from the preserves of Jacobus Burnstoii at Mayence, for the confinement of recalcitrant tenants, hostile barons, and young ladies who refused to be wooed. Did it never strike you, peering into the dark ruined dungeons, and roofless torture-chambers of mediæval castles, that these horror-fraught places, these toy-shops of tyranny, these boudoirs of blood, must have been built by plebeian workmen, labouring for daily wages, forging fetters for hire, bricking up *oubliettes*, lead-sheeting *piomb bi*, for so much a week ? And did it never occur to you to reflect what fools these workmen must have been, so to fashion collars for their own necks and rods for their own backs ? I will tell you the secret of their blind, self-ruinous obedience. *They couldn't read nor write.* Such a ten thousand thousand horse-power there is in ignorance,—accruing all to the man who knows things ! And woe be to the innocent ignorant if Sapientissimus be a rogue ! Look at that man-at-arms, pacing, halberd in hand, before the iron cage in which his brother languishes on straw. Look at that besotted negro tearing his wife, his daughter, his sweetheart's naked flesh with the bloody cowhide, at the bidding of Mr. Jonathan Jefferson Whitlaw, who, in his rocking chair, smokes his cheroot, and sips his sangaree. Look at that man in the red blanketing, with the knapsack and cross-belts, risking his life for a few pence a day, rotting in hospitals, starving in trenches, tossed about in a filthy transport, crowded in a fœtid barrack, and all because Barabbas in the East cannot agree with Judas in the West; because Captain Macheath considers himself to have been lightly spoken of by Claude du Val, and Dick Turpin had a difference of opinion with Sixteen-String Jack. Look at that elephant piling logs, dragging cannon, pushing wagons, bearing palanquins, standing on his head, dancing sarabands in a circus, at the bidding and beneath the coercion of a mahout's goad, or a showman's switch. Oh! if they only *knew*, these darkened ones! knew their strength and power; what a terrible upsetting of the balance of authority, and the " relative duties of superiors and inferiors," there would be, to be sure! The monkeys know all about it; but those we see in Europe, out of menage-ries, are like the conies, but a feeble-folk, else would they turn and rend their Italian organ-grinding tyrants. The Gorilla, too, knows all about it, and in his native wilds will stand no nonsense from educated and despotic Man. I should counsel the directors of the Crystal Palace to keep a very sharp look out after *their* specimen. The Gorilla let loose is not to be imposed upon; and would think no more of smashing all the panes of the palace with the fury of a pauper in the refractory ward of a workhouse, or of clearing the refreshment counters of Messrs. Sawyer and Strange, than of cracking a cob-nut.

To return to Eppo of Eppstein. He paid neither architect nor contractor for his castle. He paid neither for the masonry from the quarry, for the bricks from the field, nor for the gas-fittings. nor for the encaustic tiles in the entrance-hall. He didn't even pay for the stamps and parchment of the conveyance of the castle and domain to him and his heirs for ever; yet he continued to accept, with many thanks, the pecuniary offerings of the peasantry, who had been his hosts, and soon found themselves his tenants—and at a very stiff rental, too; nay, when the castle was brought to completion, he was entertained at a grand banquet in the castle hall, at which the *pfarrer* took the chair, at which Eppo made a neat speech, full of references to a bold peasantry, their country's pride, and crammed with quotations from Niebelungen Lied. For the banquet, or for the strong beer and sparkling Rhine wine, Otto the knight did not pay, not he. Don't you know people who are always going through life never paying, but being paid for, and getting people to present them with things? Eppo, however, did some work for his money, and while he ruled the roast at his eleemosynary castle, the countryside enjoyed a tranquillity and prosperity it had not known for years.

Eppo was a bachelor, and abided by the adage of "early to bed and early to rise." He was quietly reposing on his turn-up bedstead one summer evening, thinking what a remarkably nice investment he had made in building lots, when he heard a tremendous clattering above his head. Horror! The vaulted roof was tumbling in. Presently the walls began to shake and fall in too; Eppo had but just time to leap out of a window—(he slept on the first floor)—when the whole castle fell with one frightful crash into a heap of ruins. But no architect, no builder, no foundations were at fault, as at the Brunswick Theatre or Fonthill Abbey. *It was the grim giant Rackrent* who had come post-haste from Alsace, having made a composition with the besieging brewers, and who had battered Eppo's fine castle to fragments with his iron mace, laughing, Homerically, meanwhile. "Build on my land, Hey!" cried the giant Rackrent. ".Oho! we'll see!" And down went the castle walls like overripe Stilton cheese.

Eppo, unable for the time to contend with the giant, left that part of the country, taking with him, so report said, a very considerable per-centage of the sums that had been subscribed by the credulous peasantry. And there was weeping in the valley of Eppstein, for the Giant carried on worse and drank harder than ever; ground the noses of the villagers quite flat to their faces, and wouldn't let even so much as a pig-stye be built without hammering at it with his iron mace. They sighed for the halcyon days of the politic knight Eppo to come again; and their hopes were at last gratified. Even as the last of the Tribunes, driven from Rome by the Colonnas and the Orsinis, caused these ominous words to be placarded on the great staircase of the Capitol—"*Rienzi ritornera*," so did Sir Eppo one fine morning ride boldly back to Eppstein, accompanied by half-a-dozen servants, driving before them mules laden with heavy sacks. Eppo would by no means tell the villagers what these sacks contained, and strictly enjoined his servants—who were sweet-faced men, vigorous of limb and heavy of muscle, wearing leather aprons, and in all things resembling blacksmiths—to observe strict silence as to what the sacks contained. But on the next afternoon, which happened to be a very sultry summer one, Sir Eppo hied him to his dismantled castle, where the giant, never having taken even so much trouble as to have a new roof put on, still abode, and lay, like an old bear, among bones and blood. The monster was in the habit of taking his after-dinner nap within an open space enclosed by the walls; and here the knight found him, stretched on the broad of his back—he had drunk half an anker of

Johannisburg at his meal—with only a few ells of sailcloth to screen him from the heat of the sun, and snoring till the half-dislodged blocks of stone in the wall trembled again. Forthwith the wary Eppo made a sign to his followers. Forthwith the sacks were opened, and a multitude of strong iron rings taken out and linked together with the greatest caution and despatch. Rackrent, stupified with his brutish orgies, never stirred, and Sir Eppo and his merry men were enabled deftly to encircle him with a heavy network of iron rings. Some unavoidable clanking, however, ultimately woke him, but only to find himself as completely taken in the toils as a hare in its springe. How he swore! How he raved! How, after that, he roared and whined for mercy—the big, blustering coward! It was rare sport for Eppo and his blacksmiths, who stood by, holding their sides for laughter; and they laughed louder when the enshackled giant, seizing the horn that hung by his side, blew a prodigious blast upon it; for its only effect was to bring the old men and husbandmen, the peasant lads and lasses, from the neighbouring village, who all fell to shouting and clapping their hands for joy to see their old enemy thus taken in a trap. The end of it was, that they all clambered to the top of the highest wall that was standing, and hurled stones and fragments of rock upon the prostrate form of Herr von Rackrent, giant, till that immense and wicked devastator gave up the ghost. In gratitude to Eppo for their delivery, the grateful people immediately commenced rebuilding his castle, which, when completed, yielded to no Schloss in Germany for beauty and strength. In order to remind future generations of the wonderful circumstances which had led to its erection, the bones of the giant were fixed over the entrance-gate, *à la mode de* Newgate, London; and when they mouldered away, effigies thereof were carved in stone, as undeniable testimony to the truth of the story—evidence, I think, as irrefragable as was the brick in the chimney to prove the identity of Jack Cade's house. Sir Eppo thenceforth became Lord Eppo, of Eppstein, and ruled the peasantry most aristocratically. In his latter days he had a weakness for the rack and the spiked collars, as applied to tenants who talked about their rights; but he was always a highly-respectable lord, and his numerous offspring (for he married soon after he had come to his property, or rather after his property had come to him) contracted matrimonial alliances with the very first families, possessing illimitable heraldric quarterings. The Eppos von Eppstein became, indeed, one of the richest and most powerful baronial families in Rhenish Germania, and were utterly rooted up and driven to extinction during the thirty years' war.

"Is this Hombourg, I wonder," the stout gentleman asked, waking up from among the folds of his gray wrapper, and rubbing his eyes.

"Hombourg, *Ja*," answers the *conducteur*, understanding nothing of the query but the name of the town, and becoming polite all at once (he had been surly three-quarters of the way) in hope of *trinkgeld*.

"Hombourg, by Jove!" echoed the slim gentleman and the M. I. C., who had both been fast asleep while I was telling you the story of Eppo and the giant Rackrent. Aha! the artful device of getting over those eight miles from Frankfort, when all was as dark as pitch, and I could not describe the surrounding scenery. "Why, it's like a Cumberland village."

The *post-wagen* was dragging (for the four miserable Rosinantes that drew it were well-nigh spent by this time) through a narrow, crooked street, with tumble-down-looking houses, heavily timbered, with projecting eaves, like clumsy Swiss châlets. Not a soul was to be seen abroad, not a light was to be seen in any of the latticed windows. It seemed either a village of barns or a village of dead men. A hideous old church, with a ruinous bulging steeple (the moon, hitherto coy, had begun to show herself by this time), like a sugar-loaf with pieces knocked out of its sides, suddenly loomed in sight as they turned the corner, together with its graveyard, full of fantastic tombstones, and surrounded by walls of masonry, so thick they seemed like ramparts, to prevent, I suppose, the dead people from tumbling out into the road. One distant cock, and he must have been an idiot, for it was not yet ten p.m., kept up an incessant crowing, under the mistaken idea that it was morning.

"Upon my word this is a pretty place to bring people to," the stout gentleman remarked, half humorously, half savagely. "This comes of knowing red-nosed men, who pick up promiscuous acquaintances in stable-yards, dwarfs and monsters, and pig-faced ladies and children with two heads. I see it all now. Hombourg is a mere country village. We shall have to put up at the 'Travellers' Joy' or the 'Half Moon and Seven Stars,' where we shall sleep in beds with white dimity curtains, and have eggs and bacon for breakfast. We can spend the evening in the tap-room, and hear Farmer Wutts sing 'Grunters half-a-score,' and I daresay there is some nice trout-fishing in the neighbourhood, and that the parson of the parish will call upon us for contributions to the coal and blanket distribution club. Why, what the deuce do you mean by it, sir?" he continued, turning to the red-nosed man with sudden ferocity.

"It isn't my fault," remonstrated that much badgered individual. "He told me it was a most sumptuous place."

"Told you!" echoed the stout gentleman. "Yes; and Hope told a flattering tale."

"Besides," urged the M. I. C., "this may be only a suburb of Hombourg. We may come to something better presently."

"Yes," replied the slim gentleman with withering irony, "to the pound, no doubt, and the stocks and the whipping post, and the ducks in the pond. Upon my word, sir, you've brought your pigs to a remarkably fine market."

This unkind and decidedly unparliamentary expression had scarcely escaped from the slim gentleman's lips, when the narrow, ill-paved little street merged into the smooth, powdry *chaussée* again. Then succeeded a range of—as well as the moon would allow them to see—kitchen gardens, then a grove of tufted trees, and then—

THEN a broad, handsome, well-paved street, of seemingly interminable length. No gas-lamps on the pavement, but a profusion of big oil *reverséres* hung from ropes stretched high across the thoroughfare: plenty of shops, however, brilliantly lighted with gas —shops, too, gaily decorated and handsomely stocked. There were jewellers, watchmakers, milliners, staymakers, confectioners, tobacconists, stationers, printsellers, venders of toys and knicknacks. Jewels gleamed, waxen "dummies" simpered from hairdressers' shops; the air was redolent of the fumes of expensive cigars, the odour of genuine *eau de-Cologne* and patchouli; and the foot pavement was thronged with groups of dandies, in waxed moustaches and patent leather boots, and ladies with ravishing bonnets and cavalier-hats, and whose crinoline rustled in the autumn night breeze. So many large white buildings, too, with jalousied windows, on whose entablatured friezes you might read " Banque de Commerce," " Banque du Landgrafschaft," " Banque d'Escompte," " Banque et Bureau de Change."

" Why, I've passed three Rothschilds already,"

the stout gentleman called out in amazement. "We shall come upon the statue of the Golden Calf next."

Midway in this grand street the road receded some hundred paces, forming a quadrangular area. Bounded by a gravelled carriage-drive, the area itself was laid out in grass-plats, and parterred, and was pierced in the midst by a broad avenue, lined by a double row of splendid orange-trees in tubs, and laden with fruit. And at the bottom, parallel with the street, was a vast and sumptuous edifice—a *corps de logis*—and wings of Grecian architecture. The lofty windows were blazing with gas; and before the portal stood carriages, while liveried lacqueys, and more dandies, and more ladies, in crinoline and cavalier-hats, hurried in and out.

"KURSAAL," said the postilion, pointing as usual with his whip.

"What's Kursaal?" asked the stout gentleman. "The club, I suppose?"

"A concert and ball-room, perhaps," suggested the slim one.

Little did these three unsophisticated travellers know that the Kursaal was the chief booth in Vanity Fair.

So many vast, lofty, handsome mansions there were too, with large court-yards and *portes cochères*, and whose lower floor seemed to be occupied as *cafés*, for the travellers could see bearded and moustached loiterers smoking, drinking—card, domino, and billiard playing. The balconies, too, were full of idlers, ladies and gentlemen, puffing, cool-drink sipping, and flirting in the calm evening. What could these mansions be?

"Hodel di Bavière," growled the postilion, pointing with his whip to a very large house.

"Ha!" said the stout gentleman.

"Hodel des guadre Zaizons," the postilion next deigned to designate.

"Dear me!" observed the stout gentleman.

"Hodel di Rome, de la Belle Edoile, de l'Embereur, de l'Eurobe, de la Gouronne di Brusse, Hodel Hesse, Hodel Royar, Hodel di FRANCE," the postilion went on in rapid succession, shifting his whip from right to left.

"You don't say so!" was the acute and pertinent remark of the stout gentleman.

They halted for a moment as these sage words escaped him, and were suddenly aware of the presence of a large white poodle, which advanced to the horses' heads as though to greet them. He was a very nice poodle, duly shaven, oiled, curled, trimmed, and frizzled up to the perfection of canine dandyism. He elevated his moist black muzzle to the Three—a highly-educated, accomplished, sophisticated, abominable beast. He seemed to say, "I am here—behold me. I am civilisation—I am Vanity. You are welcome—Evoc!"

"Why, this is Paris!" said the Three with almost unanimity.

"*Paris, ja. sehr schön*," the postilion chimed in, "*aber Hombourg ist also schön, O! wunderschön.*"

'Tis one of their idiosyncrasies in Germany, when you travel by stage-coach, to insist upon carrying you from post-station to post-station. They don't like you to join the *wagen* after its departure, and can't bear you to alight before it has reached its full point of destination. Thus the postilion insisted (if driving one without paying the slightest attention to remonstrances and arm-tugging can be taken as insisting) on proceeding at least a hundred yards beyond the Hotel de France, where the travellers (acting under the recommendation of the dwarf to the M. I. C.) had arranged to "descend," as the continental term is. To the complexion of the Post-Bureau at Hombourg, having started from the Post-Bureau at Frankfort, the postilion was determined to come, and the travellers had nothing to do but to submit. So they were taken to the post, their luggage landed, *trinkgelds* distributed to driver and conductor; and some ten minutes afterwards, having made the necessary retrograde march, they were safely housed in three several bedchambers at the Hotel de France at Hombourg-von-der-Höhe.

THE KURSAAL, HOMBOURG, FROM THE GARDENS.

CHAPTER VI.

THE TRAVELLERS "MAKE THEIR GAME" IN EARNEST.

"Hombourg-von-der-Höhe," I find, in the diary of the slim gentleman, "lies in the midst of a charming and fertile plain between Frankfort and the Taunus, and at the foot of a bold eminence, crowned by a white tower, which dominates the country for many miles round—the castle and palace of the Landgrave of Hesse-Hombourg. It was founded by the Romans, who have left a circumvallated camp, and many other interesting remains in the neighbourhood. Where, indeed, on the earth's surface, have that astonishing people not left durable traces of their presence? Its 'traceable' history commences in the twelfth century, at which time the Counts of Hanau sold it to Godfrey of Epdstein. Concerning this Epdstein, or Eppstein family, certain wild and improbable legends exist" (wild and improbable, indeed! after the pains I have been at to tell you the most accredited version of the story of Eppo and the Giant Rackrent in the last chapter), "but much reliance cannot be placed thereupon. One legend sets forth that the Schloss of Hombourg was built on Roman foundations by Eppo of Eppstein, great grandson of him who slew a certain giant, and delivered a beautiful maiden called Bertha from his clutches." (I find no mention of any young woman of that name in my legend.) "I don't believe in knights or giants at all myself, and it is just as probable that the town and castle of Eppstein derive their name from the ivy, which grows hereabout in great abundance, and whose name in German is *Ep-pich* or *Ephen*.

"A.D. fourteen hundred and something, Hombourg was 'sold again' for nineteen thousand gold florins to the Count of Hanau; and about a hundred years afterwards, during the reign of the Emperor Maximilian, it fell under the sovereignty of Hesse. The Kaiser 'enfeoffed' Wilhelm II. as Landgraf of Hesse, and the feof was confirmed by the Diet of Worms. In 1518, Philip the Magnanimous inherited the whole of 'Hessia'—superb patrimony! could 'all the Russias' equal it in magnificence and extent?—and in the next century the little fief of Hombourg became a matter of bitter contention between the houses of Hanau, Eppstein, Hombourg, and Hesse-Darmstadt. Indeed, the Katzenellbogens even are said to have put in a claim at last; but the Hombourgers proper had the best of it, and the honour of seeing their town and castle sacked, first, by the Imperialists, and next, by the Swedes, during the thirty years' war. Since then a succession of Ludwigs, Friedrichs, Karls, and Wilhelms, have reigned as Landgrafs over Hombourg. The sovereignty, indeed, suffered a temporary eclipse during the wars of Napoleon the Great, that distinguished promoter of 'order at home' and of anarchy abroad, who quite snuffed out, temporarily, Landgrave Friedrich the Fifth, in 1806. The lackland Landgrave had to dodge about Europe, one of the then large community of insolvent sovereigns, till the Congress of Vienna, which proved itself so remarkably liberal in giving away what didn't belong to it, confirmed him in the full possession of his ancient rights, adding thereto, by way of bonus, the province of Meisenheimer beyond the Rhine. The grapes, however, grown at Meisenheimer did not prove to be of very first-rate quality, and the wine made therefrom has never commanded an extraordinary price in the market. The present Landgrave rejoices in the appellations of

Ferdinand-Heinrich-Friedrich. He has been an Austrian Field-Marshal Lieutenant, and fought in Italy. He has never been married; he is seventy-four years old; and at his death the principality of Hesse-Hombourg, and the suzerainty of the Feldsburg, the Schloss, and the Kursaal, will revert to the house of Hesse-Darmstadt. How sings the poet of the equity courts?

> " ' This fertile pasturage—these branching oaks,
> Were once the property of John-a-Nokes.
> Fortune on John-a-Nokes no longer smiles,
> The land is now the property of John-a-Stiles.'

" Such is the way of the world, in the tenure of land as in other matters. Hombourg, the town, is six hundred feet above the level of the sea. The streets are well paved, and scrupulously clean, though not the slightest apparatus for purposes of drainage appears to exist. But there are plenty of pumps and fountains; and the air seems to be particularly clear, bracing, and salubrious. The amount of romantic prospect—including the blue and purple Taunus in the extreme distance—that you may see with the naked eye, is extremely refreshing. The inhabitants, and the surrounding peasantry, male and female, are very ugly, but not very healthy. The ancient name of the district was, I believe, Hohenburg or Höhnbourg. There is an old town and a new town, and the population of the two is computed at about six thousand. It has increased, and does increase, every year at a prodigious rate. The main street is called the *Luisen Strasse*, running from south-east to north-west; there are two public squares, and at the lower end a fountain called *Pompejibrunnen*—'from its resemblance,' the guide-books say, 'to a fountain dug out of the ruins of that city.' I boldly tell Mr. Schick, the publisher of the guide in question, that this resemblance is fancied; and that the fountain is much more like Barber Beaumont's pump in Piccadilly,

than any relic of Pompeii with which I am acquainted.
Besides the Luisen Strasse there are the Promenade
and the Dorothean Strasse, the Haingasse, and the
Oberthor; and half way up the main street is the
finest building in the town, finer than church or
barracks, palace or public offices, the KURSAAL.   It
is is also called 'Kurhaus;' behind it is the 'Kur-
garten;' it has also a 'Kur-Bank,' and a 'Kur-Polizei-
Direction;' but more of it, and them, and all the
Kurs in Kurdom, anon.

"The state religion of the principality of Hombourg is Protestant, and there is a remarkably hideous
building, which I suppose I must call a cathedral,
and which is devoted to the worship of the Lutheran
persuasion.   It is called the Stadt Kirche.   There is
also a Roman Catholic church; and in the Juden
Strasse—for this little mite of a capital has also its
Ghetto, its Jews' Street—there is a synagogue.   The
communicants of the different persuasions live together in great harmony; the *odium theologicum* seems
suspended in order to avoid giving offence to the cos-
mopolitan visitors on whose presence the prosperity
of Hombourg depends; and the Lutherans are toler-
ant enough to admit of the celebration of divine
service, according to the rites of the Church of England, in the Stadt Kirche.   There is a Hofprediger
and a Consistorial-Rath (Lutheran), and a Gross
Oberpfarrer, and Stadtpfarrer (Calvinist).   There is
a town school, attended by about six hundred children, and taught by eight masters; and since the
'regeneration' and 'revival' of Hombourg by means
of the Kursaal, private boarding and day schools are
springing up everywhere, and greatly flourish.   There
is an orphan-house, a poor-house, also an hospital
supported by voluntary contributions, a ladies' benevolent society, a police-office called the 'L. H. Ver-
wallungsamt,' a court of justice, or 'L. H. Justiz-
Amt,' presided over by a 'Regierungsrath;' there is

a Commissaire du Gouvernement for the Kursaal, and a special Commissaire of the Kursaal for, and belonging to, the Kursaal itself. There are *three lawyers*,—one more than Peter the Great possessed when he visited England in 1691, and told the English nobleman that he meant to hang one of them when he got back to Moscow. The number of physicians cannot be determined with exactitude, for they increase every day. There are three public newspapers, the Government 'Gazette,' or 'Regierungs-Blatt,' which only appears periodically; the 'Amts-und-Intelligenz-Blatt,' a journal of general news, which comes out every Sunday; and the 'Kurliste,' or 'Fremden-Blatt,' which is published from twice to five times a week, according to the business of the season, and which contains a more or less accurate record of the arrival and departure of visitors. These visitors in 1834 amounted to one hundred and fifty-five, and in 1856 to the prodigious number of *ten thousand one hundred and five*. This astonishing augmentation is due to the establishment and development of the Kursaal. *Magna est Cursala, et prævalebit.* There are hotels—on the grandest scale, and not by any means unreasonable in their charges—by dozens. There are furnished lodgings, billiard-rooms, livery-stables, shooting clubs, a theatre (in the summer, and in the garden of a *restaurant*), plenty of banks (all more or less connected with the Kursaal), and a 'Lombard,' or *Monte de Piété*, otherwise a national pawnbroking establishment, which is more intimately connected with the aforesaid and so often mentioned Kursaal, than any other institution in the town or principality of Hombourg-von-der-Höhe. There !"

" For my part," breaks in the stout gentleman in *his* report, " I think that, besides the Lutheran, the Calvinist, the Anglican, and the Romish churches in Hombourg, they ought to have a Mahometan mosque, a temple of Juggernaut on a small scale, a Puseyite chapel, a Russo-Greek basilica, an Armenian church, a Quaker's meeting-house, a Buddhist joss-house, a Confucian pagoda, a temple of Zoroaster, together with convenient edifices for the followers of other creeds, such as the Arians, the Iconoclasts, the Muggletonians, the Unitarians, the Particular Baptists, the Plymouth Brethren, the 'Free-lovyers' or Agapemonians, the Brownists, the Johanna Southcotians, the Howlers, the Jumpers, the Groaners, the Shakers, and the Mormons or Latter-day Saints. Who shall say, too, that the worshippers of Mumbo-Jumbo, Bohwanie, Ahriman, and Thaducer, do not, in these days of universal tolerance, require tabernacles at Hombourg? For *I* never saw such a sweeping and raking together of people from all the five corners of the earth, and from the uttermost ends thereof, in my peaceful, but not altogether devoid of experience, days. Russian boyards, Wallachian waywodes, and Moldavian hospodars; Servian kaimakans, Montenegrin protospathaires, Bulgarian Bey-oglous, Turkish pachas, effendis, naiks, and reis (strict fact, all in their national costume, consisting of ill-made European clothes, patent leather boots, white kids, and red fezes with blue tassels, which [the former] make them look like poppies in a field of corn); Tartar khans and Livonian Ritterschaft-Herren; North German counts and barons *ad infinitum;* Lubeck and Bremen burgomasters and ship-chandlers; Dantzic spruce merchants; Berlin glovers; stalwart Austrian and Prussian lifeguardsmen; French marquises, viscounts, and chevaliers of industry and of idleness; New York stockbrokers and dry goods importers (tremendous dandies these); New Orleans and South Carolina cotton and sugar planters (ineffable and haughty exquisites these, with exuberant coats of arms on their visiting cards and cigar-cases, claiming descent from ancient English families, indulging, not unfrequently, in covert sneers at republicanism, and not caring to mix much with

the men from the north); West Indian creoles,
shivering in the genial autumnal sunshine; swarthy
Spanish dons, from old and new Spain, livid, as to
their finger nails, with the *sangre azul*, and smoking
paper cigars eternally; vivacious Swedes—the French-
men of the north, those blue-eyed, hospitable, cour-
teous, much-bowing Swedes; sententious Danes; gesticulating Italians; silent and expectorating Dutchmen; and GREAT BRITISH people! Oh, for a muse
of fire, or the pen of a professor of Ethnology, to
describe the varied species of Great Britons who
partook, last September, of the hospitalities of
Hombourg, from the Duke of Ninniver, fresh from
Sardanapalus House, to Thomas Tabbwell, military
accoutrement maker, of Albemarle Street, Piccadilly,
formerly his lordship's valet; from the terrible Sir
Judex Damnatur, Lord Chief Justice of the Uncommon Pleas, to simple-minded Billy Whaler, barrister-
at-law of the north-western circuit; from Sir Cow-
deroy Dawkesbury, formerly H.E.I.C.S., and now of
the new India Council, to young Shinders, of the
Pagoda and Pice department, Leadenhall Street!
But stay, I think I can give you a more definite
notion of the universal character of the Hombourg
visitors by the following extract from the 'Fremden-
Blatt' of September —th. My slim friend and the
man with the iron chest (he had better) will vouch
for its having been copied, *verbatim et literatim*,
English orthographical errors and all."

J. F. H. Fürst von Dwemmuch . aus Wien.
Graf von Vallarolling   . . . „ Leycester Square.
Herr Smith (mit suite) . . . „ England.
Herr Jones (und sohn) . . . „ „
The O'Doo and Mr. De Detters. „ There.
Herzog von Tapisvert . . . . „ Frascatis.
Conde di Manca . . . . . „ Spanien.
Le vieur pere Manque . . . . „ Marais.
Captain Borrow of the Spanish)
  Legion . . . .) „ Nag and famish Club.

Reigning Duke of Zeroburg . . . aus No domaines.
Monkey, Lord, und Apesley Lar=
  ronnette . . . . . . „ Hyde Parker Street.
Le Kaimakaun'te Rougelia . . „ Bucharest.
Le Hospodar de Boirelia . . . „ Belgrade Square.
Madame de Borotinne . . . . „ Blumsbury.
Grafinn von Rottenrowstein . . „ Rue des Quatrevingts.
Count Shakehiselbow . . . . „ St. James's Street.
Wr. Dyce Hombourg (mit familie) „ Bury Street.
Mr. Owl . . . . „ Stok Erchange.
Mademoiselle Virginie Breda . „ Rue Notre Dame de Lorette
Mademoiselle Manon l'Escaut .
Mademoiselle Marguerite Gautier „ Terra Incognita.
Fraulein Schlafmitganzenwelt .
Mademoiselle Ninon de l'Encles „ Athenes.
Mademoiselle Aspasie de Lais .
Lord de Reege . . . . . . „ Burlington Arcade
Captain Rip van Winkel, of the
  Backaback Local Militia . „ Raffstown, Ireland.
Le Comte d'Epingle . . . . „ Rue de Cranbourn Street.
M. Descartes, philosophe . . . „ Hades.
Marquis de Shufflecard . . . „ Bilk House.
Die Honourable Sir Charles Muck „ Baden und thereabouts.
Sir Chickenhazard Winn, Bart.. „ Spa, Ems, Kissingen, and so on.
Little Nick . . . . „ London.
Baron Punt . . . .
M. Croupe . . . . „ Soho.
Mr. Harris and fifty daughters . „ Gravesend.

N.B. The man with the iron chest declares this to be an insolently liberal paraphrase of the contents of a page of the " Fremden-Blatt." He says that the list contained many highly respectable names, including his own: that the stout gentleman, avowing that German typography was a dead letter to him, entreated him, almost with tears in his eyes, to read the names out to him; and that either from carelessness or through design he perpetrated the atrocious libel on the Hombourg visiting list, of which the foregoing extract is a specimen.

"The army of Hombourg," continues the stout gentleman, seemingly desirous of emulating the fame of Baron Haxthausen as a writer on the military resources of the continent, "is said, nominally, to consist of six hundred men, this being the amount of the Hesse-Hombourgian contingent, fixed by the Germanic confederation. The landlord of the Hotel de France assured me, with an unblushing countenance and a confident manner, that this number of men was absolutely under arms, and that the great body of the

THE STOUT GENTLEMAN SURVEYS THE ARMY OF HESSE HOMBOURG.

Hombourg contingent were at that moment doing duty, nay, had been reviewed only the other day on a plain near Frankfort. But when I came to cross-examine the head-waiter, his eye assumed the nearest approach to a wink of which the torpid Teutonic organization is susceptible, and, with guttural sarcasm, he observed, 'Papier!' As I imagined, the army exists on the army-list and in the commissariat returns; but, bodily, its strength is woefully exaggerated. Wishing to render justice where justice is due, I should say that, reckoning the available forces of Reuss-Schönhausen at three hundred and seven, rank and file, and of Schaumburg-Lippe at one hundred and three. I don't think I am understating matters when I assume that of Hesse-Hombourg to be ninety-seven and a half. I count a diminutive drummer-boy, whom I have frequently met 'skylarking' with some bloused urchins of his own age, about the town-pump—but who is an inveterate smoker, and makes love to the fat market-woman—as the half. There is a very big barrack behind the Kurgarten, full of windows, but I never saw any of the usual slovenly gentlemen in shirt sleeves and short pipes sprawling therefrom. A Tom Thumb sentinel, with a tremendous helmet, and a spike a-top, like one of the posts thus wickedly designed for juvenile impalement in Burton Crescent, London, and wearing a long gray greatcoat, in whose skirts the poor child was for ever tripping himself up, was pacing up and down, evidently fatigued by the weight of the musket he had to carry, and, ever and anon, ran into an absurdly striped sentry-box, like a guinea-pig into his hutch. Unhappy little fellow! I pitied him. On the other hand, the Hombourg army has a plethora of officers. They are of tremendous stature, wear plumes on their helmets, and their breasts are covered with decorations. One herculean hero pervades the Luisen Strasse with his martial presence. He was so big, so fierce-looking, his figure was so handsome, that I stood for some days, not only in vast admiration, but in secret awe and terror of him. The bullion on his clothes would have been regarded with avidity for melting-down purposes by the 'fences' of Field Lane and Saffron Hill, when crucibles were 'hot i' the fire,' in those picturesque but nefarious localities. He would have made the fortune of a perfumer for bear's grease, odonto, and pomade Hongroise. His moustaches were three-storeyed. The ground floor was bent downways—an arch to support the superstructure; the first floor stuck out horizontally; and the top, or attic floor, curled upwards to the heavens like the bell-gabled roof of a Buddhist pagoda. I imagined him to be the Hof-Feld-Mareschall, and commander-in-chief of the army of Hombourg: but I saw him one day receiving a tremendous wigging from a little tawny woman, with bistre eyes like plover's eggs, and a red handkerchief round her head, who addressed him as '*Du*,' and intimated, with a virulence of emphasis which looked very much as though there were a well-supplied and old-established fishmarket in Hombourg or its vicinity, that he was a *schaffskopf* (sheepshead), and a *spitzbube* (blockhead). I became acquainted shortly afterwards with the humiliating fact that my fancied field-marshal was only the drum-major of the contingent. I had fallen into a mistake similar to that of the Parisians, who imagined the Lord Mayor's huntsman to be the very greatest man amongst the civic deputation sent over to compliment the Prefect of the Seine. Such are the errors of which our infirm nature is susceptible."

"This place," writes the man with the iron chest, dipping his pen in the bitterest ox-gall obtainable at Messrs. Winsor and Newton's, "is only a suburb of the Kursaal. In Hombourg the Kursaal is everything, and the town nothing. The extortionate hotel-keepers, the 'snub-nosed rogues of counter and till,' who overcharge you in the shops, make their egregious profits from the Kursaal. The major part of the Landgrave's revenue is derived from the Kursaal: he draws five thousand a year from it. He and his house are sold to the Kursaal; and the Board of Directors of the Kursaal are the real sovereigns and landgraves of Hesse-Hombourg. They have metamorphosed a miserable mid-German townlet into a city of palaces. Their stuccoed and frescoed palace is five hundred times handsomer than the mouldy old schloss built by William with the silver leg. They have planted the gardens. They have imported the orange-trees, they have laid out the park and enclosed the hunting-grounds; they board, lodge, wash, and tax the inhabitants; and were I, without the slightest attempt at punning, to say that the citizens are all Kurs——"

Away, atrabilious man! Silence, snarler! All three critics of Hombourg affairs shall be hushed for awhile; it is time that in my proper person I should tell you of the real bearings and attributes of this Kursaal; if for no other reason, then for this, that you should cease, henceforth and for ever, from wondering at, and asking perplexing questions as to the relation borne to this narrative of the Rhine by the apparently enigmatical title of

MAKE YOUR GAME.

I know not what strange fascination of reluctance it was that prevented the travellers for two whole days after their arrival at Hombourg from passing the threshold of the Greek edifice, with wings which loomed large and white, opposite the Hotel de France, the structure which was approached by an avenue of orange trees, and before whose portals carriages were for ever standing. They lingered round its walls, they sniffed, so to speak, about its precincts; they saw its windows gaily lighted by night; they even wandered up in its magnificent gardens, and mingled with the

gay and motley throng who flirted in its bosky
avenues, strolled on its verdant grass-plats, and put
the myriad flowers in its jewelled pastures to shame
with their resplendent toilettes. There was in the
afternoon and evening an orchestra in the garden,
somewhat akin in appearance to the wooden contri-
vance with shell-shaped sounding-boards, in which the
cocked-hatted fiddlers were wont to scrape, and the
comic vocalist to quaver his dreary songs with the
intercalary prose, in days before you, oh, my member of
Parliament with the chintuft and the pegtop-trousers,
were breeched. Yes; the Hombourg Garden orchestra reminded one at least of those travellers of home
and Vauxhall Gardens. The "Saturday Review"
(whose contributors, on the principle of chastening
whom they love, are very fond of the present writer)
object to the practice of apostrophizing inanimate or
absent objects; or to a man's mind recurring, abroad,
to those domestic *lares* and *penates* which offer points
of analogy with foreign fetishes. No embodiment of
fancies; no cockney reminiscences! cries the "Saturday Review," pointing significantly to the cupboard
where the ferula and the fescue are kept; and as I
bow to the hebdomadal pedagogue, and am content to
abide amid the ambrosial essence of its periwig, to
"sit under the arches of the *Pons asinorum,* and
listen to the mystic numbers of the *As in presenti,*"
I will refrain from telling you what thoughts passed
through one of the travellers' mind as he gazed on the
rickety orchestra in the Kurgarten, and remembered
Vauxhall and the days of youth; how he pondered on
the time—so long since, it seems *multis annis ante
Romulum*—of Mr. Green's balloon and Mr. Monck
Mason; of the immortal Simpson, silk small-clothed
and crushed-hatted master of the ceremonies; of the
buttery-hutch beneath and at the back of the orchestra, whence, from brown jugs of quaint though simple
pattern, the brownest, most foaming stout was

quaffed. As the rapid train on the South-Western Railway bears me past Vauxhall, now on my way towards Kingston, I gaze downwards at the dingy palings, the blackened trees, the trumpery-looking gate, painted an emerald green, of the Royal property. A new generation is springing up—new Pharaohs that knew not Joseph, or Vauxhall in its glory. They will talk of Cremorne—of the Crystal Palace—of North Woolwich. They must pull my dear old place down in a year or two, and build Cockney villas on the site where once the Italian walk, the circus, the orchestra, and the long covered corridors of supper-boxes exhibited. This is the way of the world, and the fate of great cities. Pull down, build up; destroy the remembrances, even of the Vauxhall suppers. The boxes themselves painted by Hogarth; and Hayman, the chief carver, who boasted that he would cut slices so thin as to cover the whole garden with one ham ; the wondrous compound that the waiters called rack punch ; the fifty thousand additional lamps ; the hermit's cave ; all, all shall dissolve,

> " And like this unsubstantial pageant faded,
> Leave not a rack behind."

Only can I imagine the hermit, grown to be a very old and toothless man—toothless and drivelling— obtaining a holiday sometimes from his dark retreat, in the neighbouring Lambeth workhouse, and wandering like a ghost among those once hallowed precincts, till he is driven away by busy bricklayers.

Thus, like moths fluttering round about a candle, our three travellers had hovered about the precincts of the Kursaal, without venturing into its confines. But the time was come for them to be drawn within its all-absorbing vortex.

"There's a concert there every night, I know," said the slim gentleman. "The Administration put out bills advertising the singers' names :—Signor Stuffato

of the Pergola, and Madame Gosier of the Opéra
Comique, are staying at the Hotel de France. They
say the lady gets a thousand francs a night."

"I remember the Gosier a chorus-singer at the
Buffes Parisiennes," interrupted the M. I. C. "She
no more belongs to the Opéra Comique than do I to
the Honourable Artillery Company."

"And very badly she sings, too," remarked the
stout gentleman. "I heard her trying 'Rendez moi
ma patrie,' from the 'Pré Aux Clercs,' as I was smoking my cigar last night in the garden. It was like a
sparrow suffering from diphtheria. As for Stuffato, he
is choked with macaroni and risotto. The fellow eats
beefsteaks and fried potatoes for breakfast, and calls
himself a tenor! Why, Sims Reeves lives on nightin-
gales' tongues and distilled dew. That's the regimen
for a tenor!"

"Gentlemen," resumed the slim individual, speaking with great earnestness, and applying a term he
did not often use to his companions, "*Can you tell me
what is the cause of that eternal clanking of money we
hear whenever we pass by the Kursaal windows?*"

"I can hear silver rattle plainly," the M. I. C.
added affirmatively.

"And gold chink, too," thus the stout gentleman.

"There's a little waiter at the hotel," continued the
slim gentleman; "you know. The one with the
scrubby head, the hump back, and the two-inch tail
to his coat, whom we christened Robson."

"The fellow that looks as if he slept on sand, and
made his bed with a rake?" ejaculated the stout one.
"I know him. Good."

"Well, I asked him yesterday what the meaning of
all that money chinking over the way was, and what
do you believe the fellow did? Why, he thrust his
tongue in his cheek, winked and grinned in the most
impertinent manner, slapped his left trousers pocket
with one hand, laid the forefinger of the other by the

side of his nose, and said, ' *Faites le jeu.*' Now, I've forgotten most of my idiomatic French, although I can read Racine with as much facility as ever. What's the meaning of *Faites le jeu?*"

"MAKE YOUR GAME," cried the stout gentleman and the iron-chested man in unison; for both were anxious to display their proficiency in French.

"And when I asked him what *that* meant," continued the slim gentleman, "he went on with '*Rouge perd et couleur gagne.*' What does *that* mean?"

"I don't know, I'm sure," replied the stout gentleman, scratching his right ear-lobe. " ' Red loses and colour wins;' that's the translation; but what red and colour have to do with making your game, and what game, I can't understand."

"*I* know," cried the man with the iron chest, eagerly; and then, as if abashed at the precipitancy of his avowal, his cheek vied with his nose in blushes, and he spake no more.

"I believe, sir," resumed the slim gentleman, "that you know a great many things which you have no right to know anything about. Perhaps you will be good enough to retire to the *salle à manger*, and write a humourous description of our journey up the Rhine in Latin dactylics. That task accomplished, a few hundred Greek hexameters on the ancient history of Hombourg will employ you profitably till we return from the exploration of the interior of the Kursaal."

" I'll see you smothered in the embraces of the Lorelei, tolled to death in the pit of Falkenstein, eaten by Hatto's rats, and pounded to pieces by the Giant of Eppstein's mace, before I set pen to paper for the next fortnight, save to post up my diary, and write those perpetual hyperboles which Lord Bacon ——"

" Whom you never read, save at a book-stall, furtively, in the fourpenny box, an odd volume with one cover flapping loose by a tag of string, like a rudder

whose helmsman is asleep, the book-stall-keeper looking on anxiously, the reader looking too poor to buy,
and not too rich to purloin," interpolated the slim
gentleman.

"Which Lord Bacon,—whom I have read through,
from the 'Novum Organon' to the essay on 'Regimen of Health,' and am now copying out for the
second time —— "

"What a crammer!" exclaimed the stout gentleman.

"Which hyperboles Lord Bacon, who is not only
truthful himself, but inspires truth in others, declares
are excusable in love, but only and barely excusable
therein. The Rhine is not, thank heaven, a river of
ink. The fat plains of Nassau and Hessia are not
streets of papyrus—and vines, not goose-quills, grow
on the mountain sides. Dactylics nor hexameters
will I not write till I am bound to the mill-post in
Fleet Street again, to grind for you Philistines. Take
care I don't bring the pillars tumbling about your
ears at one of your way-gooses. So I will even go
with you to the Kursaal; and, if you will take my
advice, you will put money in your purses, but not
much."

They listened to the advice of that red-nosed man :
the slim gentleman to the extent of locking up the
bulk of his money in his portmanteau, and carrying
but one modest five-pound note in his waistcoat
pocket. But the stout gentleman, who was a favoured
child of Fortune, and a rich orphan, who ground
sometimes in the Fleet Street mill for pleasure, but
cared not for the profits accruing therefrom, had a
habit of fanning himself with hundred-pound notes,
and taking pinches of peculiar Amsterdam snuff from
screwed up cheques for vast amounts. As to the man
with the iron chest, nobody ever knew how much
money he had or where he kept it, if not in that iron

coffer of his. Some said in the lining of his hat, others in his boots, others in his umbrella (but he was always losing that)—others at Coutts's. When called upon to pay large sums he screamed agonizingly, and declared that he was ruined. "He hides millions," said the stout gentleman. "We shall have to bury him." predicted the slim gentleman. "How much can one get a diamond spray for at Hunt and Roskell's?" asked the M. 1. C.; "I want to buy one for Julia." And as he spoke he would produce, in mistake for a visiting card, a debenture bond for blucher boots.

They went over the way, even from the Hotel de France, and through the avenue of orange-trees, to the Kursaal. They remained there from eleven a.m. till eleven p.m. They neither lunched nor supped.

They came, they saw, but did they conquer?

Through a vast and lofty vestibule, a carved and panelled ceiling supported on Scagliola columns. Lightly fall the footsteps of the many passers-by. Solemnly hushed are the whisperings of vanity and the murmurs of folly. Distinct above all is heard the chinking of money. Be reverent, O ye worshippers! for this is the vestibule to the temple of Mammon— the ante-chamber where is set up on high the effigy of the Golden Calf.

A solemn lacquey stood by a grove of coats and umbrellas, inscribed above with the word " *Vestiaire.*" Other lacqueys, his fellows, wandered about the sumptuous halls. This was a brawny, big-boned fellow. with high cheek-bones, hollow eyes, a cropped head, and a thickset tawny moustache—a Prussian heavy dragoon metamorphosed, by the touch of Plutus's magic wand, into "Jeames of Buckley Square."

"He has gaiters on—he is a game-keeper," whispered the man with the iron chest.

"He has a red waistcoat—he is a coachman; a white neckerchief—he is a clergyman; an aiguillette —he is an aide-de-camp," murmured the others.

He was not powdered; he had no calves, he had no whiskers; but he was German Jeames of the Kursaal, Hombourg. nevertheless. Grave, solemn, mute, impressed with the awful responsibilities of his position, repellent of even the fancy of familiarity, there he stood, grandiose and imposing—a compromise between Michael Angelo's horned Moses and the figure of a beefeater at a wax-work show. With a slow, solemn finger, he pointed to the travellers' hats, and made signs that they must remove them. One must be uncovered before Mammon !

"That majestic flunkey," the stout gentleman observed, " reminds me of one of the Cent Gardes I saw behind the scenes of the Paris Grand Opéra on the occasion of the state visit of my friend Louis Napoleon, and my gracious sovereign Queen Victoria, in the year when people believed in the ' Alliance,' fifty-five. He was the most immobile mass of bright cuirass, buckskins, jackboots, plumed helmet, gold lace. buff-leather gauntlets, waxed moustaches, and skyblue tunic, that I ever saw. He stood in the *coulisse* on the prompt side as motionless as the Colossus of Rhodes, or the Mannikin at Brussels, in his gala dress, and magnified by two hundred and fifty. The demons of the ballet jostled him with their pitchforks and fire braziers, but he never stirred. The little *rats d'opera* hung about his varnished legs. but he made no effort to shake them off. He was the statue of the Commendatore in ' Don Giovanni ' dismounted. At last one pert little *coryphée*, with about a fig leaf and a half in white muslin, spangled, by way of drapery, but blooming in pink fleshings, went up to him, stared at him for full two minutes, her plump little arms akimbo, and her roguish mouth screwed up, and had then the superlative impudence to chuck the giant under the chin, pull one of his terrible moustaches, poke one rosy finger against the midst of his shining gorget, and say coolly to her companion, a *figurante* as impertinent as she, '*Tiens, Toinette, c'est vivant!*' '*It's alive!*' The giant did not eat her up. He was *galant homme*, and smiled grimly till his moustaches became twisted like the Furies' serpents. But, hush!

hark! what a magnificent apartment! What is that inscription above the door?"

"*Inveni portam: spes et fortuna valete*," murmured the M. I. C.

"It isn't. It's ' *Hic habitat felicitas.*'"

"Say, rather, Ye who enter leave all hope behind," retorted the man with the iron chest. "For yonder solemn flunkey was Charon, and this is HADES."

"Oh, bother! what nonsense you're talking," broke in the slim gentleman impatiently. "I can read the inscription well enough, though I don't quite see its bearing. It's something about the Administration of the Kursaal of Hombourg, and the highest *mise* being eight thousand florins. What's a *mise?*"

"A stake."

"And 'the roulette being played with a single zero.' What's roulette?"

"The wheel of fortune."

"And 'zero'?"

"Just nothing at all—a Peruvian Bond—a midshipman's half-pay—*Nil.*"

"It's my implicit belief, my children," said the stout gentleman, when they had been in the great hall some ten minutes, "that this place is neither more nor less than a gambling-house."

In the Kursaal is the ball or concert room, at either end of which is a gallery, supported by pillars of composition marble. The floors are inlaid, and immense mirrors in sumptuous frames are hung on the walls. Vice can see her own image all over the establishment. The ceiling is superbly decorated with bas-reliefs in *carton pierre*—like those in Mr. Barry's new Covent Garden Theatre; and fresco paintings, executed by Viotti of Milan and Conti of Munich; while the whole is lighted up by enormous and gorgeous chandeliers. The apartment to the right is called the *Saal Japanese*, and is used as a diningroom for a monster *table d'hôte* held twice a day, and

served by the famous Chevet of Paris. When I say
that this room is more splendid in its decorations
(the work of Belgian artists) than the great *salle à
manger* of the Hotel du Louvre at Paris, you may
form some idea of its magnificence. There is a sumptuous reading-room, warmly carpeted, and on whose
inlaid tables lie the chief newspapers and periodicals
of the civilized world, from the " Clamor Publico "
and the " Ruski Invalide " of Spain and Russia, to
the " Times " and the " Daily Telegraph " of London ;
for censorship does not exist at Hombourg-von-der-
Höhe, and so long as you do not inveigh against the
Kursaal, you may say anything, politically or socially,
that pleases you. The Administration would adver-
tise in, and subscribe to, a journal edited by the
Prince of Darkness, if they thought it was extensively circulated, and that their patrons wished to see
it lying on the table. Indeed, I don't know but that
they would be rather pleased than otherwise to give
their old crony and auxiliary a lift. There is a huge
Café Olympique for smoking and imbibing purposes
—private cabinets for parties ; the monster saloon,
and two smaller ones, where *from eleven in the fore-
noon to eleven at night, Sundays not excepted, all the
year round*, and year after year—the " Administration " have yet a *jouissance* of eighty-five years to run
out, guaranteed by the incoming dynasty of Hesse-
Darmstadt—knaves and fools, from almost every
corner of the world, gamble at the ingenious and
amusing games of " Roulette," and " Rouge et Noir,"
otherwise " Trente et Quarante."

There is one table. Long, covered with green-
baize, tightly stretched as on a billiard-field. Lighted
—but it was by day our travellers made their first
acquaintance with it : they came to know its night
and its day phases soon—not so much by the gorgeous lustres as by bright oil-lamps, their glare
shaded, and coming so lown down as two feet from

the table. Oh! but you must be able to see every number on the wheel's compartments, every piece of money that is staked on the board, when gambling is your intent. In the midst of the table there is a circular pit, coved inwards, but not bottomless, and containing the roulette-wheel; a revolving disc, turning with an accurate momentum on a brass pillar, and divided at its outer edge into thirty-seven narrow and shallow pigeon-hole compartments, coloured alternately red and black, and numbered—not consecutively—up to thirty-six. The last is a blank, and stands for Zero, number Nothing. Round the upper edge, too, run a series of little brass hoops, or bridges, to cause the ball to hop and skip, and not fall at once into the nearest compartment. This is the regimen of roulette: the banker sits before the wheel—a croupier, or payer-out of winnings to and raker-in of losses from the players, on either side. Crying in a voice calmly sonorous. "*Faites le jeu, Messieurs,*" "Make your game, gentlemen!" the banker gives the wheel a dexterous twirl, and ere it has made one revolution, casts into its maelstrom of black and red an ivory ball. The interval between this and the ball finding a home is one of breathless anxiety. Stakes are eagerly laid, but at a certain period of the revolution the banker calls out, "*Le jeu est fait. Rien ne va plus,*" and after that intimation it is useless to lay down money. Then the banker, in the same calm and impassible voice, declares the result. It may run thus :—

"*Vingt-neuf, Noir, Impair, et Passe.*"
"Twenty-nine, Black, Odd, and Past the Rubicon" (No. 18).
Or,
"*Huit, Rouge, Pair, et Manque.*"
"Eight, Red, Even, and *not* Past the Rubicon."

Now, on either side of the wheel, and extending to the extremity of the table, run, in duplicate, the schedule of *mises* or stakes. The green baize first offers just thirty-six square compartments, marked out by yellow threads woven in the fabric itself, and bearing thirty-six consecutive numbers. If you place a florin (one and eightpence, no lower stake is permitted), or ten florins, or a Napoleon, or an English five-pound note, or any sum of money not exceeding the maximum whose multiple is the highest stake which the bank, if it loses, can be made to pay, in the midst of compartment twenty-nine, and if the banker, in that calm voice of his, has declared that twenty-nine has become the resting-place of the ball, the croupier will push towards you with his rake exactly thirty-three times the amount of your stake, whatever it might have been; you must bear in mind, however, that the bank's loss on a single stake is limited to eight thousand francs. Moreover, if you have placed another sum of money in the compartment inscribed, in legible yellow colours, " Impair," or odd, you will receive the equivalent to your stake, twenty-nine being an odd number. If you have placed a coin on *passe*, you will also receive this additional equivalent to your stake; twenty-nine being past the Rubicon, or middle of the table of numbers—eighteen. Again. if you have ventured your money in a compartment bearing for device a lozenge in outline, which represents black, and twenty-nine being a black number, you will again pocket a double stake, that is, one in addition to your original venture. More, and more still, if you have risked money on the columns—that is, betted on the number turning up corresponding with some number in one of the columns of the tabular schedule, and have selected the right column —you have your own stake and two others; if you have betted on either of these three eventualities, *douze premier*, *douze milieu*, or *douze dernier*, otherwise first dozen, middle dozen, or last dozen, as one to twelve, thirteen to twenty-four, twenty-five to thirty-six, all inclusive, and have chanced to select *douze dernier*, the division in which No. 29 occurs, you also obtain a treble stake, namely, your own, and two more which the bank pay you: your florin or your five-pound note—benign fact!—metamorphosed into three. But woe to the wight who shall have ventured on the number "eight," on the "red" colour (compartment with a crimson lozenge), on "even," and on "not past" the Rubicon; for twenty-nine does not comply with any one of these conditions. He loses, and his money is coolly swept away from him by the croupier's rake. With reference to the last chances I enumerated in the preceding paragraph, I should mention that the number eight would lie in the second column—there being three columns, —and in the first dozen numbers.

There are more chances, or rather subdivisions of chances, to entice the player to back the *numbers*, for though the stations of the ball are as capricious as womankind, it is of course extremely rare that a player will fix on the particular number that happens to turn up. But he may place a piece of money *à cheval*, or on horseback, on the line which divides two numbers, in which case (either of the numbers turning up) he receives sixteen times his stake. He may place it on the cross-lines that divide four numbers, and if either of the four wins, he will receive eight times the amount of his stake. A word as to Zero. Zero is designated by the compartment close to the wheel's diameter, and Zero, or blank, will turn up on an average about once in seventy times. If you have placed money on Zero, and the ball seeks that haven, you will receive thirty-three times your stake.

So this is the merry game of *roulette*. The wheel has all but ceased to revolve in moral England. Surreptitiously, sometimes, the ball falls into the parti-coloured disc; we are enjoined to "make our game," but *rouge et noir* is played no more; and the knell of chicken-hazard has been sounded. I have done my best to explain to you the mysteries of the wheel of fortune, and have, very probably, only succeeded in producing an imbroglio of figures and sums, to which an exposition of Indian finance from a minister who stutters would be clear and lucid.

" *Faites le jeu, Messieurs,*" the banker cried, for about the fiftieth time, as the Three looked on with a grim eagerness; and the gold and the silver, the *rouleaux* and the bank notes, poured for the fiftieth time on the table. " I think—I think," said the stout gentleman, with something like a blush on his expressive countenance, " that there would be no harm in risking a florin—just for fun, you know."

He nudged the M. I. C. with his elbow as he spoke, but that individual was busy asking a croupier for change for a five-pound note, and did not hear him. " *Le jeu est fait. Rien ne va plus,*" cried the banker.

CHAPTER VII.

CONTAINS THE HUMOURS OF THE KURSAAL, AND THE CURIOUS PONDERINGS THEREUPON OF THE THREE TRAVELLERS.

THE intricacies of the merry game of *Roulette* have been dwelt upon, and it is now time to say something about its twin, or rather elder, brother, *Trente et Quarante*, otherwise called *Rouge et Noir*. There is the ordinary green-cloth-covered table, with its brilliant down-coming lights. In the centre sits the banker, gold and silver, in piles and *rouleaux*, and bank-notes before him. On either hand, the croupiers as before, now wielding the rakes and plying them to bring in the money, now balancing them, now shouldering them, as soldiers do their muskets, half-pay officers their canes, and dandies their silk umbrellas. The banker's cards are—as throughout all the Rhenish gaming-places—of French design : the same that were invented, or at least first used, for crazy Charles the Simple, with pictures of Alexander the Great, Julius Cæsar, Romulus, Remus, Semiramis, nay, for aught I know, the Pope and the Pretender into the bargain. These cards are placed on an inclined plane of marble, called a *talon*. The dealer (*Monsieur qui donne les cartes*) first takes six packs of cards, shuffles them, and distributes them in various parcels to the various punters round the table to shuffle and mix. He then finally shuffles them, and removes the end cards into various parts of the three hundred and twelve cards, until he meets with a court one, which he must place upright at the end. This done, he presents the pack to one of the punters to cut, who places the pictured card where the dealer separates the pack, and that part of the pack beyond the pictured card he places at the end nearest him, leaving the court or pictured card at the bottom of the pack.

The dealer then takes a certain number of cards, about as many as would form a pack, and, looking at the first card, to know its colour, puts it on the table with its face on the table. He then takes two cards, one red and the other black, and sets them back to back. These cards are turned, and displayed conspicuously, as often as the colour varies, for the information of the company.

The gamblers having staked their money on either of the colours, the dealer asks " *Votre jeu est-il fait ?*" Is your game made? or " *Votre jeu est-il prêt ?*" Is your game ready? or " *Le jeu est prêt Messieurs.*" The game is ready, gentlemen. He then deals the first card with its face upwards, saying " *Noir;*" and continues dealing until the cards turned up exceed thirty points, or pips, in number, which number he must mention as *Trente et un*, or *Trente-six*, as the case may be.

As the aces reckon but for one, no card after thirty can make up forty; the dealer therefore does not declare the tens after thirty-one or upwards, but merely the units, as one, two, three; if the number of points dealt for *noir* are thirty-five, he says " *Cinq.*"

Another parcel is then dealt for *rouge*, or red, and with equal deliberation and solemnity; and if the player's stake be on the colour that comes to thirty-one, or nearest to it, he wins, which happy eventuality is announced by the dealer crying " *Rouge gagne,*" red wins, or " *Rouge perd,*" red loses. These two parcels, one for each colour, make a *coup.*

The same number of parcels being dealt for each colour, the dealer says " *Après,*" after. This is a " doublet," called in the amiable French tongue, "*un refait*," by which neither party wins, unless both colours come to thirty-one, which the dealer announces by saying "*Un refait trente et un*," and he wins half the stakes posted on both colours. He, however, does not take the money, but removes it to the middle line, and the players may change the venue of their stakes if they please. This is called the first "prison," or *la première prison*, and, if they win their next event, they draw the entire stake. In case of another *refait*, the money is removed into the third line, which is called the second prison. So you see that there are wheels within wheels, and Lord Chancellor King's dictum, that walls can be built higher, but there should be no prison within a prison, is sometimes reversed. When this happens the dealer wins all.

The cards are sometimes cut for which colour shall be dealt first; but, in general, the first parcel is for black, and the second for red. The odds against a *refait* turning up are usually reckoned as sixty-three to one. The bankers, however, acknowledge that they expect it twice in three deals, and there are generally from twenty-nine to thirty-two coups in each deal. The odds in favour of winning several times are about the same as in the game of Pharaon, and are as delusive. He who goes to Hombourg, and expects to see any melo-dramatic manifestation of rage, disappointment, and despair in the losing players, reckons without his host. Winners or losers seldom speak above a whisper; and the only sound that is heard above the suppressed buzz or *chuchottement* of conversation, the muffled jingle of the money on the green cloth, the "sweep" of the croupiers' rakes, and the ticking of the very ornate French clocks on the mantelpieces, is the impassibly metallic voice of the banker as he proclaims his "*Rouge perd*," or "*Couleur gagne*." People are too genteel at Hombourg-von-der-Höhe to scream, to yell, to fall into fainting fits, or go into convulsions, because they have lost four or five thousand francs or so on a single coup. I have heard of one gentleman, indeed, who, after a ruinous loss, put a pistol to his head, and discharging it, spattered his brains over the roulette-wheel. It was said that the banker, looking up calmly, called out "*Triple zero,*" treble nothing,— a case as yet unheard-of in the tactics of roulette, but signifying annihilation,—and that a cloth being thrown over the ensanguined wheel, the bank at that particular table was declared to be closed for the day. Very probably the whole story is but a newspaper *canard*, devised by the proprietors of some rival gaming establishment, who would have been delighted to see the fashionable Hombourg under a cloud. When people want to commit suicide at Hombourg, they do it genteelly; early in the morning, or late at night, in the solitude of their own apartments at the hotels. It would be reckoned a gross breach of good manners to scandalize the refined and liberal Administration of the Kursaal by undisguised *felo-de-se*. The devil on two *croupes* at Hombourg, is the very genteelest of demons imaginable. He ties his tail up with cherry-coloured ribbon, and conceals his cloven foot in a patent leather boot. All this gentility, and varnish, and elegant veneering of the sulphurous pit, takes away from, if it does not wholly extinguish, the horror and loathing for a common gaming-house, with which the mind of a well-nurtured English youth has been sedulously imbued by his parents and guardians. He has very probably witnessed the performance of the "Gamester" at the theatre, and been a spectator of the remorseful agonies of Mr. Beverly, the virtuous sorrows of Mrs. B., and the dark villanies of Messrs. Dawson and Bates. He has read how, during the great French war, at Verdun, among other means resorted to in order to ease the English prisoners of their loose cash, a gaming-table was set up for their sole accommodation; and, as usual, led to scenes of great depravity and horror. For instance, "a young man was enticed into this sink of iniquity, when he was tempted to throw on the table a five-franc piece: he won, and repeated the experiment several times successfully, until luck turned against him, and he lost everything he had. The manager immediately offered him a rouleau of a thousand francs, which, in the heat of play, he thoughtlessly accepted, and also lost. He then drew a bill on his agent, which his captain—he was an officer in the English army—endorsed. The proceeds of this went the way of the rouleau. He drew two more bills, and lost again. The next morning he was found dead in his bed, with his limbs much distorted, and his fingers dug into his sides. On his table was found an empty laudanum bottle, and some scraps of paper on which he had been practising the signature of Captain B——. On inquiry, it was found that he had forged that officer's name to the two last bills. Another circumstance also occurred at Verdun, the atrocity of which was tempered by the ludicrous. A clerk named Chambers, losing his monthly allowance, which was his all, at the gaming-table, wanted to borrow from the managers; but they knew the state of his affairs too well to lend without security, and therefore demanded something in pawn. 'I have nothing to give,' replied the infatuated youth, 'but my ears.' 'Well,' said one of the humorous demons, 'let us have them.' The infatuated youth immediately took out of his pocket a knife, actually cut off all the fleshy part of one of his ears, and threw it on the table, to the astonishment of the admiring gamesters. The managers lent him two five-franc pieces, and he gambled on, and even managed to win a few pieces that evening; but on his adventure being reported to the commandant of Verdun, this more than Spartan gamester was sent to the *carcere duro* of Biche."

Such stories as these, naturally sinking into the mind of an ingenuous youth, combined with other terrible tales of defrauded "Heirs of Lynn" from the agricultural districts, fleeced young sprigs of nobility, ruined prodigals, "cleaned out" fathers of families, bankers' clerks driven to dishonesty by the seductions of the gaming-table, and so forth, his first visit to the Kursaal is usually paid in fear and trembling. He is with difficulty pursuaded to enter the accursed place. When introduced to the saloons— delusively called *de conversation*, he begins by staring fixedly at the chandeliers, the ormolu clocks, and the rich draperies, and resolutely averts his eyes from the serried ranks of punters, and the Pactolus whose sands are circulating on the green cloth of the table. Then he thinks there is no very great harm in looking on, and so peeps over the shoulder of a moustached gamester, who perhaps whispers to him in the intervals between two coups, that if a man will only play carefully and be content with moderate gains, he may win sufficient, taking the good days and the evil days in a lump, to keep him in a decent kind of affluence all the year round. Indeed, I once knew a croupier— we used to call him Napoleon, from the way he took snuff from his waistcoat pocket—who was in the habit of expressing a grave conviction that it was possible to make a capital living at roulette so long as you stuck to the colours and avoided the Scylla of the numbers and the Charybdis of the Zero. By degrees, then, the shyness of the neophyte wears off. Perhaps in the course of his descent of Avernus a revulsion of feeling takes place, and, horror-struck and ashamed, he rushes out of the Kursaal, determined to enter its portals no more. Then he temporizes; remembers that there is a capital reading-room, provided with all the newspapers and periodicals of civilized Europe, attached to the Kursaalian premises. There can be no harm, he thinks, in glancing over "Galignani" or the "Charivari," although under the same roof as the abhorred *trente et quarante;* but, alas! he finds "Galignani" engaged by an acrid old lady of morose countenance, who has lost all her money before lunch time, and is determined to "take it out" in reading; and the "Charivari" slightly clenched in one hand—in the hand of the deaf old gentleman with the dingy ribbon of the Legion of Honour, and the curly brown wig, pushed up over one ear, who always goes to sleep on the soft and luxurious velvet couches of the Kursaal reading-room from eleven to three every day, Sundays not excepted. The disappointed student of home or foreign news wanders back to one of the apartments where play is going on. Perhaps he does not care about smoking on the terrace, sipping iced beverages, or walking in the Kur Garten. He has read all the English books at the circulating library. He would rather not retire to the grim solitude of his hotel bed-room. In fact, he does not know what to do with himself until *table d'hôte* time. You know what the moral bard, Dr. Watts, says: "Satan finds some mischief still for idle hands to do." The unfledged gamester watches the play more narrowly. A stout lady in a maroon velvet mantle, and a man with a bald head, a black patch on his occiput, and gold spectacles, obligingly make way for him. He finds himself pressed against the very edge of the table. Perhaps a chair—one of those delightfully comfortable Kursaal chairs—is vacant. He is tired with doing nothing, and sinks into the emolliently cushioned *fauteuil.* He fancies that he has caught the eye of the banker, or of one of the gentlemen of the *croupe,* and that they are meekly inviting him to try his luck. "Well, there can't be much harm in risking a florin," he murmurs. He stakes his silver piece on a number or a colour.   He wins, we will say twice or thrice.   Perhaps he quadruples his stake; nay, perchance, hits on the lucky number.   It turns up, and he receives thirty-five times the amount of his *mise*.   Thenceforth it is all over with that ingenuous British youth.   It would be all over, under similar circumstances, with the reverend Mr. Spurgeon.   The Demon of Play has him for his own, and he may go on playing and playing until he has lost every florin of his own, and as many of those belonging to other people as he can beg or borrow.   Far more fortunate would it be for him in the long run if he met in the outset with a good swinging loss.   The burnt child *does* dread the fire as a rule; but there is this capricious, almost preternatural feature of the physiology of gaming, that the young and the inexperienced generally win in the first instance.   They are drawn on and on, and in and in.   They begin to lose, and continue to lose, and by the time they have cut their wise teeth they have neither sou nor silver wherewith to make their dearly-bought wisdom available.[*]

---

[*] Pardon a dull foot-note.   When I was a boy, not so very long—say twenty years—since, the west end of London swarmed with illicit gambling-houses, known by a name I will not offend your ears by repeating.   On every race-course there was a public gambling booth and an abundance of thimble-riggers' stalls. These, I am happy to state, exist no longer; and the fools who are always ready to be plucked, can only, in gambling, fall victims to the commonest and coarsest of swindlers; skittle sharps, beer-house rogues and sharpers, and knaves who travel to entrap the unwary in railway carriages with loaded dice, marked cards, and little squares of green baize for tables, and against whom the authorities of the railway companies very properly warn their passengers.   A notorious gambling-house in St. James's Street —Crockford's—where it may be said, without exaggeration, that millions of pounds sterling have been diced away by the fools of fashion, is now one of the most sumptuous and best-conducted dining establishments in London—the "Wellington."   The semi-patrician Hades that were to be found in the purlieus of St.

I am not at all apprehensive, my dear reader, that this imperfect description of the games of *roulette* and

---

James's, such as the "Cocoa Tree," the "Berkeley," and the "stick-shop," at the corner of Albemarle Street—a whole Pandemonium of rosewood and plate-glass dens—never recovered from a razzia made on them simultaneously one night by the police, who were organized on a plan of military tactics, and under the command of Inspector Beresford; and at a concerted signal assailed the portals of the infamous places with sledge-hammers. At the time to which I refer, in Paris, the Palais Royal, and the environs of the Boulevards des Italiens, abounded with magnificent gambling-rooms similar to those still in existence in Hombourg, which were regularly licensed by the police, and farmed under the municipality of the Ville de Paris ; a handsome per-centage of the iniquitous profits being paid towards the charitable institutions of the French metropolis. There are very many notabilities of the French Imperial Court, who were then *fermiers des jeux*, or gambling-house contractors ; and only a year or two since Doctor Louis Véron, ex-dealer in quack medicines, ex-manager of the Grand Opera, and ex-proprietor of the "Constitutionnel" newspaper, offered an enormous royalty to Government for the privilege of establishing a gambling-house in Paris. But the Emperor Napoleon—an ex-member of Crockford's as he is—sensibly declined the tempting bait. A similarly "generous" offer was made last year to the Belgian Government by a joint-stock company who wanted to establish public gaming-tables at the watering-place of Ostend ; and who offered to establish an hospital from their profits, but King Leopold, the astute proprietor of Claremont, was as prudent as his Imperial cousin of France, and refused to soil his hands with cogged dice. The lease of the Paris authorized gaming-houses expired in 1836-7 ; and the municipality, albeit loath to lose the fat annual revenue, was induced by governmental pressure not to renew it ; and it is asserted that from that moment the number of annual suicides in Paris very sensibly decreased. "It is not generally known," as the penny-a-liners say, that the Rev. Caleb Colton, a clergyman of the Church of England, and the author of " Lacon," a book replete with aphoristic wisdom, blew his brains out in the forest of St. Germains, after ruinous losses at Frascati's, at the corner of the Rue Richelieu and the Boulevards, one of the most noted of the *Maisons des Jeux*, and which was afterwards turned into a *restaurant*, and is now a shawl-shop. Just before the revolution of 1848, nearly all the watering-places in the Prusso-Rhenane *rouge et noir* will induce you next summer or this autumn to pack up your travelling chattels, procure a

---

provinces, and in Bavaria, and Hesse, Nassau, and Baden, contained Kursaals, where gambling was openly carried on. These existed at Aix-la-Chapelle, Baden-Baden, Wiesbaden, Ems, Kissengen, and at Spa, close to the Prussian frontier, in Belgium. It is due to the fierce democrats who revolted against the monarchs of the defunct Holy Alliance, to say that they utterly swept away the gambling-tables in Rhenish-Prussia, and in the Grand Duchy of Baden. Herr Hecker, of the red republican tendencies, and the astounding wide-awake hat, particularly distinguished himself in the latter place by his iconoclastic animosity to *roulette* and *rouge et noir*. When dynastic "order" was restored, the Rhine gaming-tables were re-established. The Prussian government, much to its honour, has since shut up the gambling-houses at that resort for decayed nobility and ruined livers, Aix-la-Chapelle. A motion was made in the Federal Diet, sitting at Frankfort, to constrain the smaller governments, in the interest of the Germanic good name generally, to close their *tripots*, and in some measure the Federal authorities succeeded. The only existing continental gaming houses authorized by government are now the two Badens, Spa (of which the lease is nearly expired, and will not be renewed), Monaco (capital of the ridiculous little Italian principality, of which the suzerain is a scion of the house of "Grimaldi"), Malmöe, in Sweden, too remote to do much harm, and HOMBOURG. This last still flourishes greatly, and I am afraid is likely to flourish, though happily in isolation; for, as I have before remarked, the "concession" or privilege of the place has been guaranteed for a long period of years to come by the expectant dynasty of Hesse-Darmstadt. "*C'est fait*," "It's all settled," said the host of the Hôtel de France to me, rubbing his hands exultingly when I mentioned the matter. But, *Quis custodiet custodes?* Hesse-Darmstadt has guaranteed the "Administration" of Hesse-Hombourg, but who is to guarantee Hesse-Darmstadt? A battalion of French infantry would, it seems to me, make short work of H. D., lease guarantees, Federal contingent, and all. I must mention, in conclusion, that within a very few years we had, if we have not still, a licensed gaming-house in our exquisitely moral British dominions. This was in that remarkably "tight little island" at the mouth of the Elbe, Heligoland, which we so queerly possess —Puffendorf, Grotius, and Vattel, or any other writers on the *Jus gentium*, would be puzzled tell why, or by what right. I passport, and betake yourself to Hombourg. The passion for gambling is, I believe, innate; but there is, happily, a very small per-centage of the population in England who are born with a propensity for high play. We are speculative and eagerly commercial; but it is rare to discover among us that inveterate love for gambling, as gambling, which you may find among the Italians, the South American Spaniards, the Russians, and the Poles. Moro, baccara, tchuka —these are games at which continental peasants will wager, and lose, their little fields, their standing crops, their harvests in embryo, their very wives, even. The Americans surpass us in the ardour of their propitiation of the gambling goddess; and on board the Mississippi steamboats, an enchanting game, called "poker," is played with a delirium of excitement whose intensity can only be imagined by realizing that famous bout at "catch him who can," which took place at the horticultural *fête* immortalized by Mr. Samuel Foote, comedian, at which was present the great *Panjandrum* himself, with the little round button at top, the festivities continuing till the gunpowder ran out at the heels of the company's boots.

---

was at Hamburg, in the autumn of 1856, crossed over to Heligoland one day on a pleasure trip, and lost some money there, at a miniature *roulette* table, much frequented by joyous Israelites from the mainland, and English "soldier officers" in mufti. I did not lose much of my temper, however, for the odd, quaint little place pleased me. Not so another Roman citizen, or English travelling gent., who losing, perhaps, seven-and-sixpence, wrote a furious letter to the "Times," complaining of such horrors existing under the British flag, desecration of the English name, and so forth. Next week the lieutenant-governor, by "order," put an end to *roulette* at Heligoland; but play on a diminutive scale has since, I have been given to understand, recommenced there without molestation. And now I have bored you quite enough; and I hope the small type in which these necessary remarks are printed has been sufficient to deter the ladies from reading them at all.

We gamble in England at the Stock Exchange, we gamble on horse-races all the year round; but there is something more than the mere eventuality of a chance that prompts us to the *enjeu;* there is mixed up with our eagerness for the stakes the most varied elements of business and pleasure; cash-books, ledgers, dividend-warrants, indignation meetings of Venezuelan bond-holders, coupons, cases of champagne, satin-skinned horses with plaited manes, grand stands, pretty faces, bright flags, lobster salads, cold lamb, fortune-telling gipsies, barouches-and-four, and "our Aunt Sally." High play is still rife in some aristocratic clubs; there are prosperous gentlemen who wear clean linen every day, and whose names are still in the Army List, who make their five or six hundred a year by whist-playing, and have nothing else to live upon; in east-end coffee-shops, sallow-faced Jew boys, itinerant Sclavonic jewellers, and brawny German sugar-bakers, with sticky hands, may be found glozing and wrangling over their beloved cards and dominoes, and screaming with excitement at the loss of a few pence. There are yet some occult nooks and corners. nestling in unsavoury localities, on passing which the policeman, even in broad daylight, cannot refrain from turning his head a little backwards— as though some bedevilments must necessarily be taking place directly he has passed—where, in musty back parlours, by furtive lamplight, with doors barred, bolted, and sheeted with iron, some wretched, cheating gambling goes on at unholy hours. Chicken-hazard is scotched, not killed; but a poor, weazened, etiolated biped is that once game-bird now. And there is Doncaster, every year—Doncaster. with its subscription-rooms under authority, winked at by a pious corporation, patronized by noble and gentlemen supporters of the turf, and who are good enough, sometimes, to make laws for us plebeians in the Houses of Lords and Commons. There is Doncaster, with policemen to keep order, and admit none but "respectable" people—subscribers, who fear Heaven and honour the Queen. Are you aware, my Lord Chief-Justice, are you aware, Mr. Attorney, Mr. Solicitor-General, have you the slightest notion, ye Inspectors of Police, that in the teeth of the law, and under its very eyes, a shameless gaming-house exists in moral Yorkshire, throughout every Doncaster St. Leger race-week? Of course you haven't; never dreamed of such a thing—never could, never would. Hie you, then, and prosecute this wretched gang of betting-touts, congregating at the corner of Bride Lane, Fleet Street; quick, lodge informations against this publican who has suffered card-playing to take place, raffles, or St. Leger sweeps to be held in his house. "You have seen a farmer's dog bark at a beggar, and the creature run from the cur. There thou might'st behold the great image of authority: a dog's obeyed in office." You have—very well. Take crazy King Lear's words as a text for a sermon against legislative inconsistencies, and come back with me to Hombourg Kursaal.

Gay gatherings I have seen in my time—gay and curious, for I have been a wanderer all my life, and have been thrown into the strangest company; but much I doubt if my three travellers (they are backing the red at *roulette* by this time, might and main) ever saw a sight at once so gay and curious as this Kursaal presents. Yes; I have seen the Great Lord Mayor of London in his golden coach, likewise his feast under the shadow of Gog and Magog's jovial countenances; the real turtle, the loving cup, and a supper laid out in Guildhall crypt. I have seen one Louis Napoleon Bonaparte at an evening party in England, very soberly, quietly dressed, very sad and silent (he had not many coats or many prospects in 1838), and I have seen him again on a fleet Arab, riding in front, far ahead of his staff, on the awful

Thursday in December '51 that followed the massacres of the *coup d'état*. Pale his face, but not with fear, with grim resolve rather. Iron-welded those muscles, inscrutable those eyes, looking far, far ahead, thousands of miles away into Shadowland perchance, seeing in the distance—what? A purple covered chair, sown with golden bees, over against the high altar of Nôtre Dame; incense curling, music pealing, the pontiff of the Christian church to place a crown upon his brow? A bloody bivouac, before some smoking town in a country where the fields had been fat and green, the cattle strong and plenteous, and where the peasants speak with English tongues? Or perhaps saw those eyes, by moonlight, there, as the portion of to-morrow, the plain of Grenelle, or the ditch of Vincennes; a firing party, and a bareheaded man with bandaged eyes, who had been shrived by the priest, who was to drop a handkerchief and give the word? Who knows? Who can ever know? The man with the Eyes rode on, farther and farther, though, for aught he knew, from every pane in every window in the many-storyed Boulevard houses a deadly carbine might be pointed at his heart. So he rode, farther and farther, stooping at last to pick up a diadem of empire, which a republic, drunk with vanity and stupefied with much speechifying, had let fall in the mire. I saw him again—years afterwards—and for the only time in my life radiant and smiling, and even flushed, entering, as the Queen's guest, that London where he had formerly dwelt a disreputable, penniless, out-at-elbowed adventurer. The people ran after him, and cheered him to the echo. Where shall next I see him, I wonder? Where shall we all see him, when his time comes, and if we live to see it?

At least one-half of the company may be assumed to be arrant rascals—rascals male and rascals female—*chevaliers d'industrie*, the offscourings of all the shut-up gambling houses in Europe, demireps and *lorettes*, and single married women innumerable. But they are quiet, well-behaved, and remarkably well-dressed! The ladies are really splendid; not in the dreadful garish, gewgaw finery, the slatternly magnificence, that blots gaslight life in England—no paint, no sham jewellery, no broken feathers, no tarnished bonnets, no rich dresses and mantles stained by wine, or cauterized by hot cigar-ends. The "ladies" dress positively *like* ladies. In the morning, in elegant *négligées* and wrappers, their hair symmetrically arranged, lustrous in bands confined within those provoking little fillet-nets of silver beads, which are now becoming the fashion. Marvels of dainty linen 'broidery garnish their slender necks and wrists and the hems of their snowy under-garments; great diamonds and sapphires glitter in *rivières* or *solitaires*, sprays and bracelets, by night. Slender gold chains meander over satin and velvet-clad bosoms; tiny, tight-gloved hands hold the imprisoning rake, flutter the crisp bank-note, push the glittering stake on to the oft-times fatal colour; pretty feet tap the ground impatiently when the banker proclaims the ominous "*perd.*" Sometimes, on ball nights, these ravishing creatures wander in from the adjacent ball and concert rooms, in full evening dress, their white shoulders struggling like imprisoned doves in the meshes of lace and tulle; flowers rustling, the little *clinquants* of the *cachepeignes* (I don't know their English names) jingling. They lean over the players, and brush their hot faces with their pendulous curls—the blondes are, for the most part, in ringlets; they ask in the prettiest voices what number has last turned up; their little hands venture between the burly, broad-clothed arms of the croupiers. They win, and allow their stakes to remain and remain accumulating, till they lose all, principal and interest. Then they make a provoking *moue*, utter some sparkling little objurgation of unkind Fortune—risk more, double, treble their stakes, lose again, sometimes all they have. Never mind : the Prince is generous ; the Marquis has plenty more *rouleaux*. But alas ! it may be that red has had an unheard-of run against the Prince, who is vainly endeavouring to borrow fifty francs from the croupier, or the Marquis has just lost his last napoleon backing the numbers. No aid from those sources, and away trip the ravishing little creatures, smiling and lively, twirling their fans, and saying pert things to the cavaliers in moustaches. But there is a cold rage and despair in many sacred young hearts—their owners almost children. To-night the belle of the Kursaal, the sought-after by foreign noblemen, decorated with many orders (which very likely do not belong to them), the gaped-at by raw young English bumpkins of fashion—newly-fledged ensigns, spending a quarter's pay in one *mise* on the red—and smock-faced undergraduates, making good use of the long vacation, in which they assured their parents and guardians they intended to read so hard;—to-night this radiant creature will retire to the garret of the second-rate hotel, where the rent has not been paid for so long, nay, nor the charges of the matutinal meal and vesper *table d'hôte*—where the landlord is dunning, and where, when every one is in bed, even the inebriated Englishman who won so largely on the numbers, and insisted on treating the waiters to sparkling Moselle at one o'clock, a.m., there will sit on a mean pallet a very haggard, careworn woman, reckoning how much the pawnbroker will lend on the few gewgaws that remain to her; for there are pawnbrokers in Vanity Fair—ay, and there is death occasionally, and a little suicide sometimes ; only, *on ne parle pas de ça*, we keep these little trifles as quiet as possible ; and, according to the stout gentleman, the funerals, even of the native inhabitants, take place very early in the morning, that the nerves of the visitors may not be shocked. Very different this from Ventnor, Isle of Wight, where, if you happen to arrive, looking somewhat like an invalid, you may chance, ten minutes afterwards, to perceive a sleek man, in raven black, beneath your window, in earnest conference with your servant or your landlady, and who you may be almost certain in conjecturing to be an undertaker; and where even the landlady who lets the lodgings, as she expatiates on the charms of the apartments you are engaging, points significantly to the convenient breadth of the staircase, and hints that there are no awkward corners to prevent the coffin coming nicely and comfortably downstairs, and that she always expects a week's rent in advance: for accidents will happen with the best-doctored invalids.

What more of men-folk can be discerned throughout the gambling day and night in Hombourg Kursaal? The rogues I have glanced at—they deserve but a cursory notice. A scrap of red riband the more, an extra twist to the waxed moustache, an additional dash of lacquer to the worn boots, and they are the same shabby rascals you meet in the *coulisses* of the Paris Bourse, or about the *café* Leblond and Passage de l'Opéra (till warned off by the *sergens de ville*), the same battered scamps who hang about cheap eating-houses and cigar-shops near Leicester Square, or hover fitfully about that Tattersalian ring, that Mammon-worshipping Capel Court, within whose precincts as defaulters and "lame ducks" they dare not show their noses. Roguery is very catholic. Rascaldom is of no citizenship but the world. Guzman de Alfaruche and Mr. Dando, the oyster-eater, claim cousinage; Pontis de St. Helène, *alias* Coignard the convict, and Tom Provis, the sham baronet, real forger, are related, both by the father and mother's side. There is freemasonry among knaves—a system of signs, a code of laws, an universal language; and he who would cheat at the *roulette* wheel here, if he could, and sometimes does manage to claim a stake that is not his, is the same swindler who would decoy you, Mr. Greenhorn, into a skittle-alley in Shoreditch, and plunder you of your last shilling—is the same Mr. Softroe who would meet you at the liquor-bar of a Mississippi steamer, inveigle you to play "poker," cheat you, ay, and quickly bowie-knife you, if you discovered that it was through cheating you had lost your dollars; who would degenerate into a pure thief and pilferer, as a Neapolitan or a Chinese; and who, at Singapore or Manilla, would insinuate himself into your bed-room at night, nude, his body copiously and completely anointed with palm-oil—as slippery a thief and as difficult to lay hold of as a fraudulent bank-director—and steal the very teeth out of your head, in addition to your watch, clothes, and loose cash, while you slept.

"More man: plague! plague!" cries cynic Timon, as Alcibiades comes by beating his drum, or snarling Apemantus crawls up to carp at him. O noble Timon, wert thou in this Kursaal, what force might thou add, what additional bitterness might thou impart to the malediction with which thou smotest the men of Athens, and not only them but all mankind! For here indeed are those who would swear into strong shudders and to heavenly agues the immortal gods that hear them; here are the "curl'd-pate ruffians," become bald with much dicing and carousing; here the "unscarred braggarts of the wars," and those who "thatch their poor thin roofs with burdens of the dead," some that were hanged—no matter; here is the "Flamen that rails against the quality of flesh and not believes herself;" for here—do my eyes deceive me?—no, 'tis really he—the Reverend Hugo Hollow-penny, formerly of St. Ignatius College, Camford, relegated from thence in consequence of that ugly affair in which Lord Swandown was pigeoned in his second term by Maggs of Barabbas Hall and Scurff of St. Sepulchre's, and in which nefarious transaction— (the lad was not eighteen, and his losses were as enor-

mous as his debts)—the Rev. H. H. was (of course
innocently) implicated. Hugo was in orders at the
time; he would have been ruined (though nothing
could be proved against him) but for the kindness of
Mrs. Bifrons, Lord Bishop of Bosfursus's wife. the son
of whose butler, indeed, he was: who mercifully
brought about his nomination to the colonial chaplaincy in the Island of Hoopdedoodendoo, which, as all
old Africans know, is on the Dooda coast. I can't
exactly make out how it was, a week after this, that
Hugo was seen at the " Blue Posts " very late, treating
a negro prize-fighter to champagne cup. That sable
gladiator may have been, it is true, one of the potentates of the Dooda coast. How was it, too, that a month
afterwards he was gazetted to the curacy of Pottlyd-
dyian, close to the Land's End, Cornwall? It is certain, however, that the Reverend Hollowpenny came
to London in the year following that of the Great Exhibition, without any curacy, and almost without any
clothes at all ; that ever since that period he has been
leading what by the greatest stretch of courtesy must
be called a sadly Bohemian life ; now editing the
" Boanerges Broadsheet," a low-church weekly journal.
which was expected utterly to demolish the Puseyites.
but broke down instead lamentably at the third number, driving Burjoice, the printer, into the " Gazette,"
and Hollowpenny himself into Horsemonger Lane
Jail; now lecturing on the " Comicalities of Calvinism," in London and the provinces. Piccolo, the
music-seller, " hired him," or " farmed him," as the
slang professional phrase goes now-a-days, took him
out of prison, clothed him, gave him handsome terms
and a three years' engagement, and expected to make
a fortune out of him; but, alas! Hugo turned out a
total failure. That ugly story of Lord Swandown and
the pigeoning got abroad again; people wouldn't
listen to his comicalities or his Calvinism. and Piccolo
was glad to pay him forfeit and cry off. I declare that

soon after this I heard that the Reverend Hugo Hollowpenny, B.A., Cam., was keeping a betting-shop. Was it not also he who was mixed up with Voules and Nimblethimble, the sharpers, who got up the fictitious "Distressed Trousers-makers' Association," and collected large sums from the benevolent, which they applied to their own nefarious purposes? There was not so much harm in Hugo's attempting to earn an honest living by waiting every Sunday morning, at the Surplice Coffee House, St. Paul's Churchyard, with a complete suite of canonicals and ready-written sermons, in three different shades of doctrine, in a carpet bag, in case any metropolitan clergyman should be taken ill, or have an engagement anywhere out of town for fly-fishing purposes, and who would wish his pulpit filled temporarily by a qualified clerk in orders, happy to perform "Sunday duty" for a half-guinea fee. Not quite so unexceptionable was Hugo's opening a select boarding-school at Ealing, and flogging five-eighths of his scholars away before the first scholastic quarter was ended. After this, his friends and creditors (he had many of both, for the man, though unprincipled, was genial) lost sight of him for many moons; and now, lo! he turns up in the Kursaal of Hombourg-von-der-Höhe. Clerical as ever is the cut of his long-skirted clerical coat, his M.B. (Mark of the Beast) waistcoat; his low, white cravat, pepper-and-salt trousers, and cloth-topped boots. Clerical still, but rusty exceedingly, is the Rev. Hugo Hollowpenny. Why is he wandering here, I pray? What does he seek? What will he do with it—or would he do with it if he had it? The English chaplaincy at Hombourg is already occupied by a worthy and efficient divine. Baden, Wiesbaden, Ems, Kissengen, Nassau, Nauheim, Aachen, Spa, Cologne, Bonn, have all their English congregations, and their indifferently-paid English pastor. There is no room, ecclesiastically, for Hollowpenny anywhere. Shall I tell you what the man does? He punts! he gambles! He makes his daily bread and cheese out of the black and the red; to him the *pair*, or the *manque*, the *impair*, or the *passe* of the *roulette* tables are board, lodging, and washing—yea, and the garments, even, to his back. He plays his little double-florin piece, and loses. Well; he goes away and pinches and spunges for the remainder of that day. He plays and wins. Keeps on winning till he has netted, say, a couple of napoleons. Then Hugo Hollowpenny is a gentleman for the rest of the twenty-four hours; and goes away, not striving to win more, rejoicing. But woe betide the unhappy wretch if risking, as he sometimes does, a florin upon the fatal criss-cross network of numbers, and the one he backs turns up in the wheel. At once he goes mad. Dines at the *table d'hôte*; drinks much Burgundy; takes *chásses*, and *aprés chásses*; comes back to the accursed table, plays wildly, wildly, and more wildly still, loses all but a few pieces, risks them all, and is about—nay, sure to retrieve himself; when eleven o'clock tinkles from one of the little golden timepieces on the consoles, and the poor slave is bankrupt and penniless. Some of these days, as sure as fate, Hugo Hollowpenny will hang himself, or blow his brains out. It is a pity, you will say, to know Latin, and Greek, and conic sections, and come to the risking of stivers on the green-baize of a common gaming-table. To be a man of capacity and learning, and a Christian priest to boot, and end so. What would you have? It were better even that he were here harming only himself, than in another country, or under other circumstances, doing harm, perhaps incalculable, to other people. Better Hollowpenny in this Hades, than Hollowpenny in the pulpit or on the platform, telling lies to honest folks. At home the man might have stolen, forged, strychnined somebody for the sake of a dividend warrant, and have made his exit at Portland, or by the Debtor's Door.

Let him alone at Hombourg-von-der-Höhe, then, and grudge him not the *visa* to his Foreign Office passport. Let him play his few remaining stakes. We shall hear no more of him; and if he misbehave himself abroad, there are foreign *bagnes, polizei præsidiums,* and *ergastoli* enow, where he will be taken care of.

There is a gentleman who has written a book all about Bartholomew Fair, in times ancient and modern. He had better have stayed his hand, and come first to Hombourg Kursaal. The glories of "Bartlemy," past and present, could have been nothing to the great fair that goes on here "all the year round." Look at them, Mr. Morley; look at them, Mr. Thackeray—you have looked at them once before, and to a purpose, in your "Kicklebury on the Rhine." Look at them, ghosts of John Bunyan and William Hogarth. See them flitting, flirting, gossiping, ogling—poor deluded mortals—round and round these fatal tables that are to them as the candle is to the moth. The grave English families, the decorous English dowagers, the starched and prim young English misses that come sailing at first into the Kursaal, marshalled by pater and mater-familias as demurely as though they were coming to church! They walk round and round the tables, first, half-contemptuously, half-pityingly regarding the eager gamesters; but still passing on, and whispering comments that bear equally on the folly and sinfulness of gaming, and upon the "astonishing run of luck that some people seem to have." Then they will grow more familar, and remain stationary for awhile at the back of some player, who is playing adventurous and complicated *coups;* or, which is more probable, they will recognize some acquaintance who has thrown his surplus stock of morality—how many of us go out in ballast!—overboard, and is playing for the dear life. Him they will congratulate upon his luck, or condole with on his evil fortune. Generally, the ice is broken, the first adventurous plunge is taken,

by some scapegrace of a boy, or boarding-school romp
of a girl, who, heedless of the stern prohibition of
the elders, steals away to the table of forbidden
delights, and risks half-a-dollar. They win. Children
—the young at least, as I have elsewhere remarked,
although, for the matter of that, any *habitué* of Hombourg will bear me out in stating that "little Toddlekins," in a very tender state of juvenility, is by no
means an unfrequent punter at the Kursaal play-
table *—almost always win. 'Tis a way Satan has of
persuading them to become inveterate gamesters when
they grow up. Papa, and mamma, and elder sisters—
elder brothers have been away playing in a frenzied
manner these many days past—first look grim, chide,
reprehend, and threaten departure and punishment;
but Master Jacky has won a napoleon; Miss Fan
comes bounding up with her little hands overflowing
with florins. Upon my word, within a week afterwards you may see the whole family at hard, steady,
persistent play. Papa, who ought to have been in his
counting-house in Pope's Head Alley this week agone,
is pricking the turn-ups at *rouge-et-noir* on a card.
Mamma, who at home goes three times to church on
Sundays, and has the Reverend Jumping Owler to tea
three times a week, is planting florins all over the
roulette table, as though she were sewing coins on a
network *cachepeigne*. The young ladies have spent
six months' pocket money in advance, and are deep in
the governess's debt. She is a Frenchwoman, and
has a sly turn at the red on Sundays, when the family

---

* In 1716, the barrow-women of London used generally to
carry dice with them, and children were induced to throw for
fruit and nuts, as indeed was any person of a more advanced age.
However, the pernicious consequences of the practice beginning
to be felt, the Lord Mayor issued an order to apprehend all such
offenders, which speedily put an end to street gambling. For
that time at least; but in our own days we have seen the gambling pieman, with his cry of "Toss or buy—up and win 'em."

are attending service at the Chapelle Anglicaine.   As
for the elder brothers, they are in the hands of the
Lombards and the Jews by this time; all the jewellery,
with which they can conveniently dispense without fear
of its being missed, is safely housed at the Mont de
Piété, in the Haingasse; and many a snug little bill
has been done, without paterfamilias's knowledge, at
the Commercial Bank, or at one of the establishments
of the numerous Hebrew money-changers of Hombourg. The only lucky individual of this party of
now desperate gamblers—a week ago so tranquil, so
contented, so virtuous—is little Master Jacky. That
young rogue wins continually, and his pockets are full
of napoleons, which his elder relatives, from materfamilias downwards, are not ashamed to borrow from
him, threatening to box his ears soundly if he winces
at the imposition of these " forced loans."

CHAPTER VIII.

IN WHICH THE **THREE PILGRIMS** FIND THE DESCENT OF AVERNUS AS EASY AS LYING.

THE three travellers whom I have left in the lurch for such an unconscionable period, while endeavouring to explain to you the mysteries of *roulette*, &c., according to the Cocker of the Kursaal, and while expatiating on the humours of that delightful establishment—these three individuals were but mortal men. If you pinched them, they squeaked; if you tickled them, they laughed; if you angered them, they bellowed; if you insulted them, they struck and kicked. They were, in fact, flesh and blood: nothing more. So, as has been elsewhere dimly hinted, being thus mortal, and having come to Hombourg for the express purpose of disporting themselves among the humours thereof, the stout gentleman, the slim gentleman, and the man with the iron chest, all began to play; and when they had once begun, they went on. The man with the iron chest remarked, after the first day's punting, that he had not risen so early, lived so temperately, or worked so hard for years; and that if he only continued the numerical combinations in which he was engaged, the infallible result must be his acquirement of some knowledge of long division and the rule of three, arithmetical problems of which he had been hitherto entirely ignorant. Unhappily, it was only to the extent of the rule of " Reduction " that this iron-chested person was fated to pursue his researches into the recondite mysteries of the Tutor's Assistant. The stout gentleman proclaimed that play-

ing at *roulette*, as a manly and invigorating exercise,
beat billiards, quoits, pulling against tide, and jumping in sacks; and quite threw partridge-shooting and
the dumb-bells into the shade. The slim gentleman
said nothing, but his looks were oracular, and his
brow was " sicklied o'er with the pale cast of thought."
The principal nourishment he took between breakfast
and dinner-time appeared to consist of the small limp
cards on which the odds at the game are pricked down,
and which he tore into small pieces, and masticated
with great apparent relish. He was evidently much
pre-occupied, and his companions whispered that his
hair was coming off. Of course our Three all played,
or said at least that they played, according to the
dictates of some " infallible systems " known to them,
and to them alone. They were not so communicative
now, as of yore, and saw very little of each other out
of business (play) hours, nay, rather prepared to
separate in the Kursaal itself, and make their game
in different saloons; but as I am merely the Editor of
these papers, and happened to turn up " promiscuous "
at Hombourg while my three heroes were there, I
am enabled to describe to you their several acts and
deeds. And, to tell the truth, that which I didn't
see (for I wasn't ubiquitous) was narrated to me by
the three men in their subsequent moments of peni-
tence. It was for a considerable period that they dwelt
in sackcloth and ashes. They howled and grovelled a
good deal before they left the Landgravate of Hesse.
What yelpings and whinings there have been in secret
cupboards of, and recesses of, that joyous little carni-
val town, to be sure.

Now, first of the " infallible system " of the man
with the iron chest. He had learnt it, he said, of a
Polish Jew, who had it from a Russian Chamberlain,
who had extracted it by torture from a Tartar horse-
dealer, who had brought it from the Great Wall of
China, where it was the means of replenishing the

coffers of the Mandarins with many millions' worth
of sycee silver per mensem. The red-nosed man played
this system with prodigious assiduity. To myself and
the bystanders, it appeared chiefly to consist in ac-
cesses of raging madness, accompanied by extreme
ferocity and hoarse mutterings in an unknown tongue,
which he afterwards stated to be Romaic or Modern
Greek, a dialect in which (although I have only his
personal statement to prove it) he had been an adept
in the sunny days of youth. I will say little of this
strange man tearing his hair, clenching and unclench-
ing his fists, beating diabolical tattoos with his feet,
viciously rubbing that empurpled proboscis of his, and
squinting horribly, because these were physical and
facial peculiarities germane to him in his normal
morose-imbecile state. One part of the " infallible
system " he pursued, was to change English bank-notes
into florins, to tear those fat white coins from the
blue cylindrical envelopes in which they were confined, and to stuff with them the many pockets at the
hips, breast, and flanks of his stableman's-looking
coat. I have never known so short a coat to have so
many pockets. Being thus well-ballasted with silver
dross, he continuously flung florins from his pockets
on to the table, and, with amazing frequency (in the
beginning), drew back heaps of argentiferous coinage,
sometimes intermingled with single, and even double,
Frédérics d'or—large, dull, corpulent, orange-tawny-
coloured pieces of money, these latter, and somewhat
resembling Spanish doubloons. The man used to lose
now and then (in the beginning), whereat he would
mutter more hoarsely than ever in the unintelligible
jargon he affected; but he must have won constantly
and considerably, for I used to see the skirts of the
stableman's coat positively and visibly swelling with
dollars before my eyes, even as swole that young
woman whom the elder Mr. Weller watched as she
drank seventeen cups of green tea at the Anniversary

Festival of the Brick-Lane Branch Temperance Association. When he had won an uncommonly good *coup*, the red-nosed man was accustomed to mutter "Julia! Julia!" in a tone of strident exultation; and, for the moment, stuffing his latest winnings into his cap, he would rush out on to the terrace, meet, as if by preconcerted signal, the stout gentleman, exchange some telegraphic signals with him, relating apparently to numerical computations; smoke, in rapid puffs, the largest regalia (or the nearest Frankfort imitation of one) that could be procured; swallow a tankard full of Bavarian beer, or a half flask of Rhenish, and rush back to the table, where he would continue playing more desperately than ever. Thus for many days did the man with the iron chest make his game. By dinner time his hands were black as negro's by continually fingering of dross, and greasy notes of the Landgravate or de Banque de France, which to his great distaste he was sometimes compelled to take when the tables had been hit unusually hard. His hair, never very elegantly disposed, became hideously dishevelled; his eyes glared; hectic spots appeared on his dun cheeks; his tongue lapped thirstily from his mouth; and the regular *habitués* of the gaming-table, who were ruined or enriched every day in the week, always with the same imperturbable quietude and *nonchalance*, looked with amazement, not unmingled with alarm, upon this wild man of the Kursaal, who played so fiercely, and gave utterance to such strange noises. When the bell rang for the *table d'hôtes*—and when six o'clock strikes in Hombourg, every house seems to have set up a *table d'hôte* and a bell as sonorous as Great Tom of Lincoln, which ding-dongs astoundingly—the man would retire and reappear, washed and kempt. He devoured large quantities of food at dinner, brandished his knife and fork to the alarm of decorous maiden ladies— to all of whom, however, he was scrupulously polite—sitting by, and with gurgling sounds in his œsophagus, disposed of mighty potations. Afterwards, in *cafés* and in garden arbours, he smoked like Etna, and drank tumblers of punch that steamed like Hecla, and at unholy hours volunteered songs in harsh polyglot, which but for their resemblance to the general dirges of the Waitongos, and the war-songs of the Woowoos, might have passed current for convivial ditties.

The slim gentleman kept himself to himself. Indeed, he half hinted to his less philosophical companions, that the less he saw of them for the next ten days the better; that he wished them every success in their play, but advised them to be cautious, and that when he had netted a hundred thousand francs, or four thousand pounds sterling, he intended to run over to Frankfort (in a barouche drawn by six greys, with postilions in pink and silver, and outriders in green and gold), and give a *fête alfresco* to the Germanic Confederation represented at the Frankfort Diet. Till then, mealtimes always excepted, he begged to be excused from holding any further communication with his fellow-travellers. He played nothing but gold—utterly despising florins and double florins—and "made his game" in a quiet and cat-like manner. It was a sight to watch him sitting patiently, hour after hour, the fore-finger of his right hand pressed to that forehead which was doubtless full as the steward's cabin of a steampacket with the most abstruse mathematical calculations. That fore-finger was only withdrawn when the whole puissant right hand was required to lay down a stake. The palm of the remaining hand lay outstretched on the field of the cloth of green. It held a long, sinuous, snaky cordon of gold:—the money he had won. The money he played *with*, or staked, was arranged before him in shining piles. He never spoke, he seldom moved. He never rushed out like those sensual creatures, his fellow-travellers, to smoke or drink. He counted his money with his eyes, never with his fingers. He was there—tranquil, immoveable, vigilant,—the Napoleon of *roulette;* and Marengos and Austerlitzes succeeded each other in his victorious progress, as if Moscow and the Beresina were phantoms—as if to-morrow would never come.

To-morrow ; aye that dread to-morrow that comes to all : the fateful "*Demain*" of Victor,

> "Demain est la sapin du trône,
> Aujourd'hui c'en est le velours."
> *   *   *   *   *

Yes, to-morrow is the coarse deal, with its ten sacks, that forms the frame-work of the throne, as to-day is its velvet and gilding.

> "Demain c'est le coursier qui s'abat plein d'écume ;
> Demain, O conquérant, c'est Moscou qui s'allume
>   La nuit comme un flambeau :
> C'est not' vielle garde qui jonche au lointain la plaine
> Demain c'est Waterloo! Demain c'est St. Hélène!
>   Demain c'est le tombeau !"

But the slim gentleman troubled himself very little about these things, and only looked upon to-morrow as a day when he should win more Frédérics d'or.

The stout gentleman's mode of "making his game" was volatile, erratic, fugacious—not to say fidgetty. He was by no means the Napoleon, but rather the Figaro, of *roulette* and *rouge et noir.* He was here, there, and everywhere. He was everything by turns, and nothing long. He flung down a handful of silver—very frequently as large a handful of gold—on a number on the *roulette* table, and, with an airy smile, sauntered away, and left his *peculium* to take its chance. Then he would wander away to the *trente et quarante* and back the *couleur* for a couple of Naps. Then he came back to *roulette,* found he had won what he jocosely designated a "pot of money," and let his money—stake and winnings—remain on the *tapis vert*. Sometimes as the whim—the prudent whim —seized him, he would pocket his stake. Then he would skip away to the reading-room; glance over the last week but one's "Punch;" find he had lost; elope to the terrace; meet the man with the iron chest; cigar and beer with him; perhaps indulge in a sardine or two, or a light sandwich of ham or German sausage —for the stout gentleman's appetite was always of the healthiest. He made multitudes of impromptu acquaintances—he was always of a familiarly affectionate disposition, and would, I dare say, have addressed the judge who sentenced him to penal servitude for life as "My chick," had such an unpleasant conjuncture in his affairs arisen—and called numbers of be-whiskered and be-ribboned foreigners *Mon cher*, or *Moi caro*, or *Mein lieber freund*—which ever happened to turn up first. He avowed, subsequently, his impression that there did not exist a greater set of rogues unhung than the frequenters of the Kursaal at Hombourg-von-der-Höhe.

Within four days of "making the game" having commenced, the three travellers began to be weary of staking silver pieces, and flung *rouleaux* of forty pounds apiece with supreme disdain upon the verdant board.

A rumour ran abroad that the man with the iron chest had been seen to light a cigar with a thousand-franc note.

"We shall break the bank," whispered the three over a bowl of punch à la Romaine, in an arbour of de Kurgarten.

"They will break the bank," muttered in secret conclave, and in their inmost strong room, the Administration of the Kursaal: "They will break the bank: *ces Anglais. Hundert tausend teufeln!*"

And how about the "infallible system" played separately or collectively by the Three?

I have said that they were penitent afterwards, and confessed. Thus much did the man with the iron chest admit. That, on his departure from England he was really in possession of a so-called mathematical system which had occurred, or had been, so to speak, "revealed" to him while laid up with a fit of the rheumatism at Brussels, years before. He had studied this system very deeply; applied it in theory at home, both to *roulette* and *rouge et noir;* then essayed it, as he termed it, with "blank cartridge," using haricot beans in lieu of money, and carefully debiting and crediting himself with the loss and profit; he had worked out hundreds of diagrams on paper, entirely to his own satisfaction, and at one time stood to win no less than seventy-nine thousand six hundred and three haricot beans; and, finally, he arrived at the mature conclusion that his system was really infallible. and that, properly played, it must as infallibly bring him in a large fortune. The munificence of his intentions, at this stage of his enthusiastic castle-building, with respect to the already mentioned Julia, could only be equalled by the Monte Christo-like extravagance of his plans for purchasing landed estates in Devonshire, baronial titles in Germany, and for releasing the sumptuous diamonds of his family from the tribulation under which they had so long laid at the hands of certain commercial firms of Lombard extraction. The red-nosed man, in fact, had secretly determined, so soon as his fortune was made, to "have his rights," and "show the world what he was made of." But on his arrival at Hombourg, the M. I. C. frankly confessed that the chandeliers and the money-chinking got into his head, somehow, and confused it. Some essential part of his system, with which, when he left the banks of the Thames, he was elaborately crammed, suddenly and vexatiously became missing, and the remaining portions got inextricably mixed up with another system, quite as infallible, but also irreducible, through confusion, to action, which had been departed to him by an ancient *portier* at an hotel in the *Quartier Latin*, who had formerly been a *croupier* at Frascati's in the old days of the Paris *ferme des jeux:* while, to make confusion worse confounded, there constantly intruded themselves on his mind some scattered particles of another system he had once dreamed of after a lobster salad—a system which appeared irrefragable while the dream lasted, but which, like many other things that pass through the ivory gate, turned out to be perfectly irrational and preposterous when he was wide awake. Whereat the man with the iron chest becoming desperate, and finding his gambling faculties one hopeless imbroglio of chaotic ideas, wildly determined to " back his luck," staked money according to the dictates of chance, cabalistic words that occurred to him, always let his winnings remain during three *coups* after the event, and generally played the game of an insane person. As has been recorded, his gains [in the beginning] were enormous.

Now of the system pursued by the slim gentleman. That, too, of course, was infallible; but I feel bound to state that on my applying for information to the meagre person in question, he flatly refused to give me the slightest information as to the features of his system, unless indeed that my name happened to be Laplace, Professor de Morgan, or Mr. Babbage, the anti-organgrinder; or, in the second place, that I at once consented to invest a thousand pounds sterling in working the infallible system, for the common good of himself and friends—myself standing in. Thus much the slim one maintained, and was prepared to make his affidavit concerning it in any court of justice or record in Europe. That his system was so far infallible, that so long as he adhered strictly to his laws, his gains had exceeded two hundred and fifty pounds per diem; and that had his capital been a little more elastic, he would indubitably have broken the bank within a fortnight.

It only remains to glance at the infallibilities as exemplified in the system of the stout gentleman. When first questioned on the subject, the stout individual blushed, next he cried " boder," and devoted all infallible systems to irrevocable perdition. Finally, he made a clean breast of it, and acknowledged that his infallible system was just no system at all, and that it consisted no further than in backing the play of the prettiest lady near him.

And I am not quite certain whether the stout one's was not as good a system, not only as those pursued by his companions, but as the three thousand and three, all warranted infallible, which the ever fresh recruited army of dupes at Hombourg are continually breaking their teeth, and fortunes, and hearts against. I say, that my certainty is not *quite* complete; for it need scarcely be hinted that I, too, have a system—an infallible system of my own—of which I have not yet imparted the secret to one living soul, and that some of these days I intend that infallible system to make me as rich as Rothschild.

It is very curious, and very ludicrous, to think of the infinity of devices, half puerile, half shrewd, and sometimes wholly superstitious, by which gamesters endeavour to bind chance in bonds, to make a certainty of the odds, and to tempt fortune to their side of the *tapis vert*. Sometimes a player carries a pack of cards about with him; cuts them furtively beneath the table, and stakes his money on the colour opposed to that which he has turned up in cutting. In the numbers at *roulette* he will back the numerals of the day of the month, of the years of his age, or that of his grandmother, or of the days he has been in Hombourg. Some gamesters will dream of a number, and back it faithfully for a certain time. Others—and this is an old English gaming tradition—have an idea that pawnbroker's money is luckier than cash got in the ordinary way, and will positively pledge some article, in order to begin the day's campaign with cash that has issued from the coffers of mine uncle. There are those who will go up to a total stranger, and ask him to mention any number he may think of, above ten or under ten, as the case may be, and forthwith go and back that number, just as the lazzarone speculators in the Neapolitan lottery will rush up to a person who has been run over, or has been thrown from his horse, and importune the perhaps dying wretch to mention, with his dying groan, a number for them to back. I have known players fill their pockets with white and coloured counters—white for red, and colour for black—and regulate the direction of their stake by the hue of the counter they thus drew out hap-hazard. In short, there is no end to the silly little devices by which the votaries of play endeavour to propitiate that goddess, who, so far from being blind, as she is usually represented, strikes me as being, so far as Hombourg is concerned, the farthest-seeing and clearest-sighted deity in all Olympus.

Thus act the men who speculate on chance, and mere chance, and who have their lucky and unlucky days—rigidly abstaining from play on the latter:—as when it rains, or when such and such a croupier is not present, or when they have had their nails cut. Then there are the gentlemen who delight in fantastic combinations—who will back such a particular column of numbers; who will go through the whole abacus of thirty-six from first to last, or backwards from last to first; who will back all the evens, and then all the odds; who will back all the tens, and leave the units alone; who pitch upon one number and continue to bet upon it, through fair and through foul weather, throughout an entire day; who will back so many numbers on the board in such degrees of juxtaposition, that the pieces they lay down may form the points of a square, a triangle, an oblong, or a cross; or will proceed from the top to the bottom of the schedule of numbers in parallel rows of three. There are those who place their entire faith in a colour, red or black, and will stick to that colour, constant as the needle to the pole, for a week together. Others will have nothing to say but to "odd" or to "even," or to "*passe*" or to "*manque*" (above eighteen and below eighteen). Others confine themselves to operations on the vertical column—that is, to the numbers in any one longitudinal row of the table; and a larger proportion of players—the apostles of the principles of negation—will have nothing to say to any other chance but "number nothing,"—Zero. You know that if the *roulette* ball enters the compartment allotted to Zero, he who had backed it raises thirty-five times his stake; and in the hope of this eventuality the disciples of Zeroaster will go on backing "nothing," which nonentity lies at the head of the number-table, close to the tire of the *roulette* wheel, with amazing patience and perseverance. Sometimes a player, whose system compels him to double, triple, quadruple, or quintuple his stakes, to "recoup" himself for a run against the chance he is staking on, will, when his investments have grown very heavy, and there is alarming prospect of being broken if the run continues much longer, begin to "insure in Zero"— that is, he will pop a couple of florins, or perhaps a half-Frederic, into "no man's hand," every time he passes his larger and more serious stake. Others devote a certain per-centage of all their winnings to the nourishment of Zero; and it is astonishing what balm for a wounded spirit is derivable from the sudden efflorescence of Zero into substantial wealth, and all from some chance florin, which you had discarded, perhaps, because it was a little cracked or tarnished, and the probation of which, in the latitude of Zero, you had three-parts forgotten.

The bank is stronger than all the systems, fallible and infallible, than all the combinations, mathematical, superstitious, or simply capricious. Every arithmetician knows that there are certain combinations both at *roulette* and at *rouge*, by steadily pursuing which, never deviating one iota from the rule laid down, and progressively increasing your stakes, you *must* eventually win. But, unless your capital be enormous, your gain, even in the end, will leave but a very small surplus above your original outlay; and, in the majority of cases, your capital is *not* strong enough to carry out the combination in the face of a heavy run against you—as when you are backing red, and black turns up eighteen, or, as it did once at Geneva, twenty-seven times; and you are broken and cleaned out—it may be, irremediably ruined, on the very eve of success. Consider that you are but one man, and that the bank is a Pyrrhic phalanx; that you have to oppose a limited to an unlimited capital; that if to reimburse yourself for a heavy loss, you are in a position to secure almost a certainty of winning if you can stake a certain sum, but that the bank cunningly puts a limit to its possible loss, and tells the player, " *You* may stake what you like; but eight thousand francs is *our* maximum, and above that sum we decline to play." Consider the numerous " pulls " possessed by the bank, in the Zeros, which after all are not very extensively backed—hours sometimes elapsing without number nothing turning up, and the process of insurance thus becoming wearily stale, flat, and unprofitable; in the limitation of the hours of play—for the clock may strike eleven just as you are about to make your fortune; in the bank being, from chime to chime, *always* at it, always gambling, whereas you can only devote a certain number of hours per diem to making your game; in the bank, in its *personale* of dealers and croupiers, being always calm, collected, sober, and indifferent as to gain or loss, whereas you, the player, are generally nervous and excited, never indifferent, and frequently, after the vesper bell has done chiming, considerably flushed with champagne. Consider all these things, my son, and be wise ere you steam up the Rhine towards Hombourg-von-der-Höhe; for if you go there, and be made of ordinary flesh and blood —I am not writing for oysters or icebergs—you must play, and will in all human probability leave your skin behind you.

Of course there are the people who have won, do win, and will win at Hombourg, and at Baden, and elsewhere. There are the tremendous, and almost superhuman runs of luck, such as no bank can foresee or withstand; such as enriched the notorious Baron de Warens, and gave a hundred thousand francs of clear profit apiece to two players who did not in the least need such a bonus—the late Prince Lucien Bonaparte, and the Austrian General Haynau, of detestable memory. Then, there is no use in denying it—there are the people who are born to be lucky at games of chance, and who, at whatsoever game they play—loo, poker, *roulette*, or blind hookey, can almost be certified to come off the winners. But, *en revanche*, these lucky ones generally outstep the boundaries of their luck, by greedy persistence, or by audaciously rash speculation. They ride the free horse to death, tire out the patience of Fortune, and are ruined in the long run. There are people who can make a decent, albeit painfully-acquired livelihood at *rouge et noir*, because, being of a phlegmatic and cold-blooded constitution, they have strength enough to abandon the play-table immediately after they have won or lost a certain sum. They are the philosophers who follow the croupier's advice, and *se contentent de peu*. And generally there are the people who, by a chance "fluke" or "spurt," win a large sum of money, and are wise enough to put it in their purse, forthwith pay their hotel bill, and quit Hombourg for ever. But the names of the people who act with such sapient discretion, or have so acted in the course of one summer season at the Kursaal, could be written on my thumb-nail; whereas the names of those who, by winning, are enticed again to play, in order to win more, and end by losing all, are Legion.

CHAPTER IX.

MORE GOLDEN GAINS.—THE THREE VISIT THE SCHLOSS OR CASTLE OF HOMBOURG.—PRINCESSE ELEEZA-BETH.—POOR OLD GEORGE.

THE campaign of cards continued.

The stout gentleman declared publicly, that he had won so much lately, that he had some intention of frying his gold watch. He asked in a casual way the price of good-sized diamonds, and mentioned that he considered ten florins a very moderate fee for a waiter who brought you a pipe-light. He burst into the apartment of the M. I. C. one morning, and informed him that if things went on, and he continued winning at this rate, he should buy a gold coat and a silver bootjack.

The slim gentleman said nothing: but it was reported that he staked nothing now but rouleaux. Not rouleaux of florins, but compact little columns of bright napoleons and tawny louis d'ors, holding fifty in a rouleau, and rolled up as tightly as sausages in their cerulean envelopes.

"How does he look," asked the M. I. C., "when he has those stakes risked on a single *coup?*"

"Green!" answered the stout gentleman.

"*Mais non!*" ejaculated a foreign gentleman (they were dining at Chevet's *table d'hôte*). "*Monsieur est plutôt jaune. Je vous assure qu'il est jaune comme ma——*" I think the foreign gentleman, who was profusely decorated with legions of dishonour and other unornamental crosses and ribbons, was about to say "*Jaune comme ma chemise*"—"as yellow as my shirt," when he recollected that the undergarment was never of the liveliest of hues. Indeed it looked as though it had been carefully boiled in pea-soup. So the foreign gentleman contented himself with saying: "*jaune comme un orange*"—"as yellow as an orange"—instead.

It is certain that for five successive days the travellers won a vast amount of money. I was never, however, with any degree of certitude, enabled to ascertain the exact figure of their gains. The stout gentleman —who looked upon everything *couleur de rose*—stated, when interrogated on the subject, that they made "thousands an hour," a statement I am inclined to think must be taken with some degree of circumspection. Their nationality was descanted on. Their individuality was keenly disputed. There was a party who stoutly maintained the stout gentleman to be Omar Pacha in plain clothes; and little Baron von Ichwartzlegg, who had been gambling about the German watering-places since the year '17, was ready to take his affidavit—though goodness knows *that* wasn't worth much—that the slim gentleman was no other than the famous Count Gogglestein, "*l'homme aux lunettes d'écaille*"—the "man with the tortoise-shell spectacles," supposed to be the celebrated "double million magnifiers," spoken of in the trial of Bardell *v.* Pickwick, whose appearance at Aix-la-Chapelle caused such a sensation in that resort of decayed gentility during the year in which the Congress of Sovereigns, who afterwards joined what is called the Holy Alliance, was sitting, and who, by the power of those same terrible spectacles with the tortoise-shell rims, was enabled to discern secret marks on the ornamental backs of the cards used at *écarté*—all the cards having emanated from one manufactory at Cologne, of which the head engraver was in confederacy with the unscrupulous Count Gogglestein. Be it as it may, he won seventy-five thousand francs

in two months at *écarté*, and was only at last discom-
fited by accidentally knocking off his spectacles, one
very hot night, while in the act of wiping his forehead with a handkerchief. The spectacles fell to the
ground—it was at a ball and card party, given by
Pozzo di Borgo to Metternich—and were at once
trampled into a thousand fragments under the military heels of Captain Prince Gangrenoffski III. of
the Imperial Russian Guards.

Concerning the man with the iron chest, opinions
were divided; but all concurred that no good could
come out of so very red a nose. Still the company
at Hombourg were unanimous in declaring that our
three travellers were making a fortune; and the gifted
French journalist, Paul de la Canarderie, who was
staying at the Hôtel Bellevue—where he had run up
an enormous bill—wrote to the little Paris periodical,
in which he indited a weekly *feuilleton*, that there
were three *insularies* at Hombourg—one a *milord,
bien gros;* another a *banquier qui avait l'air affamé,*
with a hungry look; and a third with a prodigiously
red nose, who appeared to officiate as "*jockei*" to his
companions.

It is not to be supposed that the travellers neglected to indulge in those multifarious recreations
provided by the Administration of the Kursaal at
Hombourg, in addition to the seductive *roulette,* and
the fascinating *trente et quarante.* While playing
and winning with extreme industry, they appear to
have found time to fare sumptuously every day at the
gorgeous *table d'hôte,* held within the walls of the
Kursaal itself; to pay frequent visits in open carriages
and four to the neighbouring and fair city of Frankfort; to make one grand excursion, which lasted an
entire day—but I rather think this must have been at
a period when they were not winning quite so rapidly
—to the Felzbourg in the neighbouring Taunus range

of mountains; to take the waters at the divers brun-
nens or springs adjacent, with great zeal and regularity:
to indulge in hot, cold, douche, hip, wave, and plunge
baths; to try the grape cure, and the *molken*, or whey
cure; and to take several sound and salutary walks in
the adjacent villages. I am not at all prepared to say
whether the slim gentleman did not also find leisure
enough to write a treatise on the "Doctrine of
Chances," utterly confuting the laws laid down by
Laplace, Democvri, and de Morgan; whether the
stout gentleman did not fall violently in love with a
lady who wore yellow ringlets, and a cockatoo's
feather in her bonnet, and led a curly poodle by a
rose-coloured ribbon; and finally, whether the man

THE STAHL-BRUNNEN (STEEL WELL) IN THE KUR-GARTEN.

with the iron chest didn't quarrel with, and challenge to mortal combat, a staff-officer in the army of Hesse-Hombourg.

Searching among the papers kindly placed at my disposal by my three friends (they are all retired from public life now; and one, alas! is—but no matter), I discovered the account of a visit paid by the three to the Schloss, or castle of the Landgrave. The document is in the well-known handwriting of the stout gentleman; and I am only sorry that considerations of space compel me to condense it, somewhat, from its original amplitude. Thus writes our corpulent friend:—

"October——. Rather an ugly day's work yesterday. Forgot to transmit that odd two hundred and fifty per agency of Chartered Commercial Bank to my London banker. Red turned up seventeen times in succession. The red-nosed man borrowed a rouleau of me. Said he didn't want to change another English bank-note that night. His nose is growing mauve-colour, shot with pink madder. Curiously, I didn't want to change notes either, so borrowed two rouleaux from the slim one. His face looked a lively pea-green in hue as he handed over the frederics— reflection from the green baize, no doubt. Champagne not good at the hotel. Sparkling Moselle worse. Burgundy shameful. An intolerable lot of vulgarians on the strangers' list of the hotel. I think it will rain to-morrow. After all, this Hombourg is, I consider, a very much overrated place. There is nothing like one's own country, after all this gallivanting about foreign parts. As for the Landgrave, he is a regular old humbug." (I hope it is not treason to transcribe this opinion of the stout gentleman at this time of day, and in the present complicated position of continental affairs.) "Would you believe it, that the old curmudgeon won't live in his own palace, but passes his life in a poky little hole of a keeper's hut on the road to the Taunus, and kills game for his own dinner? Landlord of the hotel says that he is '*un homme sauvage.*' Perhaps he was disappointed in love some sixty or seventy years ago, and that soured him for the rest of his life. Poor old chap! I know, myself, what the feeling is too well. Heigho! . . . By the way, we all went to this same palace, or schloss, or château, or whatever you may like to call it, this morning. Very queer old place, very rum old establishment indeed. It's at the top of the Leusenstrasse. At least, you don't turn to the right when you get to the top of it, as if you were going to the Pawn—the Mont de Piété—the 'Lombard' I mean, but to the right up the Herrngasse, and there is the old tumble-down barrack of a place right before you. There are some little boy-sentries at the gate, and a guard-house, with more little boy-sentries, crouching on beds and squatting on forms, inside it and outside it; but, bless you, they didn't warn us off, or challenge us. I daresay that they were too much afraid of us; or, perhaps, they thought we might fling them some coppers to scramble for. In we went, through a shabby court-yard with whitewashed walls, into another yard quite as shabby, but much larger, and in which stands a huge, hulking Martello sort of a place, of tremendous height, called the 'White Tower.' We were staring up at this tower, and wondering whether there were any state prisoners inside it, shut up there for hinting that the Landgrave's government didn't manage the *roulette* wheel quite fairly, or that the cards used at the *trente et quarante* had been doctored, when a sly, sleek, comfortable old gentleman, in a long blue frock-coat, and a white head exactly like the top of a twelfth-cake, whom I had observed dodging about ever since we passed the entrance, came up and made a low bow, with a sly smile on his old, wrinkled, weazened, pippin face, that gave him very much the appearance of an urbane ourang-outang.

"'Princesse Eleezabeth!' remarked the blue-coated old gentleman, with another smile, and another bow.

"'You mean Queen Elizabeth,' I condescended to explain, correcting the benighted foreigner. 'Yes, she was a very great sovereign. She built Tilbury Fort, was the first to eat roast goose on Michaelmas Day—I wish she had been the last, for it always kills me with indigestion—and invented starch for ladies' collars. I will trouble you not to talk any scandal about her, if you please.'

"'No, no!' persisted the old gentleman. 'Princesse Eleezabeth. Here. Schloss Hombourg.'

"'I tell you it was Queen Elizabeth,' I retorted, with some heat, 'and she never was at Hombourg in her life. She wouldn't have been seen in such a disreputable place. She was the friend of Lord Burleigh, Amy Robsart, the Earl of Kenilworth, and Lord Chancellor Bacon. Don't tell me, sir. She patronized the immortal Swan of Avon. Do you recollect Doctor Johnson's celebrated lines about Shakspeare's plays—

'Which so did take Eliza and our James.'

She was Eliza. By the way, where is Eliza?'

"'I think you had better shut up,' grumbled, in his usual discourteous manner, the red-nosed man. 'Ben Jonson wrote the lines you speak of, and the Princess Elizabeth was no doubt a German princess who lived all her life on Sauerkraut, and waltzed herself to death.'

"'No, no!' reiterated the old gentleman in blue, "Princesse Eleezabeth Englische princesse. Born Schloss Vindsor. Aha!'

"'You're both wrong,' that cynical slim man observed, 'and the old fellow is quite right. The Princess Elizabeth was a daughter of George the Third, who married a landgrave of Hesse-Hombourg about the time that Prince Leopold married our Princess

Charlotte. She must have lived here. Suppose we go in and see the place.'

" The old gentleman seemed perfectly to understand the latter part of the speech; and producing a large bunch of bright keys from one of the ample pockets of his blue coat, led the way for us towards the right-hand corner of the court-yard, bowing and grinning unceasingly, and never leaving off a muttered mention of ' Princesse Elizabeth.'

" We saw, going in, a coach-house to the right, from which two stablemen or keepers—I'm sure they would have been discarded from any genteel mews in England—were drawing a rickety old shandrydan of a carriage, with big wheels, from which the paint was very

THE COURTYARD OF THE SCHLOSS, HOMBOURG.

nearly worn off; heavy springs, and a huge, rusty leathern hood. When they had got it out, another stableman in a white blouse emptied about a pint of water from a pipkin on the off-wheel, and dabbled it about the spokes with a paint brush. Then he retreated a few paces, and contemplated his work with great, though silent, admiration. A lean black dog, like a turnspit come down in the world in consequence of the invention of machinery, and the introduction of roasting-jacks into kitchens, came up, wagging his ears and tail in great admiration likewise. The keepers, who had seen him in the blouse spill the water over the wheel, then clapped him on the back, and called him 'Karl,' and all three presently proceeded into the coach-house, sat on a bench, and lighting their pipes, fell to smoking with great composure. The dog, I daresay, would have liked to smoke a pipe also ; but reasons connected with natural history interfering, he went on wagging his ears and tail instead. Just as we passed under the verandah of the portico, we heard the three stablemen striking up a little part song, so I conclude the Landgravial carriage was considered washed for the day.

"The entrance-hall of the Schloss is about as good a one as you would expect in England in a country-house at about a hundred and fifty pounds a year rent. The walls are whitewashed, and there is a plaster cast or two stuck about on brackets. There was an infantine sentry in the passage, who was literally leaning on his musket; for I am sure without its aid he would have fallen to the ground, through the weight of his accoutrements. I expected to see him every moment impaled upon his bayonet's tip, like those old Roman fellows who used to throw themselves on the point of their swords. How the deuce did they manage it ? Were Brutus and Cassius a couple of Ramo Samees ?

"Going up a mean sort of a staircase, with a flimsy banister, the stairs bees-waxed and polished in the usual abominable continental fashion, we entered a plain room, filled with 'Roman antiquities,' that would not have been out of place in a provincial museum at home. Most of these were dug up at the Saalburg, and the neighbourhood of the Roman camp in the Taunus. There were urns, saucers, bricks, votive tablets, channels for hypocausts, and especially one measley old stone, on which I read the following inscription :—

IMPCA

HADRII

RAHPA

N.P. DIV

PRONEP

HADRI. A

There, my excavators of Uriconium! There, my sages of Wroxeter! There, Mr. Roach Smith! I think it will puzzle you to decipher this inscription. I should like to know, for instance, what, in your great learning and sagacity, you make 'HADRI. A' stand for.

["The man with the iron chest says that I am a ninny, and that the letters mean, of course, Hadrian Augustus. Some people are remarkably wise; but I don't see any 'of course' about it. At all events, I have thrown down the gauntlet, and there it must lie, till some adventurous Roman antiquary picks it up again.]

"In the centre of this room, on a table, there is a great heap of Roman money, of which 550 pieces were picked up on the road to Usingen in the year 1816. I wish I had been there at the time. The money looks very rusty, and is all over verdigris, but it is a decidedly superior coinage to the disgraceful and detestable kreutzers which they give you here in change for your florins. Mem., to bury a kreutzer in every one of the orange-tree tubs on the left-hand side of the avenue going up to the Kursaal to-morrow morning. I left half a florin in my second-best trousers pocket the day before yesterday with the same intention; but there was a hole in the confounded calico, and I daresay one of the Landgrave's army picked up my half-florin, and carried it to his Serenity, or Transparency, whatever his title may be, as tribute—if, indeed, he didn't spend it in tobacco and beer.

"There are some portraits on the staircase, of about the same degree of artistic excellence as you may see in English country town halls, and large taverns where they give public dinners. There is Frederick Duke of York, with a bald head and a large jowl, in his scarlet uniform and hessian boots. By the way, were 'hessians' so called and introduced into my native land from the fact of the marriage of a daughter of England with a Landgrave of Hesse-Hombourg? There is William the Fourth as Duke of Clarence; and there is the Duke of Kent, looking as impenetrably stupid, ill-tempered, and obstinate, as I am told that revered scion of royalty really was in the flesh. At the head of the staircase is a stone statue of St. Elizabeth, Landgravine of Thuringen, and represented in the act of giving a beggar-boy some bread out of her apron, which bread was metamorphosed suddenly to flowers by her ardent prayers. A legend says of this incident, that St. Elizabeth's husband, being very angry at her uninterrupted distribution of alms to the poor, forbade her to do so any more, and commanded his servants to tell him if his wife continued to do so against his will. One day, when she was about to give alms, her husband, informed of it, overtook her, and asked her what she had in her apron? and when answered—'flowers!' (oh! the little fibber!) desired her to show them to him. Straightway she prayed as hard as ever she could; and the bread was metamorphosed, as you see sculptured in stone, into flowers. This St. Elizabeth was the daughter of Andrew II., King of Hungary, and was born at Presburg in 1207. At the mature age of eleven, she was betrothed to Ludwig of Thuringen; and at fourteen she was married, and became a full-blown landgravine. 'She disdained all comfort,' says the chronicle, 'dressed herself poorly, and ordered that she should be awakened every night in order to say prayers, and to be whipped by her servants in a secret room.' It is almost a pity that Landgraf Ludwig of Thuringen was not of the wife-beating persuasion. He might at least have saved his wife the trouble and the risk of catching cold in getting out of bed to be whipped by the lady's maid. They manage these things better in England; and connubial castigation is done on the premises."

" *Wretch!* " [I find this uncomplimentary epithet, in a delicate Italian hand, interpolated in the stout gentleman's manuscript.]

" Landgraf Ludwig," continues the S. G., " died in 1227. Elizabeth would never marry again, and died a still blooming widow at Marburg, where she had founded an hospital, and where, like the immortal Florence Nightingale, she pleased herself in performing the lowliest offices for the destitute patients, in 1231. Faith produced many wonders at her tomb. Pope Gregory IX. canonized her; Kaiser Friedrich II. crowned her corpse with gold; and there are relics of her now in the Cathedral at Breslau, and at the Elizabetheimer cloister in Vienna. God bless her, any way. She must have been a good woman.*

---

* M. de Montalembert has written a devout ultramontane sort of " Life of St. Elizabeth of Hungary :" and Mr. Carlyle, in his " Life of Frederick the Great," gives a curious episodical gloss on the life of the fair Saint of Marburg. " Conrad," writes Thomas, " younger brother of the Landgraf of Thuringen . . . was probably a child in arms when Richard Cœur de Lion was getting home from Palestine, and into troubles by the road; this will date Conrad for us. His worthy elder brother was husband of the lady since called Saint Elizabeth, a very pious

" Quite enough, I think, by this time, of St. Elizabeth, who has carried me away from the seedy old castle of Hombourg to all manner of queer mediæval reminiscences. However, she was mamma to Henry the Magnanimous, Duke of Brabant, whose wife was in her turn mamma to Henry the Child, and thus became ancestress to the 'Royal Family of Hessia.' And thus it was, also, that her statue came to be in the Hombourg Schloss.

" Curtains of white velvet (wofully shabby and discoloured by this time), provided in the 'Royal Rooms' by the Landgravine Elizabeth, in compliment to a royal guest, Queen Matilda of Wurtemburg; curtains poonah-painted, indeed, or covered with some equally silly species of floral ornamentation, by Landgravine Elizabeth's own fair, industrious hands; carrying one back curiously to odd associations of old days passed in tambour and needlework in Windsor towers, with Madam Schwellenburg and Fanny Burney—these we saw. View from windows in room to south very picturesque. Portraits of Landgravine Caroline, and Catherine of Russia, in powder and patches. A plague of family portraits!—dozens of Hesse-Hombourg Landgraves, including George the Pious, Philip the Magnanimous, and Frederick with the Silver Leg. In and out we went, through a series

but also very fanciful young woman; and I always guess his going on the crusade, where he died straightway, was partly the fruit of the life she led him; lodging beggars, sometimes in his very bed, continually breaking his night's rest for prayer and devotional exercise of undue length—'weeping one moment, then smiling in joy the next'—meandering about, capricious, melodious, weak, at the will of devout whim mainly. (See *Libellus de dictis quatuor ancillarum*—a report of the evidence of Elizabeth's four maids.) However, that does not concern us. Sure enough, her poor Landgraf went crusading, year 1227. . . . Poor Landgraf fell ill by the road at Brindisi, and died—not to be driven further by any cause."—ED.

of second-rate lodging-house-looking apartments, and mean white-washed corridors, with red tiled floors— yes, sir, red tiled floors, not half so comfortable, or indeed decent-looking, as the upper storey apartments of the Hôtel de France.

" ' Well,' said I, in amazement, ' if this is a specimen of the palace of a German sovereign prince, I'd sooner be mayor of Little Peddlington.'

" ' Wait a leetle bit,' expostulated the old gentleman in the blue coat, ' Princesse Eleezabeth.'

" So we went over the rooms of the late Landgravine, the ' English Princess,' the daughter of George the Third. I believe from all accounts that she was a most excellent, amiable, charitable woman, and that she was in every sense a real blessing to the people of the little principality of which she was the sovereign-consort. The reason is comprehensible enough. You see that our bounteous English government settled upon this young English Princess, when she espoused the Hesse-Hombourg Landgrave (who had been deprived of his landgravate during the usurpation of Napoleon, and had been fighting about in the Austrian armies, living upon what he could pick up), an income of something like eight or ten thousand a year out of the Civil List. It wasn't theirs to give away; said Civil List being at that time wrung from the vitals of an oppressed, overtaxed, unrepresented people. Only fancy ten thousand English pounds sterling being flung yearly into the vacuous Hombourg Exchequer— for there was no Kursaal then, and the surpassing virtues of the mineral waters had not been discovered. Only fancy this glorious £10,000 a year translated into florins and kreutzers! Why, it was a mint of money! Why, it must have stopped up the chinks and crannies, and new-laid the floors, and new-tiled the roofs, and new-potted the chimneys, and new-planted the gardens of the desolate tumbledown old Schloss-Hombourg for many a long day. It must have augmented the Hombourg army, and kept the civil departments of the government going to a most astonishing extent. I only wonder that, there being some largish ponds about, the Landgrave didn't affect a certain yearly sum to the creation of a ministry of Marine, and organize a Hesse-Hombourgian fleet in opposition to the squadron maintained by the Prussian government at Stettin, consisting of one gunboat and a steam-tug. I can at once realize a notion of the unfeigned grief with which the death of the Princess Elizabeth—who long survived her husband—was received throughout her small but compact territories.

"The suite of apartments which this good lady occupied during her wifedom and widowhood are situated towards the north, and command a capital view of those always picturesque Taunus mountains. There is not much to speak of in the decoration of the apartments themselves. Many an Anglo-Indian civil servant's widow is better lodged than was the Landgravine Elizabeth of Hesse-Hombourg. Still there are some interesting fragments of foreign *bric-a-brac* scattered about. There is a model of the castle of Schwarzburg, and one of a castle where Mary Queen of Scots was imprisoned: an ebony casket, once belonging to Queen Elizabeth; a model of the porcelain tower at Pekin; antique watches; portraits and pictures painted on china; the workbox and portrait of Maria Theresa of Austria; the model of a man-of-war skilfully enough made in silver by Louis XVI. of France—poor fellow! if he had been born a working silversmith, he might have kept his head on his shoulders; a timepiece made by the same mechanical sovereign, a present from the Duchesse d'Angoulême; a dressing-box of Saxon porcelain; a picture of Mary Stuart and Rizzio harping melodiously together; a pair of malachite consoles, presents from the Czar Alexander of Russia—these were things that I found, not 'in the drawer of the cook,' as Mr. Hood's

THE GREAT GRIMGRIBBER GATEWAY OF THE LANDGRAVE'S PALACE.

ballad has it, but in the apartments of the dead Landgravine—all commented on by the old man in blue as
having been special favourites with his beloved ' Princesse Eleezabeth.'   He had been in England, the old
gentleman informed us, years and years ago, when
the Princess had been on a visit toh er Royal relatives
in that country.   He preserved reminiscences—copi-
ous enough, but also sufficiently confused—of Windsor
Castle and Brighton Pavilion.   Indeed, he had seen
his late Majesty George the Fourth; and the poor
old fellow distended his cheeks, tried to protrude his
pendulous old abdomen, and essayed to brush up the
few remaining hairs on his powdered twelfth-cake
head, in order to give us a graphic idea of the corpu-
lence and the curly wig of potent monarch."

Here ends the manuscript of the stout gentleman;
but I am inclined to think he has omitted some minor
points of detail in his description of the Schloss at
Hombourg.   He has not said a word about the gardens attached to the palace, which are very prettily
and picturesquely laid out; and it is from the after-
statements of the slim gentleman that I was enabled
to give a view of the Great Grimgribber Gate in the
inner courtyard, surmounted as is that triumphant
archway (apparently constructed in pale gingerbread,
which has been grievously nibbled by many generations of rats) by an equestrian statue of Landgrave
Frederic II., surnamed " of the silver leg," who, in a
complete suit of armour, a monstrous periwig, and
whose nose is of the orthodox Slawkenbergian pattern,
is mounted on a raw-bone steed, with a flowing mane
and gorgeously caparisoned, gallantly galloping from
an elliptical cavity above the archway, and leaping
into nothing at all, just as you see him in the accompanying engraving.   The slim gentleman states that
he immediately passed through the archway, and looked
up at the wall to see whether the tail of the silver-
legged Landgrave's horse were sticking out behind.

But he could discern nothing, and the sculptor had
probably forgotten it, as Mr. Beasley the architect
forgot the gallery stairs to the Lyceum Theatre, and
Sir Francis Chantrey was oblivious of the necessity
of stirrups when he made George the Fourth ride
that stone cock-horse in Trafalgar Square. I never
found the man with the iron chest very communicative on the subject of the Schloss. He expressed his
opinion once that the whole palace was a " humbug,"
and over and over again declared his persuasion that
the old gentleman in the blue coat, with his head
powdered like a twelfth-cake, was no other than
Ferdinand-Henry-Frederick, reigning Landgrave of
Hesse-Hombourg. He was, he said, confirmed in his
conviction when the old gentleman accepted, with an
infinity of bowing and scraping, the small sum of one
florin fifteen kreutzers, presented to him by the party
as a *douceur*, or gratuity for showing them over the
Schloss. It was *so* like a German potentate, he
added; and when a discrepancy in his theory was
pointed out to him, in the fact that at one period of
their passage through the palace, an ancient female,
of morose and acid appearance, and clad in rusty
black, had appeared in a violent, albeit spectral manner,
from a secret door in a corridor, fallen on the old
gentleman in blue, furiously vilipended him in rapid
but quite incomprehensible German, and even made
a considerable show of wresting his bright bunch of
keys from him—arguing from this, that the old lady,
to assume such apparent authority over him, must
have been at least the wife of the old gentleman in
blue—the man with the iron chest sternly replied
that you never knew what women were up to; and
that, although the Landgrave Ferdinand had never
been married, he might have been, at some time or
other of his long life, " a gay man," and kept his
morganatic *chère amie*, as Front de Bœuf kept Dame
Ursula in the turret of the castle of Torquilstone.

Besides, urged the M. I. C., there is a dowager Landgravine already in the castle, and the Landgrave's
sister. Might this not have been the morose and
acid-looking old lady in rusty black. The slim gentleman denied this, stating that he had seen the rusty
shandrydan carriage, alluded to at an earlier period
of this narrative, drawn by two attenuated horses of
grave and reserved mien, and driven by a long-bodied
coachman, wearing a shabby livery, and crowned with
a prodigious cocked-hat, much battered, and worn fore
and aft, like that of the admiral in the pictorial illustrations to the charming and pathetic ballad of "Billy
Taylor," emerge from a side door of the castle, and
take the road to the Taunus; and, furthermore, the
slim gentleman averred that in that carriage sat a
majestic fat lady, in a black silk pelisse and a huge
coalscuttle bonnet, whom a passing schoolboy (demanding a kreutzer, by the way, for the information)
assured him was the Dowager Landgravine Louisa.
She was accompanied by a demure young person in a
plain cotton print, with a straw hat and blue ribbon,
who must have been either the dowager's youngest
daughter, another Princess Elizabeth, or an inoffensive
dame de compagnie.

I have been myself more than once over the Schloss
of Hombourg, and can vouch for the general accuracy
of my three travellers' descriptions; but I found in
the English Princess's apartments some articles of
furniture—mere nicknacks as they were—far more
interesting and suggestive of curious reminiscences
than the Emperor of China's porcelain pagodas, or the
Emperor of Russia's malachite consoles. Yes, I liked
better to dwell on some scraps and oddities the good
woman had here preserved, full of kindly, genial,
homely memorials of her beloved England. There
were little faded pigtail and powder-patched portraits,
miniatures, and medallions—even down to tiny black
profiles, cut out with scissors, and shaded with bronze

in the old Tunbridge Wells and chain-pier at Brighton style, of all her royal brothers and sisters. There was a little bad water-colour drawing—it might have been done by an itinerant artist on Ramsgate sands—representing the Princess Victoria, when a child, standing by the side of the Duchess of Kent. In a low-browed, panelled room was a fair library of English books; the huge Bensley edition of the Bible, in monstrous tall copies that stood shoulder to shoulder, like Frederick-William's regiment of Potsdam grenadiers; Annual Registers, Tatlers, Spectators, Sherlock on Death, Voltaire's Charles XII. (the infidel must have been contraband ware, smuggled into the library of a daughter of the orthodox George III.); Brooke's old maudlin sermon-novel, "The history of Henry, Earl of Morland"—no other, indeed, than the "Fool of Quality," which has recently been republished in England, with a preface by the Reverend Kingsley:—the collection of books, in short, you would expect to find in the possession of a reputable English gentlewoman of the last century.

And there is the Landgravine's sleeping apartment; and the big state-bed, whose eider-down pillows were erewhile graced by the recumbent heads of Elizabeth of England and Frederick-Joseph of Hessia. Did they wear night-caps, I wonder, or did they carry their crowns to bed with them, like the kings and queens who lived "once upon a time," in the fairy tales? I am not quite certain whether an Anglo-Saxon tourist —a bachelor, as he who writes then was—has any legitimate business in a lady's bedroom, even if it be in the showrooms of a palace. I have always felt out of my element in Queen Mary's bedchamber, at Hampton Court. I could not help lingering here, however, and listened and gazed patiently while the old man in blue—he was my cicerone, too, and must be of no age, and for all time—pointed out and prattled about the effigies of Marlborough and Eugene, of

the "silly-Billy," Duke of Gloucester, George the
Third's nephew, and the "butcher" Duke of Cumberland (who was, after all, and Culloden notwithstanding,
a fat, good-tempered kind of man), his uncle. And
then the old gentleman took, cautiously, from underneath the counterpane, dusting it carefully, and
holding it peeringly to the light, an unframed picture
on panel, the portrait of George the Third. He only
showed it to the English, he said, and "Princess
Elizabeth" was fonder of it than of any other performance in her straggling gallery. I started. This
King George?" I exclaimed. Yes, it was that king.
King William, when Duke of Clarence, had visited
Hombourg, and seen the portrait. He pronounced it
an admirable likeness, but, with tears in his eyes, had
bidden the old man put it away, for Heaven's sake,

POOR OLD GEORGE!

and hide it. King George, as he was here represented, was not in his coronation dress, with his sceptre in his hand, and his crown on the table beside him. Nor in his colonel of volunteers' uniform—pigtailed, cocked-hatted, and booted—as you may see him, in bronze, even now, over-against Waterloo House, in Cockspur Street. Nor was he represented in the Roman manner, laurel-wreathed, bare-necked, and toga-draped, as he is represented, D.G. Brit. Hib. Franc. Rex, on the half-crowns and shillings. A very different King George was here, of a verity. A very old, wrinkled, bald, long snowy-bearded dotard; so vacant-looking! so forlorn and feeble! There was no light, it was easy to see, in those poor veiled eyes: no coherent word could ever pass those half-opened lips. It seemed almost a mockery in the painter to have shrouded that tottering form in a loose purple bed-gown, ermine-doubled, and with a star emblazoned on the left breast. What were stars and garters, crosses and ribbons, to the broken-down, sightless, senseless patriarch? But a king is a king, and I suppose they dressed him up in some regal scraps and tippets, though all who paid court to him were his doctors, and nurses, and keepers. This was King George, ætat 79, blind and mad! Poor old King! I thought, looking at the piteous effigy of his transient, fitful gleams of semi-reason—moments that must have made him miserable, for they made him conscious of his fallen state—moments when he was wont to mutter that he must bring the revolted colonies to reason, that a tight hand must be kept over the Catholics, and that he would not break his oath— no, not he. Poor old fellow! what were colonies, Catholics, royal marriage acts, Fox's swarthy visage, Bishop Hurd's sermons, apples in their dumplings, coalition ministries, Weymouth theatricals, Queen Charlotte's snuff and toupee, coronation oath, and all, to him now? I thought upon his insisting once on arranging the programme of the Ancient Concerts, of which he had been once chief patron—selecting all Handel's pieces that bore on madness and blindness, and winding up with "God save the King." Heaven rest him, and save him indeed, poor crazy Lear, with all his obstinacy and tyranny! At least they took good care of him, and suffered him not to wander up and down with beggars and naked men on the Dover road. At least his daughters were not Gonerils and Regans; but Elizabeth and Amelia, Sophia and Augusta, were all Cordelias to him, and loved him very dearly when his wits were gone, and his orbs had shot their fires into the dark abyss.

CHAPTER X. AND LAST.

OF THE DIVERS HEAVY BLOWS AND GREAT DISCOU-
RAGEMENTS UNDERGONE BY THE STOUT GENTLE-
MAN, THE SLIM GENTLEMAN, AND THE MAN WITH
THE IRON CHEST; AND THEIR ULTIMATE RETURN
TO ENGLAND, HOME, AND BEAUTY.

Come back to the Three: for, indeed, they are by
this time in a lamentable case. Why did they not continue the transmission of their winnings day by day to
England, per Chartered Commercial Bank? Colours
began to have tremendous runs against them, routing
all their abstruse calculations, and turning their infallible systems inside out. They lost vast sums.
Complaints began to be heard of the small pittances
advanced on gold watches at the Lombardian establishment in the Haingasse. The three were on conversational terms with the pawnbroker and his assistants.
The stout gentleman called the chief Lombard Von
Dobree; and declared that Hombourg-von-der-Höhe
ought properly to be called Attenboroughbourg-von-
der-Owe. He no longer flashed his diamond ring in the
admiring eyes of beautiful ladies. The temper of the
slim gentleman, although he bore his losses with Spartan fortitude, was manifestly soured. The stout gentleman avoided him, expressing his fear that his slim companion would bite him. The man with the iron chest
became frightfully morose, not to say ferocious. His
nose glowed like a fiery furnace. He took to smoking
in bed; and puffs of nicotianic vapour escaped from
his garments as he walked about. He talked of selling the stableman's coat and wearing a blouse for

cheapness' sake. He was heard bullying the waiters dreadfully, and demanding hot and peppered meats with the voice of a roaring lion. His companions fell upon him and scolded him fiercely, because (all expenses were to be divided between them) his washing bill was of such a large amount. "Twelve shirts a week!" his comrades shouted vengefully; "but where is the result? You look dingier than ever. Do you eat shirts?"

I am afraid that the three travellers had begun to *hate one another*.

The landlord went on making out larger bills than ever, *but he was not half so civil*. The morning after an unusual run of ill luck, he asked the stout gentleman, somewhat impetuously, for an immediate settlement of accounts.

"I'll go over to the Kursaal and see about it," responded the obese one.

The landlord pressed the slim gentleman on the same topic, or, it may be said, without the suspicion of a pun, on the same "score."

"Don't bother me," answered the slim gentleman tartly. "Accounts, indeed! Hoity, toity! I shall have to play nothing but *rouleaus* to-day, to retrieve an unfortunate miscalculation of yesterday."

The Host of the Hôtel de France was momentarily abashed at this Napoleonic display of cynicism and superiority to adverse circumstances; but the man with the iron chest coming down to breakfast shortly, he made a fresh onslaught on him.

"Fellow," the red-nosed individual answered, sternly and contemptuously, "when you know how to fry potatoes crisp and brown—when you make your steaks of beef, and not of gutta-percha—and when your claret is Bordeaux wine and not ink, you may prate to me about accounts. But be not cast down, Boniface," he added in a kinder tone—he had a heart, this red-nosed man—"I dreamed last night that black would turn up eleven times in succession, and I mean to back black this morning like old boots. I'll come over from the Kursaal in half-an-hour and report progress."

Unfortunately it was red, and not black, that had a run that morning—turning up not eleven but fourteen times in succession.

It was agreed on all sides that something must be done.

The "something" took for a day or so the form of preserving a manly dignity, added to some magnanimous hilarity under afflicting influences. The stout gentleman reminded his companions that Mr. Simon Legree, the slave-dealer, in "Uncle Tom's Cabin," always counselled the negroes whom he had purchased to "keep a stiff upper lip," as a remedy against giving way to despair. Accordingly, the Three put a most valiant face upon their losings; the stout gentleman swaggered, the slim gentleman was sharp, and the M. I. C. savage with the waiters; and they all went on as though they had ten thousand a year. There was no diminution, but rather a sensible augmentation, in the daily consumption of Sillery and sparkling Moselle; and the stout gentleman even gave notice of his intention to try a bottle of Esterhazy's Tokay, fifteen florins the bottle, for lunch, some morning. The traveller—I won't mention his name—who *as yet* still retained a gold watch, was instructed to draw it from his pocket and consult it continually to keep up the appearance of wealth. "Surely," the M. I. C. cogitated, "the landlord can't entertain any doubts concerning his bill, when he sees us increasing it to such an extent."

The habitual cheerfulness of the stout gentleman did not entirely desert him at this trying juncture; but his humour gradually assumed a biting and sarcastic character. He had always been somewhat proficient in poetical composition, and I have preserved

some sparse fragments of his efforts in versification
made at his gloomy period. They may be termed
Sybilline Leaves, being mostly pencilled on the backs
of the fatal little cards with the red and black dots on
which the chances are printed.

Here is a pathetic morsel—

> " A flat he would a gambling go,
>   Heigh ho! says Roulette,
>   Whether the banker would let him or no;
>   With his raky shaky croupier and cards,
>   Heigh ho! says Antony Roulette."

The next is more jocund in tone, yet painful in its
climax—

> " Dickory, Dickory Dock,
>   They began at eleven o'clock;
>   But the red had a run,
>   So no money they won;
>   Dickory, Dickory Dock."

There is a fine vein of satire running through the
following—

> " Humpty Dumpty laid on the *Noir*—
>   Humpty Dumpty lost; and he swore
>   Not all his gold watch, pin, sleeve-buttons and chain,
>   Can pay Humpty's loss at the Kursaal again."

He begins the next scornfully, but the effort is dis-
tasteful to him, and ends abruptly—

> " Bah, Bah! Blackleg, have you any cash?
>   If you have any, to play's rash."

Then how vigorous is the metrical flow of—

> " High diddle fiddle, Roulette's all a diddle,
>   When you win you jump out of your skin;
>   But the banker he laughs to see such sport,
>   *And the croupe runs away with the tin."*

The last specimen of which I shall give an extract is hopeful, sanguine, almost to desperation—

> " One on the *impair*, and two on the *manque*;
> Bet on the numbers, you're sure to break the bank."

I scarcely know which to admire most in these short lyrics : the deep under-current of satiric philosophy, or the charming and infantine mould into which they are cast, full of evidence as they are that among the stern and engrossing cares of mature life, the stout gentleman had not forgotten those happy and innocent days of childhood, when he played among the daisies, cried for the moon in a pail of water, pulled the kitten (frolic little pusskin !) about the room by her tail, and playfully bit his little sister on the elbow on some disputed question of toffee. *I, curre,* happy little infant with chubby legs ! May you never live to see a *roulette* wheel or a *rouge et noir* table at Hombourg-von-der-Höhe !

Curiously skimming over the amalgamated diaries of the three travellers, I find the following items of observation recorded, for some of which, perhaps, allowance must be made, as they were written towards the latter part of their sojourn, and amidst much financial gall and bitterness—

" People are not expected to die much in Hombourg. It interferes with the gaieties and happiness of the Kursaal, and the Administration do not like it. The native inhabitants, like good servants of their paternal Landgrave, retire to Frankfort, or to the adjoining villages, when *in extremis*, and die without making any fuss about it. When the physicians report the case of a foreign invalid to be desperate, he receives a civil note from the Administration, pointing out that he came to take the waters—not to be killed, but to be cured, gently dwelling on the impropriety of throwing gloom over a cheerful watering-place, and entreating him to go away and die some-where else. When so disagreeable an accident as death occurs—as it sometimes will do—the funeral takes place very early in the morning, and the under-taker's men are instructed to wear white favours, and say they are going to a wedding. Suicides, or rather attempts at *felo-de-se*, are rather common at Hom-bourg, among ladies and gentlemen who have been playing 'infallible systems,' there being a lake of sufficient depth, conveniently situated in the Kur-Garten : but these rash acts seldom terminate fatally, a large Newfoundland dog being retained by the Administration to pull drowning persons out of the water. The rescued persons have been known to return, all dripping wet, to the Kursaal, and win largely. *Dum spiramus speramus.*"—(*Slim Gentle-man.*) . . . . . "There are a hundred golden rules to ensure winning at *rouge et noir*. The best one is to have nothing whatever to do with that fatal game. . . . . The *Banque* will sometimes advance money to well known and desperate gamblers. They lend a *rouleau* or so, 'on parole,' pretty certain of getting it back in the ordinary way of the tables. One, who so borrowed a hundred *louis* on parole and lost them in five minutes, and said he would go and fetch some more money from his hotel, went, but forgot to come back ; being met in the street by a croupier, and re-proached with his breach of parole, he retorted, 'Well, it is a debt of honour, therefore I sha'n't pay it.' "—(*Ibid.*)

"The dwarf, who came to Hombourg with a bagful of napoleons, had to borrow a florin from a croupier, to go back to Frankfort by the omnibus."—(*M. I. C.*)*

---

* The stout gentleman evidently had the dwarfish individual in his mind when his tuneful muse incited him to the composi-tion of the lyric, "Humpty Dumpty laid on the *Noir*."

“When you describe your symptoms to a Hombourg doctor, and dwell upon nervous depression, he says, soothingly, ‘ Well; we must try a change of colour; we must win a little more!’ . . . Natives of Hombourg are not allowed to gamble. They have been known to emigrate to the British islands, become naturalized British subjects, and return to Hombourg, in order to be able to play without let or hindrance.

“Gamblers are generally affable, serene, and apparently unmoved, even under the pressure of the severest losses. I, however, once saw a losing player lose his temper. He was a burly Briton, seemingly from the manufacturing districts; and when he had made his last *coup*, lost, and the croupier was sweeping away his money, he reached his large fist over the table, and crying, ‘ There, mounseer ; take that along with it, for luck,’ hit the *employé* of the Administration a tremendous crack on the nose. Natural, but impolitic. I believe the Administration caused him to be beheaded.”—(*Stout Gentleman.*)

“ They give concerts at the Kursaal during the summer season. They pay the artistes handsomely ; but as they generally lose their salaries, and a good deal more, at the gaming-tables, they have to sing two or three times for nothing, in order to pay their expenses back to Paris or Brussels. Billiards are not encouraged by the Administration of the Kursaal. The game is in itself too amusing, and takes up too much time.

“ They should have sign-posts all over Hombourg, with polyglot directions, ‘ This is the way to the pawnbroker’s.’ ”—(*Stout Gentleman.*)

“ Few men are in Hombourg a fortnight without finding out the way to the pawnshop without any adventitious assistance.”—(*M. I. C.*) “ I have known ladies to fasten their shawls with the corking pins gratuitously distributed by **the** Kursaal 'Jeames's' to prick the cards withal. . . . ."—(*Slim Gentleman.*)

"Sometimes, the morning after a great battle, when almost **all** the habitual players have **been** 'cleaned out,' you scarcely see anybody **at** the **tables** save the bankers and croupiers. Sallow Jews **flit about** the **gardens** and reading-rooms, proffering financial assistance to those whose bills or expectations of remittances they know to be good. Ruined **French** marquises, and temporarily bankrupt German princes, are seen furtively, and by by-approaches, flitting towards the Mont de Piété, the Kursaal of **the** pawnbroking interest, where they deposit, on temporary mortgage, all their available articles of jewellery ; nay, are sometimes reduced **to pledge** travelling coats lined with fur, and covered with much embroidery and braiding, and even their not too abundant surplusage of body linen. Usurers are in great request, and **a vast** amount **of** discounting takes place before **noon.** I too, **your** humble servant, have felt **the want of a financial** accommodation from individuals of the Harpagon and Trapbois order, **concurrently** with extreme thirst brought on by unlucky runs ; **and** ringing my chamber-bell of a morning, have ordered the waiter to bring me **'a** bottle of Assmanshaüser and a moneylender,' **to** fulfil the double **purpose of** clearing my 'throat' **and** replenishing my 'chest.' Misery makes a man acquinted with strange bed-fellows, and punting at Hombourg **will** sometimes **cause you to** form the strangest alliances. I have seen **a count** of the Holy Roman Empire quite familiar with a clothesman, and submissive to **a Jew** money-changer, when his luck has taken an adverse turn; and I have known a Russian prince quite contented, when his martingale has been contrary, **to** accept an invitation to dinner from **the keeper** of a pipe-shop at Cologne. I wonder what **will become of us all if we go on** losing, and don't pay the bill. Shall we be had up before the Landgrave, and ordered for immediate execution before the Kursaal windows, as a warning to unlucky gamblers? Shall we be sentenced to a life-long captivity in that lofty white tower in the court-yard of the Schloss? Shall we be driven into the solitudes of the Taunus mountains, and left there to be devoured by the wild bears with which that hot volcanic range abounds? There is Horror in the thought!" There the manuscript breaks off; but I think that I (the editor) can enlighten the writer (the man with the iron chest) as to the treatment debtors who can't pay their hotel bills are likely to experience. There is really a debtor's prison at Hombourg, and captives are occasionally confined therein at the suit of hotel-keepers, bootmakers, and tailors, whose patience has been worn out; but the Administration—ever watchful, ever benevolent!—invariably satisfies the claims against the *détenus*, and sets them at liberty, after a moderate delay has taken place, to see whether any of the friends or relations of the locked-up individuals may not be disposed to help them out of durance vile.

My task now nearly approaches its conclusion. I have but a few more incidents to relate, and you will hear no more of my three travellers. It so fell out that a run of ill-luck having seriously, if not irretrievably, injured their finances, and being by this time heartily sick of Hombourg-von-der-Höhe, the Kursaal, the Kur-Garten, the rakes, the *roués*, the *roulette*, and the *rouge et noir;* and especially of that abominable "Administration," and all things thereunto appertaining, they determined—or, rather, I think it was the slim gentleman, as being in this respect the most muscular financier of the three, who determined—to send to England for a hundred pounds, and, settling some little demands already outstanding against them, to quit the wicked, delightful place for ever. For though money is apt to grow scarce in

Vanity Fair, credit is easily to be obtained. "You may run in debt to the tune of five hundred florins a minute," writes the stout gentleman testily. This idea, long resisted and frequently broached, was frequently postponed, on the plea that "luck might change to-morrow;" but as "luck" did not present the slightest appearance of changing on many succeeding mornings, save into something infinitely worse, the sorrowful necessity was at last recognized. Besides, the mill in England was beginning to want grist by this time. Apprehensions of "hair-combing" by female hands began to show themselves among the travellers; and the red-nosed man, with many snortings and mutterings, declared that he had been absent from his "Penates" too long. As if a man with so red a nose could have any Penates, under any circumstances! It was agreed, then, that the hundred pounds were to be procured from England, the bills paid, and the dust of the Kursaal shaken off the feet of the wearied and disgusted travellers. It is astonishing, when this idea was once started, the stout gentleman and the man with the iron chest wanted it carried into immediate execution. They gave no rest to the slim gentleman, till an embassy, composed of two of their number—one to take care that the other didn't drown himself in the river Mein, I presume—was despatched to Frankfort, and, by the intermediary of a great banking firm there, to telegraph to London for the despatch of the required sum. It was pointed out by one of the astute Hebrew *attachés* of the great banking firm in question, that the answer to the telegraphic message, advising the remittance, must come by post. For nothing could be easier than for a swindler in London to telegraph in the name of any great banking firm to the house at Frankfort, to pay some other swindler any number of pounds sterling, and by this means defraud the Frankfort house of the amount.

While the requisite funds were in process of transmission, the travellers "improved the opportunity,"
as the diplomatic's phrase goes, to take a pedestrian
journey to the Taunus mountains. These were once
volcanic mountains, and still contain many warm
mineral springs, which are still boiling, and producing
medicinal waters for the benefit of mankind, and the
greater glory of the Kursaal Administration. The
travellers did not ascend the Felzburg; but they
visited the summit of the Alt König, or " High King,"
the mountain next in altitude to that in eminence.
They also had a peep at the Pfahlgraben, or Paling
Ditch, which is a trench running to the height of the
Taunus, and extending even to more distant parts of
the country. Three noteworthy adventures marked
the expedition of my three friends to the " Alt
König." In the first place, they did not meet one
living soul in the course of their ascent; but, within
a few hundred yards of the summit, they encountered
a solitary and begrimed-looking woodcutter, in an
unclean blouse and wielding a savage axe. He could
proffer no information when addressed both in English, French, and German—which is not so very incomprehensible, when it is considered that he did not
understand either of the two first of these languages,
and very probably knew very little of the third—a
barbarous *patois* being, in many cases, substituted
for the pure vernacular. It was conjectured by the
stout gentleman that this woodcutter, who, besides
being black in the face, hirsute, and savage-looking
beyond my powers of description, had staring eyes of
a crimsoned hue, and gleaming white teeth, must be,
if not the enemy of mankind himself, at least some
awful gnome, hobgoblin, or dwarfish demon—you
have his portrait opposite—specially belonging to
the Taunus mountains, and acquainted with the
locality of the gold mines, nugget caverns, and other
auriferous deposits which tradition declares to be

abundant round about the Felzburg. The man with the iron chest proposed that they should force the grimy woodcutter by threats, blows, and, if necessary, torture, to conduct them to a cavern full of nuggets and ingots, a mine brimming with frederics-d'or, or a bin full of gold dust.

"Torture!" repeated the slim gentleman. "How on earth could we torture him?"

"Nothing easier in the world," replied the red-nosed man. "You have some German tinder fuzees with you, haven't you? well, tie half a dozen or so round the tips of his fingers, and then set light to them; *when the nails begin to frizzle below the quick,* I warrant that he'll find both his tongue, and his hoards of gold into the bargain."

I rejoice to say that this inhuman and atrocious proposition was unanimously scouted; and the travellers left the woodcutter, who glowered and gib-

THE WOODMAN OF THE TAUNUS MOUNTAINS.

bered at them, leaning on his axe meanwhile, in a most unearthly manner. Perhaps he was a demon after all, and would have entered into a compact with them to break the Kursaal bank, but that from their number—demons are not omniscient—he assumed then to be of the mystic confederacy of "Number Three." That uncanny triple guild can, as you are aware, break banks, conquer empires, storms and sunshine, winds and tides presage, give names to every mountain of the moon, and extinguish the Thames when set on fire. The Emperor N—p—l—n belongs to the "Number Three;" so does the editor of the "Morning Advertiser." So did I once; but I didn't pay my annual subscription, and they scratched me.

It is just as probable that the grimy woodcutter wasn't a bit in the gnome, demon, or hobgoblin line, but an honest peasant of the Taunus district, Hans Schaffskopf, it may be, by name, who worked cheerfully at his toilsome vocation for a few kreutzers a day.

The travellers started at about noon. It was nine o'clock at night when, wearied and footsore, they reached Hombourg again.

Some inconsiderable but very inconvenient delay took place in the transmission of the required funds to our three thoroughly belated pilgrims; necessitating several visits by one or the other of them (for their finances would not now permit a combined trip) to Frankfort, there to interrogate, and sometimes it must be admitted to remonstrate and expostulate with, and even to abuse the clerks, cashiers, office boys, messengers, even to the mighty chiefs of departments of the great banking firm—the greatest banking firm, as it is generally recognized, of Europe and of the world. Indeed, the stout gentleman threatened to bring an action for negligence against Messrs. R—— and Co.; pleading special damage;

but not being perfectly satisfied as to what country, if in any country at all, the venue would lie, he ultimately abandoned the idea.

These trips to Frankfort—reiterated and unavailing, became very dreary and spiritless affairs. The slim gentleman no longer talked of entertaining the Germanic Confederation at *al-fresco* fêtes. There were narrow-minded discussions as to the appointment of the small remaining stock of florins and kreutzers on the occasion of each embassy being dispatched to Frankfort; and it was clear that unless the remittances did not speedily arrive, the travellers, so far as ready money went, would be brought down, like the sailors who started from " Bristol Citie," to " the last split-pea." The " tick " at the Hôtel de France still continued ; indeed, it had grown into a huge double eight-day clock of credit, and threatened to strike.

One day, however, this mournful trio had mustered sufficient small change—there had been an interview with Herr Attenborough-von-der-Owe that morning— to warrant a conjoint trip to Frankfort ; and it was on this occasion that, wandering in the quaint, antiquated Judengasse, or street of the Jews, the slim gentleman, by the advice and with the consent of his stout and red-faced friends, purchased the two iron chests, or rather caskets, which you may see depicted in the engraving appended to this, the last chapter of " Make your Game." They did not exactly know why they purchased these same caskets. Perhaps as a compliment to the fondness of the red-nosed man for iron chests—whether of large or small dimensions.

Most people who have gone " up the Rhine "—and who in these tourist days has not made that delightful ascension ?—have also made the trip from Mayence to Frankfort-on-the-Maine ; and certainly everybody who has sojourned, even for a day, in that old city of the Teutonic Cæsars, has paid a visit to the far-famed

Judengasse alluded to in the foregoing paragraph. I stumble over a note respecting this celebrated thoroughfare pencilled by the stout gentleman on a fly-leaf of the Hombourg guide-book.

" Judengasse. Walked about in it. Wished we were as rich as the Jews. Met a Jew boy with a satchel—not creeping like snail unwillingly to school, but repairing thereto blithely and merrily. Jew boys like to learn. Knowledge is power, and education puts them in the way of making their fortune with greater celerity. Mem.: M. Sidonia in ' Coningsby.' He knew everything, from squaring the circle to the market price of hundred-bladed penknives, and was, consequently, worth millions before he was twenty-one. I was a very idle boy at school; hence my present poverty. The Judengasse was in the way to the Rabbinical academy where my young friend was pursuing his studies ; and he very politely consented to officiate as Cicerone, discoursing meanwhile in French —excellent as to quantity, but, as regards quality, execrable. At the southern extremity of the Judengasse there is in course of erection a magnificent synagogue : the greater portion of the funds fur-

THE JEWS' STREET, FRANKFORT-ON-THE-MAINE.

nished, I presume, by Rothschild. The famous old founder of the house was born in this old Judengasse, and kept a little shop in it, selling rubbishing trinkets, for years. Street itself long and narrow, and reminds you equally of Petticoat Lane, Holywell Street, Church Lane, St. Giles's, the 'Coomb' in Dublin, and the 'Goosedubs' in Glasgow. Mr. Hecht, of the Jewish persuasion, keeps a Hebrew *café* and *gasthaus* over against the synagogue. Near to that is a *Wechsels Comptoir*, or money-changer's shop. Curious to see the Christian stonemasons and bricklayers slaving at the walls of the synagogue for the Jews they profess to despise. Fat and florid Israelites—perhaps subscribers to the building funds—come and inspect the progress of the works, with cigars in their mouths, and smiles on their oleaginous countenances.

"Great crowds in the Judengasse. There must be some large school contiguous. Mingled with the rabble: saw groups of little girls; with blue petticoats and purple stockings, and with calfskin knapsacks on their backs, trotting to school. Marvellous iron-work in scroll and filagree about some of the houses. Doors and windows heavily barred and chained up, in significant reference to the possible visits of the bold old barons of yore, who, when they paid a visit to a money-lender, did not always leave him their bill at three months for the cash they took away. Odd, grotesque signs over shop and house doors. Sign of the 'Apple,' with old mother Eve and the old Serpent and the tree between them. Sign of a knight in armour sculptured on a lintel: might have come out of one of Albert Dürer's old cross-hatched woodblocks. Slender pilasters with capitals formed by carvings of corpulent cows. Sign of the 'Eincorn' (unicorn); his horn very prominent: the horn of Judah, doubtless. Walls of one house built apparently of oyster-shells. Sign of the 'Silver Crown,' the 'Green Hat,' the 'Ring,' the

‘ Bell,’ the ‘ Lamb ’—uncommonly well shorn was this
juvenile mutton—the ‘ Hoof,’ referring, perhaps, to
the down-trodden condition of Jewry during the middle ages.　Signs of the ‘ Golden Adler,’ or ‘ Golden
Eagle ;’ the ‘ Lion,’ the ‘ Ape.’　All these signs in
sculpture.　None painted.　The stout one said that
if the Jews in the Judengasse had possessed painted
sign-boards, they would have made their customers
take them as part equivalents for cash in the bills
they discounted.　Says that he has two Titian Venuses
(warranted), an undoubted Rembrandt, and a Cor-
reggio (formerly in the Orleans Gallery), all proceeding from Jewry, and the discounting operations
thereof, though not from the Frankfort Judengasse.
At the northern extremity is a market-place, smelling
very ‘ loudly ’ of fried onions and sour cabbage.
There is a lottery-office in the street, and you *may*
win the gross prize of 100,000 florins for an outlay of
fifteen kreutzers.　There is a Hebrew bookseller’s
shop, where many examples of Talmudical typography
are exposed for sale, mingled with some old-fashioned
English books.　Upon parole, I saw the ‘ Farmer of
Inglewood Forest,’ side by side with a tremendous
Hebrew folio, that might have been the work of the
immortal rabbi, Ben-Ayesha Ben-Jamri Ben-Haphish-
bashoth, of Aleppo.　There was a hairdresser’s shop,
but I think they must have more beards to dress
than wigs ; for the two waxen dummies in the window, though graced with tremendous moustaches,
&c., were quite bald.　General products of the Judengasse may be summed up as rags, dirt, bones, old
locks and keys (by the hundred dozen), old chests of
drawers, cabbage leaf cigars, old hats, old clothes. old
books, and old boots.　There is positively nothing
new, or even middle-aged, about the place.　Everything has the most venerable appearance of shabby
antiquity.

“ The caskets, of which the M. I. C. took a not too

graphic sketch, were purchased at one of the rustiest
shops, or rather sheds, for the sale of second-hand
ironmongery that I ever remember seeing. Buying
these chests—in the which, by the way, we expended
very nearly the entire balance of our remaining florins
—it occurred to our stout friend that we must inevitably win large sums of money at the Kursaal the
moment our remittances arrived from England. We
had at first only intended to buy one iron-bound box
—and I don't know why we bought it at all, were it
not for its quaint form and evident antiquity—but the
stout one insisted that we should have a large treasure
casket for the florins and five-franc pieces, and a small
one for the napoleons and frederics-d'or. So we
bought the two caskets, and putting one inside the
other, in the manner of Monsieur Robert Houdin and
other conjurors, we paid a Jew boy five kreutzers to
carry them to the post-bureau, whence we conveyed
them, per our usual omnibus, to Hombourg. I think
we traversed that abominable powdery road fringed
with apple-trees—traversed it backwards and forwards
—in our inquiries after the long-delayed remittance,
till we knew, not only every village, but every house,
cottage, pig-stye, stone, shrub, cock, hen, and dog on
the way. I am inclined to think that the sight of the
supplemental iron chest created for us, on our and its
arrival at Hombourg, some augmentation of consideration on the part of the landlord of the Hôtel de
France, and that he believed us to be not yet entirely
ruined, but provided with a fresh supply of funds
stored in these ferruginous boxes."

At length the money arrived, and, with a touch of
retributive justice, was paid by Messrs. R—— and
Co., of Frankfort, into the Kursaal Bank, at Hombourg. A sad and solemn duty had to be performed.
All bills were paid. The last letters at the post-office
were called for, and the word was (not very exultantly,
though) "Ho! for England!" Per omnibus to

Frankfort, per rail to Mayence, per boat to Mainz-Castel, per steamer to Neuweid-on-the Rhine.   From thence to Cologne the well-known : and thence by the old, old, hackneyed route to Ostend, whence the Belgian mail steamer took the three to Dover.   After Dover, what was there but the train to London, the autumn bills, and the Mill again, and a determination on the part of the three travellers—who are now faster friends than ever—never to "make their game" at Hombourg on the strength of an "infallible system," unless indeed they have the capital of Rothschild, added to that of Jones Loyd, to back them up withal ?

THE END.

London: J. & W. RIDER, Printers, 14, Bartholomew Close. E.C.

NEW SERIAL.

*In Weekly Numbers, Threepence; Monthly Parts, One Shilling;
and Half-Yearly Volumes On fine paper, splendidly illustrated.*

ALL ROUND THE WORLD;

An Illustrated Record of Voyages, Travels, and Adventures in all Parts of the Globe.

EDITED BY W. F. AINSWORTH, F.R.G.S., F.S.A., &c.

No. 1, *price* 3d., *and Part* 1, *price* 1s., *ready October* 15, 1860.

PROSPECTUS.

"ONCE UPON A TIME," as story tells us, there was a noble young prince, the safety of whose life and future happiness depended upon his seclusion in a remote tower, far from all human intercourse. All that could be brought together for enjoyment was placed at his command; but the Prince was always dull, and pined with weariness of soul, until the benevolent Fairy, his guardian, hit upon placing before his eyes, in airy landscapes, magic images of all that was rare, curious, and beautiful in the universe.

The object of "ALL ROUND THE WORLD" is the same as that of the good Fairy. We propose to set before the stay-at-home Traveller, pining to receive new impressions, an exact image and representation of the World wherein he lives, supplying him with that ready means of acquaintance with each country, its scenery, its vegetation, its animals, its inhabitants, and its monuments, that can only be attained by the eye, and accompanying each pictorial delight with graphic illustrations by men of celebrity in the career of travel and adventure.

We shall take our readers "ALL ROUND THE WORLD," in a long and varied traverse; opening to them, as we go on together, the great books of Geography, of Science, and of Nature.

How necessary such a work is at the present moment; how little we know of ourselves and of each other— of those even who live almost in contact with ourselves—may be judged from the fact that the interior of even our own great Colonies is as yet *terra incognita.* In Asia, the vast range of the Himalayas, with the health-giving breezes of a northern climate, looking down upon the sun-burnt plains of India on the one side, and the smiling pastures of Tartary on the other, was, until lately, unvisited; China and Cochin China, with their swarming millions of population, unfrequented; and Japan a sealed country. In America, while of the south-east we still only know

"Those vast shores, washed by the farthest sea,"

of the centre and the west we were ignorant, except that they were inhabited by savages yet untamed. It is a fact that the whole of a country, since pronounced to be the most beautiful in the world for scenery, as well as the mildest in climate, whose valleys teem with fertility, and whose mountains abound with gold and other metals, and minerals even more precious—viz., from California upwards to Vancouver's Island, and across from the Red River to the Pacific, was left for two centuries in the hands of the Hudson's Bay Company, as being a region of ice and snow, fit only for the bear, the beaver, and the trapper.

In Africa, we are but just roused to the importance, not of exploring merely, but of trading with the tribes and nations of its fertile and healthful central regions, while Commerce no longer brandishes the bloody whip and clanks the iron fetters of the slave, as she sails up the Gambia, the Binue, and the Niger, or loads her polluted decks with a human cargo from barracoons on the fatal Western coast; but, with mild Religion by her side, advances up the Congo and the Zambesi, to assure and certify a conquest more enduring than arms—intercourse in connection with the precious gift of instruction in the Religion of Christian Peace.

Wonderful, indeed, has been the progress of discovery effected within the most recent times. Whilst the exploration of the Niger, the Binue, and the Zambesi, in Africa, reveals new fields of inquiry, the navigation of the Murray and the Murrumbigee, in Australia, and of the Amur, in Russia, opens up new regions to the colonist; and that of the Yang-tse-kiang, in China, and of the Parana and Paraguay, in South America, equally extensive realms to commercial enterprise. Nor are the remarkable accessions made of late to our knowledge of the interior of Australia

—more especially the discovery effected by Mr. McDougal Stuart, of a vast extent of land available for pasturage or tillage—of less import to the future. The discovery of a whole district of lakes, and of a region of snow-clad mountains, in inter-tropical Africa, reduces, with the exploration of the upper affluents of the White Nile, the solving of that great problem of all ages—the sources of the Nile—to the same narrow compass as Arctic research had done the limits within which the north-west passage, and the relics of Franklin and of his unfortunate companions, had to be sought for, previous to McClintock's last voyage. Nor ought it to be omitted, that the determination of the existence of an available pass in the Rocky Mountains is like the last link in the great line of communication, which will inevitably be established with the lapse of time, between the Atlantic and the Pacific, through British America.

With this knowledge of the universe—with this work of universal civilization—it is the object of " ALL ROUND THE WORLD" to associate the reader. It is even hoped to see the volumes of this work on every parlour table, placed under the Great Bible, as a Family Book ; and it will be our earnest endeavour, as it is our sincere purpose, to render it worthy of that place.

These are not alone the advantages which " ALL ROUND THE WORLD" will supply to its possessors. It will serve as a Universal Guide and Reference Book to illustrate passing events, containing exact information of what is being done by contemporary travellers in all parts of the earth and seas—following them in their distant wanderings, constituting the reader, by engravings, an eye-witness of what they see, as well as, by graphic textual illustrations, a participator in their struggles, their sufferings, their privations, their dangers, and their final fortunate discoveries. Nor is this all. Whatever, in any nation, whether in its commerce, manufactures, material industry, or natural productions, may be of advantage to ourselves, will be herein set down, faithfully described, correctly delineated, and clearly recorded for future reference.

The task is a large one ; our duties comprehensive, and our devotion to them unswerving. The mine we open is deep and rich; we shall spare no pains in bringing its wealth to light. We have faith in our good intentions, and that they merit a great success. It will be for the public, by an extensive and earnest support, to prove that we have not miscalculated the good sense, the desire for practical information, the capacity, and the wants of the millions of English readers.

The nature of cheap periodical publications has been hitherto, for the most part, to stimulate and excite men's attention. All this is but a repetition of the working out of an old problem. The education of all nations has commenced with a taste for fiction. In "ALL ROUND THE WORLD" we are about to take a step in advance. We still preserve the stimulating and exciting; but we add to it the useful and the true. "Truth is stranger than fiction." Travelling has more actual dangers than the imagination of the romancist can invent. Thus, insensibly, will a more positive and direct knowledge be impressed on the mind. Shall we be mistaken in hoping for the approbation and the encouragement of the judicious? of the teacher? of the parent? and, above all, of the clergy, in such a work? Our objects are known, and such as all must deem praiseworthy. The method of our carrying them out is now open for judgment.

Every care will be bestowed in making "ALL ROUND THE WORLD" a work of intrinsic value, not only as a book, but as a work of art. The designs will not be ornamental landscapes, but drawings by travellers themselves, executed by the most able artists and engravers; while we are happy to say that the stores and libraries of the Learned Societies have been placed at our service, as well as the manuscripts and personal assistance of many eminent travellers, towards the perfecting and complete accomplishment of a work, which all pronounce to be greatly wanted, and highly commendable in its plan and execution.

Each weekly Number will consist of sixteen pages, imperial octavo, with several illustrations.

No. 1, price 3d., and Part 1, price 1s., ready Oct. 15, 1860.

OFFICE :—122, FLEET STREET, LONDON.

*In Weekly Numbers, Twopence, and in Monthly Parts, Nine-
pence.   To be completed in about 50 weekly Numbers.*

No. 1, AND PART I., READY NOVEMBER 1.

PROSPECTUS

OF THE

ILLUSTRATED UNIVERSAL GAZETTEER.

EDITED BY

W. F. AINSWORTH, Esq., F.R.G.S., Etc.

It is not necessary in the present day to enlarge
upon the claims a good Gazetteer has upon public
attention, for it is undoubtedly as useful and as indispensable to the general reader as a Dictionary.   But
it is indispensable also that a Gazetteer, to be really
useful, should be thoroughly reliable, and its information be brought down to the latest date.

Political and Commercial changes, the founding and
growth of Colonies, and the progress of Geographical
Research, have rendered many of the existing
Gazetteers in a great measure obsolete and worthless.
Change is synonymous with Time.   The New York or
the San Francisco of 1860 differs vastly from the New
York or San Francisco of 1850.   Canada, Australia,
and the United States have contributed, within the
past few years, scores upon scores of new places to the
Map of the World.   Even in our own island, where
the landmarks are so deeply planted, new towns have
arisen ; while, in consequence of the changes effected
by our railway system, old seats of activity and indus-

try have declined and dwindled away. All these mutations require to be set forth in a good Gazetteer —such an one as is now offered to public notice.

The ILLUSTRATED UNIVERSAL GAZETTEER will represent the actual condition of every place of the least importance throughout the world. This vast body of information must necessarily be given in a concise form, but none the less full, complete, and satisfactory. The increasing demands of commerce require that special attention be bestowed on the natural resources and products of every place ; and this feature, among others, has received careful attention in the compilation of the Work. Utility, apart from extraneous disquisitions, has been steadily kept in view. The latest statistical authorities, and the records of the most recent travellers, have been consulted, and no pains or diligence spared to render this ILLUSTRATED UNIVERSAL GAZETTEER the most accurate and useful of its kind yet published.

The ILLUSTRATED UNIVERSAL GAZETTEER will be embellished with upwards of Five Hundred Wood Engravings, derived, whenever possible, from Photographs of the scenes represented. This latter feature is a novel one, and must specially recommend the Work to the attention of the Public, inasmuch as it will enable the reader to obtain, perhaps for the first time, correct ideas of the aspect of places famous in the records of the present day, and in the annals of the past.

No. 1, *price* 2*d.*, *and Part I.*, *price* 9*d*, *ready Nov.* 1, 1860.

London : HOULSTON & WRIGHT, 65, Paternoster-row.

"A guest that best becomes the table."—Shakspeare.

ENLARGEMENT OF THE
WELCOME GUEST
TO
THIRTY-TWO PAGES, ILLUSTRATED,
PRICE TWOPENCE, WEEKLY.

A YEAR has now elapsed since the proprietors of the WELCOME GUEST offered their new programme to their constituents, and they think they may point with pardonable pride to the thorough fulfilment of the promises made in it. The most popular writers have in turn furnished specimens of their ability, and a publication of a perfectly original character is the result. Their experiment was a bold one, but it has been successful: The WELCOME GUEST has taken the front rank among the leading periodicals of the day, and challenges comparison with any of its compeers.

Encouraged by past success, the proprietors have determined on a bolder experiment than any which has preceded it : they have resolved on enlarging their periodical by the addition of eight pages to the present size, which will thus be increased to thirty-two pages each week instead of twenty-four as heretofore. The WELCOME GUEST will then contain the largest quantity of original literature ever before printed in a weekly sheet, and it thus becomes the cheapest illustrated periodical of the age.

The new space acquired will enable the proprietors to introduce a feature they have meditated for some time. The most popular writer of the day is

GUSTAVE AIMARD,

the great Indian hunter, whose works have been translated into almost every living language, and they derive such universal recognition, because they are the results of personal experience. There have been writers of thrilling Indian romances before now, in whose company we have scoured over the prairie ; but something has ever been lacking in their descriptions. We have felt instinctively a want of that vitality and strong human interest which can alone emanate from a lengthened residence among the wild races and singular scenes that supply both the incidents and localities of the tales. It has been Gustave Aimard's privilege to spend the greater portion of his life aloof from civilization, as the adopted son of one of the most powerful Indian tribes ; as squatter, hunter, ranger, warrior, and miner in turn, he has traversed America, from the highest peaks of the Cordilleras, to the shores of Ocean. Hence it will be seen that Gustave Aimard does not write romances; he only describes his own life.

Believing that these tales of Indian life need only to be known in England to be admired, the proprietors of the WELCOME GUEST have secured the copyright for this conntry, and they commence the new volume with

THE PRAIRIE FLOWER,

the first chapters of which will appear in No. 54, ready October 6th.

The other featnres peculiar to the WELCOME GUEST will, however, be in no way neglected. Mr. G. A. Sala is engaged on a series of papers, illustrated by McConnell, called, the

STREETS OF THE WORLD,

a snbject peculiarly adapted to his graphic and versatile pen, while a collection of sea stories, by the author of

TALES OF THE COAST-GUARD,

a weekly review of

SCIENCE AND ART,

and a series of Social

ESSAYS ON POPULAR TOPICS,

will also appear at regular intervals.

In a word, the proprietors are resolved to spaie no outlay, shun no labour, in rendering the WELCOME GUEST not only the cheapest but the best periodical of the age. They leave their cause confidently in the hands of the pnblic, for they feel assured that their efforts will be fully appreciated.

ORDER

THE WELCOME GUEST,

ENLARGED TO THIRTY-TWO PAGES.

PRICE TWOPENCE, WEEKLY.

THE LARGEST, CHEAPEST AND MOST ORIGINAL PERIODICAL OF THE DAY.

London: HOULSTON & WRIGHT, 65, Paternoster Row.

A GOOD GIFT.

This day, with Illustrations by Phiz, royal 18mo., price 3s. 6d.,
cloth gilt,

LADY CHESTERFIELD'S LETTERS TO HER DAUGHTER.

Comprising the opinions of that gentlewoman upon Fashion, Morals, Deportment, Education, and Matrimony.

By *GEORGE AUGUSTUS SALA,*

Author of "The Baddington Peerage," "Twice Round the Clock," &c., &c.

London : Houlston & Wright, 65, Paternoster Row.

Just published, with 50 whole-page Illustrations by McConnell, post 8vo., cloth gilt, price 10s. 6d.,

TWICE ROUND THE CLOCK.

By *GEORGE AUGUSTUS SALA,*

Author of "The Baddington Peerage," "Lady Chesterfield's Letters to her Daughter," "Gaslight and Daylight," "A Journey due North," "William Hogarth," "Make Your Game," "Looking at Life," &c., &c., &c.

London : Houlston & Wright, 65, Paternoster Row.

This Day, price 2s., Foolscap 8vo, Fancy Boards,

JOHN HORSLEYDOWN;

OR THE CONFESSIONS OF A THIEF.

WRITTEN BY HIMSELF.

Revised by Thomas Littleton Holt (late Editor of the Morning Chronicle.

CONTENTS :

London : WARD AND LOCK, 158, Fleet-street.